Pain of Darkness

C R Saxon

This is a work of fiction. Names, characters, places, and incidents either are the product of the author's imaginations or are used fictitiously, and any resemblance to actual persons, living or dead, business establishments, events, or locales is entirely coincidental. The publisher does not have any control over and does not assume any responsibility for author or third-party websites or their content.

First Edition
Copyright © 2022 C R Saxon
www.hcspublishing.com
All rights reserved.
ISBN: 9781955644044

Acknowledgements

To my amazing, supportive, and totally awesome husband and alpha reader: Thank you! Thank you for helping me make this book a reality. I love you oodles!

Thank you to my wonderful beta readers – my two most loyal in particular: Tammie and Kelly. And thank you to everyone who helped get this book published.

To everyone reading this, thanks for giving my story a shot. I hope you enjoy it!

Unseen Scars:

Cost of Victory

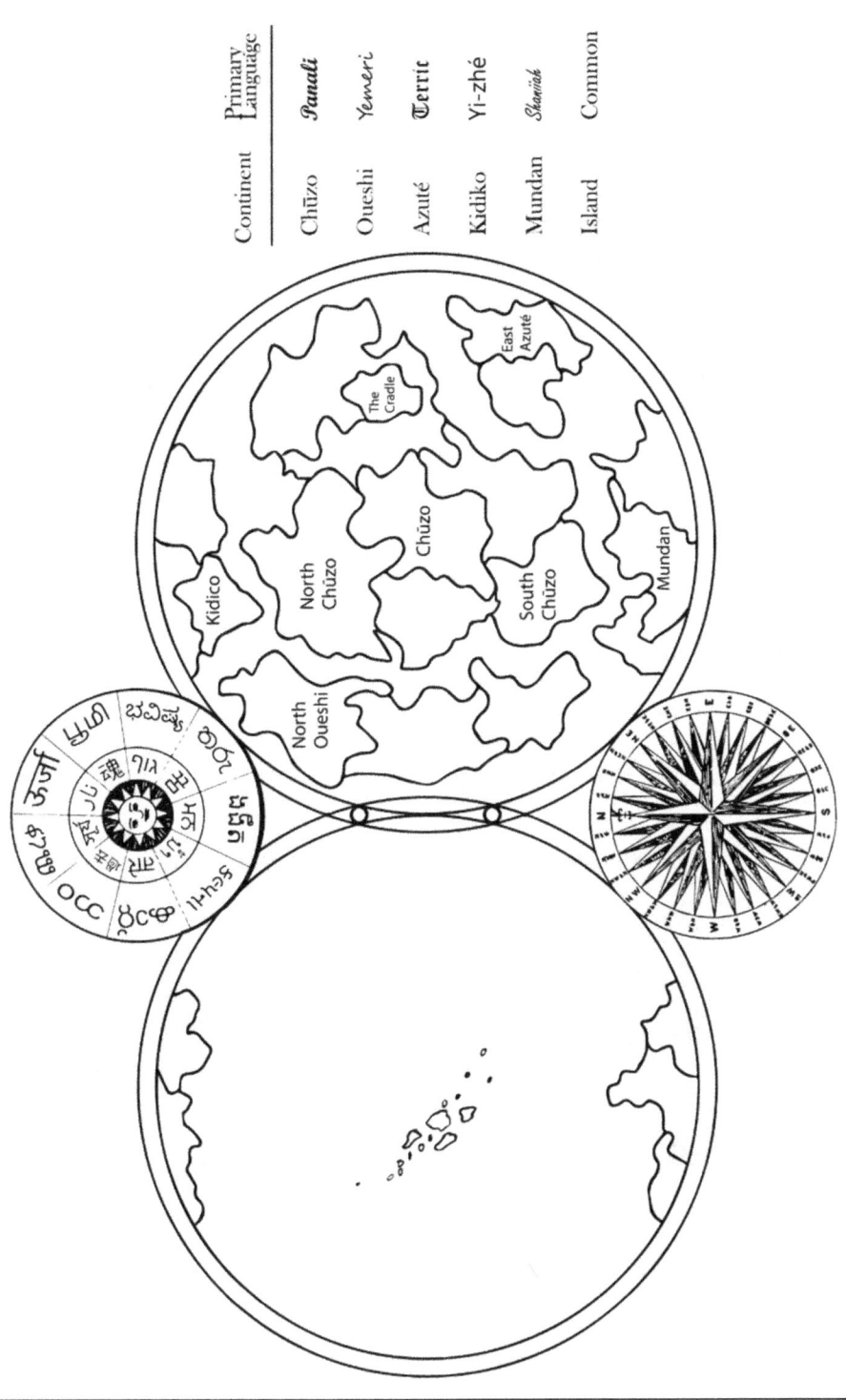

Continent	Primary Language
Chūzo	*Panali*
Oueshi	Yemeri
Azuté	𝕿errit
Kidiko	Yi-zhé
Mundan	*Shaniah*
Island	Common

THE CHARGES

 Humawit
Earth

 Zavun
Sun

 Û-ya'ïn
Water

 Iinamï
Heart

 Saikun
Fire

 Śarï-a
Body

 Shēnó
Life

 Dyzlar
Stars

 Ogani
Dreams

 Wézi
Moon

 Dashū
Souls

 Pigosa
Darkness

 Erviv
Wind

 U-Ech
Mind

 Kámua
Past

 Umbacano
Imagination

 Ajulagrá
Future

 Táqua
Energy

ABILITIES

 Athletes run faster and farther than Olympic humans. They're stronger and more agile with superhuman stamina. Athletes are often trained as Fighters to fulfill future political duties. Athletes and Fighters both are small and lean.

Fighters have less stamina than Athletes but greater fine motor control, process and react faster, and are ambidextrous. They're unable to digest animal proteins.

 Healers control the energy inside of living things. They expertly manipulate cells and encourage them to die or grow. Reading living energy allows them to "see" what's going on inside organisms and what has happened to the body.

Energists control and manipulate the naturally existing energy around them. Though they can access living energy, they risk killing the creature they pull the energy from. They're born without hair pigment.

 Artists stimulate and maipulate brains through visual stimulation using images, movement, and sculpture they create. Their art carries their intended messages to the viewer regardless of how abstract the idea or differences between viewers.

Weavers stimulate and manipulate brains through auditory stimulation. By telling stories and creating music, they seemingly alter reality for the hearer. A Weaver's voice triggers this stimulation unless they consciously choose not to. They're born with vitiligo.

 Thinkers' minds constantly work to understand the world around them to the deepest detail. Though Thinkers try to focus on one specific interest or two, they'll study and contemplate anything that grabbs their attention. Nothing bothers them more than not being able to understand.

Tinkerers are driven to use their knowledge to create. Their minds have an uncanny ability to easily figure out and understand what's needed to bring their ideas to life, but they have difficultly processing the world outside their head. They're born with unusual eyes.

 Telepaths constantly experience the minds of those nearby, making their brains more resilient against illness. They process mental stimuli at superhuman levels while engaged in everyday activities. With effort, they can access deeper parts of a person's mind and can even force simple commands.

Mind Talkers choose to access another's mind and can reach forgotten and hiddend parts. They can easily manipulate and control a mind they've accessed. They're born with hypotrichosis.

Languages:

Common – Generally used by the majority of the world

Oŭndo (Ō-ōon-dō) – Considered an extinct language; origin unknown

𝒴uchio (Yōo-chi-ō) – The Grassland's traditional language

𝓔lemental voice – regardless of the language spoken the hearer can always understand.

Titles:

Dinta (**Din**-tä) – North Oueshi "lesser prince"

Nuwa (**Nōo**-wä) – East Azuté "queen"

Nu (**Nōo**) – East Azuté "king"

Zi (**Zē**) – East Azuté "prince"

Inoa (E-**nō**-ä) – West Kidico "general's daughter"

Mwã-tonô (Mwä-**tō**-nō) – Unknown origin "heir of Tonō"

Tonō (**Tō**-nō) – Unknown origin – a name from legend

Kōjomã̀ (**Kō**-jō-mä) – Unknown origin – means nothing nice

Jinku (**Jin**-Kōo) – Oŭndo for trainee or heir

Kalj (**Kal**-j) – Heir to the Emperor of Kidico

Rã-yŭmon (**Rä**-yōo-män) – A title Oya refuses to claim

Chapter 1

Everything's dying...

First the people...

Now the land...

How badly have I cursed this world?

Hearing Madam Aguilla's report was bitter. How could so much land be dying?

"Dinner's..." Jon trailed off when boney hands gestured silence.

It hasn't been an hour... "Thank you. Please continue sending data – I'll make adjustments as needed."

"Thank you for serving in light of the Duke's absence." Age framed her warm smile.

"Apply the treatments monthly..." Ferdinan felt his ally's interest pique. *Go away.*

"Is something wrong?"

Startled, the skeleton continued, "Don't touch the fields in the south or west 'til the northern ones are producing again."

Jon's complete attention radiated at him...

Go away!

Madam Aguilla considered his words for a moment, "Why?"

"Treatments feed off the contaminants. Once clean, nourish the land for a full year. Till in the first harvest. I'll analyze samples and make adjustments 'til the harvests are determined safe to eat."

Lines dug deep across her forehead. "Two years if not more?"

"I'm sorry it's not faster." Frustration warmed nearly transparent blue eyes, forcing them downward. "It's the best I can do."

"A few years' struggle is better than dying out completely."

"Yes, Madam Aguilla." Ferdinan bowed deeply to the woman. "If there are any troubles I'll come straight away."

"Thank you, Lord Ferdinan. You're a good child."

Bitterness twisted Ferdinan's gut. *No. I'm not.*

At least this time he recognized what he saw immediately. *It's too similar to that virus...* One mutation could cause another plague. *I need to be extra cautious. More death... I can't... Not again...*

Straightening, Ferdinan gave a proper farewell and braced himself to deal with his curious ally.

"Dinner," Jon tried again. "You know Yuchio?"

Why wouldn't I? Letting out a slow breath, the skeleton walked over to the small table furnishing the cabin.

"That makes seven."

"Seven?"

"Languages. Yuchio isn't one you've reported knowing."

Not wanting another argument, Ferdinan shrugged. There were bigger worries troubling him. *What did Jon tell his family? What'll they do?* A few more hours left and he didn't know what to expect.

"'Aguilla' is an Oueshian name."

A deep ache consumed his temples. "As are 'Ozar' and 'Rigel.'"

Annoyed, Jon slid a bread plate and soup bowl over.

Despite his stomach's demands, the vegetable goulash looked unappetizing. *This would've been better raw...*

"Warm or cold, you're eating it."

Ugh... Opening the bottom compartment of his mint tin, Ferdinan swallowed a pill – ignoring Jon and his screaming muscles.

"Every day..." Jon squared his shoulders. "What are those?"

"Does it matter since I'm cooperating?"

"Yes," Jon pressed, "'cause despite feeding you, you look worse."

"There's no point eating if I get sick."

The two stared at each other. Jon looked like he was sorting through a million pieces of an unknown puzzle. While Ferdinan's perfectly crafted mask insisted his lie was truth.

"Ok." Jon pointed at the screen. "What was that about?"

"What was what about?" Boney hands grabbed the roll and tapped it against the plate - fighting the urge to cram it in his mouth.

Jon rolled up the sleeves of his silk tunic. "Soil treatments?"

"It doesn't concern you."

Jaw twitching, Jon struggled to ignore Ferdinan tearing the bread into crumbs. "If it affects my neighbors-"

"She doesn't live in Oueshi," Ferdinan rolled a piece of torn bread between two fingers - teasing himself with it. Making himself wait. Practicing the self-control that'd be crucial at Jon's estate.

"Yuchio's the Grassland's language. As their neighbor-"

"She doesn't live in Oueshi." *Stop. Last time you pushed, it nearly broke you.*

Pursing his lips to the side, Jon leaned forward. "Then where?"

"Not in Oueshi." Ferdinan's expression darkened - annoyed and grateful the Dinta hadn't memorized his allies' extended households. Dropping the tiny bread ball, the skeleton stood. He needed to move, but there was nowhere to run on the boat. Sharing a cabin... He couldn't even do drills. *Leave me alone!*

Dread set in. *Calm down. Stay in control.* In a couple of hours he'd be trapped with the entire Artimus family.

I can't do this... But he had to. He had to prove whatever Jon told his family was exaggerated.

If only he could go back to being ignored.

Back to before South Chūzo...

* * *

Sunlight kissed the water's edge, distorting the cliff face. Oya loved this climbing spot. The challenge and view were a perfect break from collecting connections. Intimate familiarity with her climbing wall was freedom itself - allowing her mind to run wild while her body moved. Even Humawit's animosity couldn't spoil it.

Though her holds randomly disappearing was particularly petty of the earth and impinged on the freedom climbing offered.

Soon I'll have no choice. Humawit, you promised me that long.

The crack her toes nestled in crumbled. Delicate hands held on. Was Û-ya'īn's rein here making things worse with the earth?

Lighted orbs moved closer. They had nothing to do with the setting sun, rising moon, or twinkling stars.

But without them...

Alien green eyes studied the woven lighted strands wrapped around her palm. It'd grown into an impressive cord, but was far from the thick rope she'd end up collecting.

Yuyu, Herrard, and Zephyr are taken care of. My dear friend was whisked away to the land of Giants. Three and a half weeks undisturbed... Can I do it? Can I get it done? Maybe...

Bare feet searched for another purchase while her mind replayed the oddity of last night's session... The layout was changing.

Or maybe she needed a break. Hour after hour of the same task... But... The change felt deliberate – orchestrated.

Crazed green eyes turned to the star strewn sky. It was amazing. Long minutes passed admiring the twinkling dots. And a small ache pricked at her heart. Then Humawit took away a handhold.

Protesting won't... I don't have the reserves you do.

Which was the problem. Oya wasn't sleepy or physically exhausted. Her very soul was tired. What little was left of it...

Winking to the glowing orbs, her free hand slid down the flying goggles sitting atop her head. No point making Humawit angrier. And right when the ledge was finally in sight... *I'm getting slower.*

Pushing off the rock face, she allowed herself to drop. The freefall was exhilarating! And it ended too soon. Activating the cuffs, she adjusted to fly feet above the water. Rocketing into the sky...!

Û-ya'īn didn't follow. Didn't leap up. Didn't play.

And it was bitter.

But her old friend was doing what she asked. And Yuyu held its transfer. Û-ya'īn would come if she called... Would obey if she forced her will and demanded it. But that'd take more strength than she currently had. Then she'd possibly have again.

4

Which Humawit realized... *What does that ultimately mean?* Flying to the top of the cliff, she was greeted by an unexpected sight.

A boy her age with darkly tanned, reddish skin and angular features stood – dark eyes wide in terror. *Why are you out this far? And all alone...? Hm...you look familiar. How do I know you?* Waving... He gasped and jumped back, fear tripling. *Odd...*

Playing with him was tempting. But she was tired, so she flew to Ferdinan's island and sat on the beach. *"Are you well, old friend?"*

Small waves danced among the rocks below. Sorrow filled her but she grinned. Û-ya'īn was right there. She wasn't losing it yet.

But one day... Each Charge deserved a keeper. Each needed one. And she needed time to let go.

"Keep having fun with Yuyu. And thank you."

* * *

It was Xhou's fault things were awkward between him and Herrard, but he couldn't do what the Healer wanted. Still, he had to do something and Jon's request seemed perfect. Breathing in deep, Xhou readied a cheery greeting and entered the common room.

"You woke up screaming again."

Startled, but unphased, the Zi gave a light chuckle. "That was hardly a scream. Besides, who isn't having nightmares?"

Herrard looked up, "telling Master Loucé about them will help."

Silence lingered too long, amplifying the awkward strain. "Um..."

The weight of sincerity in those light brown eyes crushed him. *I don't need Master Loucé. Ferdinan learned to smile – to play – after experiencing all that. I will too.* He'd become whole and useful again.

Everything he needed to be; he'd become it.

Everything he needed to do; he'd do it.

Because if Ferdinan could heal on his own, so could Xhou. "Jon asked for my help. I'm not sure how much I can do...so..."

Herrard held up a hand. "You missed a step."

What didn't I say? "Sorry. Um... Jon asked me to keep Oya entertained over break. Said Ilu couldn't handle a month of teasing."

"Ah." Herrard hid a smirk behind his hand. "He's only complained about her once this break."

"It only started."

"Fair." The Healer stretched. "Need help with home or Oya?"

"Oya. There isn't much you can do for my country." That last statement earned Xhou a frown. "Please make sure she's invited to activities? And let me know if she's stressing Ilu too much?"

"Gladly."

Xhou sighed. *Why was that so stressful?* They often asked favors of each other. "If I knew how Ferdinan kept her easily occupied..."

Herrard flinched at the Tinkerer's name.

"Um... Her teasing can get intense – if it's too much..."

Long, light brown hair swayed as Herrard shook his head. "I don't understand why you two think so poorly of her."

"She worked me nearly to death, abducted me, flew me over open ocean, and dropped me face first on a random beach just to have a short chat. And to hear me scream, I'm sure."

A less than princely snort left Herrard. "She's only nice to me."

"Lucky."

"I'll gladly help with Oya." Once again, Herrard's expression turned serious. "No headache this morning?"

Xhou rolled his eyes. The daily check-up was a headache. "If I felt any better, I'd live forever."

Disappointment blanketed Herrard, but he didn't say anything.

How do I fix what I broke? "Everything's fine. Mom wouldn't let me help if not."

"Ok." Grabbing his screen, Herrard moved toward his room, stopping when he was shoulder to shoulder with Xhou. "I'll always listen. I'll help with everything I can."

"Thanks. I haven't forgotten."

Chapter 2

Adjusting the cuff of his silk shirt, Jon studied his reflection. "I did my duty. I kept him alive. It's my family's turn."

I'm selfish... But he was tired and didn't know what more to do.

If they can't help him, no one can. I'm done.

"I'm terrible." Jon sighed. He'd hurt his family if they knew he felt this way. But they hadn't dealt with the skeleton the last...!

It's been nearly a year... It felt like ten. And...

There was something Jon couldn't figure out. Ferdinan was on edge – constantly holding himself back. Irritation and frustration were driving the gent toward something. But what? What was he hiding?

How badly was he going to devolve?

And those pills... The skeleton was lying about them. The ones for his stomach smelled of mint and Ferdinan took them randomly. But not those. He took one at the same time each day.

Blowing out a breath, Jon grabbed his bag. *Did he switch to a stronger medicine? Then...why does he look more grotesque?*

A chime announced it was time to disembark. *Finally...*

Deft hands adjusted his collar and smoothed his vest before combing through brown hair. It needed to be cut and thinned. Much longer and the curl would become prominent – and as unruly as Ferdinan's. *I hope they made an appointment for me at Terran's.*

Adjusting his bag, Jon stepped on deck. A salt breeze eased the sun's intensity. Ferdinan stood out sorely. And waiting below – dwarfing everyone else – were two men. One was a head taller than most. The other was two. *Oya would love seeing this.*

The taller one waved. *I wish I could stay forever...*

Running, Jon leapt into Ozar's arms. "I've missed you so much!"

"We've missed you too." Ozar squeezed his baby brother while Samuel approached the pale, shaking Ferdinan. "Will he ever stop being afraid of Samuel?"

"I don't know." *I don't care.* Samuel was there. Right there. *Samuel will take care of him. Samuel can take care of him.*

Whatever fears ruled the bizarre skeleton, whatever drove the Tinkerer's unfathomable behavior...it didn't matter. Not to him. Not now. His family could care for the gent now. Squeezing Ozar as hard as he could, Jon buried his face in his brother's shoulder.

Nothing mattered. Jon had his family now. Soon he'd tell mom everything. Everything Ferdinan did. Everything that happened. That terrified him. That made him feel worthless. Useless...

Soon.

But not right away. And it made him angry.

He understood. But...he had needs too. Needs which always took second place. Always second to the inconsequential nephew of an ally. Uncomfortable heat flared through his chest.

Jon knew he should feel bad thinking that. But he didn't. He was angry – bitter. Ferdinan stole his family time since that first visit.

Focus on fun and relaxing 'til we get home. I was told to...

He batted away the tears blurring his vision before Ozar noticed and took his older brother's hand.

Watching Samuel struggle to coax Ferdinan down the plank sparked guilt – cooling the fire.

He put his ally in that position. Ozar always greeted him and Jon needed Ozar's welcome. Which left Samuel approaching before the gent could prepare for time near a Healer. *Can he handle the car ride? And...why send Samuel? I know I was vague...and what happened last time. But why not Jingjing or Bastian?*

Comfort vanished when Ozar approached Ferdinan. A massive hand reached for their ally, but the skeleton backed away and bowed.

Sorrow tinged the Hei-O's smile. "Best not keep them waiting."

Jon's smile wasn't happy either. It was filled with years of animosity the gent earned.

No time was wasted slipping into the car and cuddling with his brothers – soaking in their warmth. He held them tightly for two hours until the car stopped in front of a huge, fancy building.

This wasn't home – but it was the next best place. Seeing the full might and glory of the bright, inviting sign filled Jon with comfort.

Neither did he let Ferdinan's confusion and nervous twitching steal his relief. Berago's was joy and love and excitement. He didn't care how uncomfortable Ferdinan was, because he loved it here. The gent wouldn't take this away from him too.

Annoyed, Jon gestured for his ally to hurry out of the car, but was greeted with an expression he couldn't interpret. And it didn't matter. Ferdinan was going inside, regardless of the gent's wishes.

Visibly steeling himself, the skeleton climbed out – keeping his distance. Blue crystals looked to Jon for...something...

"You need new clothes." Jon took Ozar's hand and started toward the entrance.

~

Tall doors opened wide. A pleasant scent greeted them. And Jon smiled. His hand felt tiny wrapped in his big brother's long fingers. Samuel's hand rested on his shoulder. Feeling small was wonderful.

Why do I feel like crying? He was home. He didn't have to keep struggling for the impossible. He didn't have to do anything.

But he wasn't happy.

Looking back... Ferdinan loitered near the entrance – blue crystals focused on terribly worn, too small shoes. The hems of his tattered slacks were unforgivably frayed and didn't cover his knobby ankles. And the shirts Jon gave him shortly after the fire... A few months and they were already too small in the shoulders and sleeves.

Ozar cleared his throat.

Sweat broke out across Ferdinan's skin. Every piece of ill-fitted clothing squeezed tight. Shoulders strained against seams barely holding together... Every piece was a disgrace.

"Are you ok?"

Startled, the gent stepped back. "I'll wait outside."

"I doubt you'll find another shop able to fit you. Even Rigel struggles finding pants long enough."

Blue crystals darted away from Ozar's gaze.

9

"The owner's a close friend. He's prepared every courtesy." Ozar frowned when Ferdinan started trembling. "Besides, Evelyn personally designed some outfits for you."

Nearly non-existent lips twitched. Conflicting desires flashed across Ferdinan's face. And those broad, bony shoulders slumped. Letting out a slow, controlled breath, the gent nodded.

Is there anything he won't do for her?

A joyous squeal greeted them. Jon turned to see a small man hugging Ozar's middle. Or small next to his brother. The Hei-O laughed and returned it before offering the traditional greeting.

Leoniel Kyo was a staple in Jon's life and always like this. Joyful. Energetic. Affectionate. And dripping with color. Today he hosted lavender hair and a shiny sky-blue suit. A yellow vest shined under the jacket – complementing the exceptionally poofy cravat. Ring laden fingers waved in a grand gesture before greeting each of them.

Except for Ferdinan – who hid behind Jon.

Concern flashed across Leoniel's face, but the Kyo gave his sweetest smile and disregarded Ferdinan's apology. Excitement beamed from every pore. "Ozar! Who's this adorable child?"

The Hei-O laughed. "Ferdinan Samultz. Only son of North Chūzo's main branch family and our little brother."

Ferdinan couldn't look more uncomfortable, yet Jon decided to be mean. "Don't forget, this cutie's also Evelyn's big brother."

Lavender hair bobbed. Ringed fingers took Ferdinan's hand and bowed deeply. "My name's Leoniel. I'm honored to serve you."

All color left the skeleton. Terror flashed across colorless eyes. It looked as though the gent couldn't breathe. Couldn't move.

He'd never seen Ferdinan react like that. Before Jon could step between them, Leoniel released that bony hand and straightened.

The Kyo smiled brightly – until he saw Ferdinan's panic.

Panting. Gasping. The skeleton fought for air – moving back until a wall stopped him. "You don't..."

"Are you ok, dear?" Leoniel smiled gently at the sick child.

Ferdinan bowed, "I'm sorry... I apologize. I'm tired..."

"Ah, you are precious!" Dark eyes and lavender hair bowed forward. "As expected of the Oza's beloved big brother."

Bright red and shaking, Ferdinan moved to use Jon as a shield.

Guilt twisted the Thinker's insides. *I shouldn't have been mean.*

Their colorful host pushed back the cuff of his sleeve, revealing a bejeweled gold band. Pressing a gem summoned three tailors. The two tallest greeted Ozar and Samuel then escorted them away, leaving Leoniel and the beautiful Rinie. Straight, black hair fell to her waist, emphasizing her swollen belly.

Her child's grown so much since last break! Jon smiled - head lowering to her. *Next time I'll be able to see it.*

"Rinie, Jon's yours," Leoniel instructed, "I'll help the Oza."

"Oza?" Ferdinan stumbled backward.

"What else would I call Evelyn Oza's hero?" Leoniel giggled.

Blue crystals looked away. "I'm a lesser Lord."

Jon looked at Leoniel and shook his head.

"I apologize, Lord Ferdinan. This way, please."

"Thank you." Boney fingers grasped stick arms and Ferdinan's gaze locked on to worn shoes once again.

Leoniel escorted them to a row of rooms and opened a door for the skeleton. Rinie tried doing the same, but Jon got it first.

The tuxedo fit perfectly. And the fabric - exquisite. It was impossibly soft. Exactly what you want against your skin. And it draped perfectly - giving in all the right places for comfort and unrestricted movement. It was the epitome of luxury and comfort.

Jon looked great. The best he'd ever looked. "I'm ready."

The curtain parted and Rinie entered - screen and bowtie in hand. She looked him over before taking a few notes. Adjusting the collar, she slipped the bowtie around his neck and knotted it beautifully. "How does it feel?"

"Perfect." Jon smiled, admiring himself in the mirror. It was a handsome suit. Long fingers ran through brown hair. "Once I get this tamed, I'll match."

"That's already been arranged. When you're finished, you'll be taken to Terran's."

Rinie did a few checks before telling him to take it off and dress again. He didn't want to. The suit was as comfortable as a mother's hug and he *really* liked how he looked in it. Slipping back into his travel clothes, he stepped out of the fitting room.

Choosing the most comfortable chair for Rinie, they caught up while waiting for the other two. Talking to her was always wonderful. Her smile put him at ease. But... *She's so small...* When did she stop feeling larger-than-life? When did she become so delicate?

Slightly swollen fingers rubbed her belly. Delicate. And energetic and lovely. Rich skin glowed – reminding him of Oya. But not her face. It was sweet and sincere. The opposite of crazed. And her dark eyes looked like a mother's should. Exactly like his own mom's.

"How soon 'til you see your child?" Jon reached a hand to her belly, but stopped. Touching the unborn without permission was disrespectful. But...he'd always wanted to know what it felt like. Knowing a child before you see it...

Her warm hand took his – tiny next to his own. "Would you like to meet him?"

"May I?" Jon's breath quickened and he bowed lower.

Smiling sweetly, she placed his hand to the side of her belly.

Something *thumped* against it. "Whoa! Wow!"

"You feel his little foot?"

Enthralled, he could do little more than smile. It was astounding. Her belly was warm and he felt her child moving. "Hello, I'm Jon. I look forward to meeting you."

There was a *bump* a little higher than the kick, but his long fingers still felt it. *He's saying hi back! This is amazing...* He felt euphoric. *Women really are the closest beings to a god...* "Thank you for sharing your child."

Jon's hand lingered while Rinie giggled. "I'm happy sharing my miracle with my adorable nephew."

Red flooded Jon's cheeks.

~

A *crash* interrupted their relaxing reunion. "What was that?"

Worry creased Rinie's brow. "Something shattered..."

What's he doing now? Jon should go, but he didn't want to. This wasn't his responsibility for three weeks. But... "I'll check-"

"Give them a minute," she squeezed his hand. "Ozar requested special accommodations for him."

That's why no one approached 'til Leoniel summoned them. Normally a dozen employees would dote on him until he was ready to be fitted... *How does he steal everything?*

Soon Leoniel escorted Ferdinan to the next dressing room over. Only, the Kyo didn't stay long. Door secured behind him, he turned a concerned smile to Jon. "Is he usually easily startled?"

"Sometimes..."

Nodding, Leoniel pushed a gem on his gold bracelet and called for someone to clean up a shattered mirror.

He broke a mirror? No. This isn't my responsibility anymore.

Rinie stood. "Is everything ok?"

"I scared him. Not sure how..." Leoniel frowned, worried.

A cold chill ran down Jon's spine. *They told him? Right? What else would those "accommodations" be for?* But... "Leoniel?"

"Yes, dear?" Turning on his heels, the man smiled brightly.

"You were told...how he looks?" Jon squirmed.

"Ozar explained the boy's situation." The Kyo squeezed Jon - easing his anxiety before mussing his hair. It was odd now that the man was shorter, but just as wonderful. "You normally don't let it get this long. I can have Enbert call Kiswala."

"I have an appointment."

"Wonderful!"

They chatted until the door opened. The fidgeting skeleton stood drowning in an obnoxiously large tuxedo shirt. Bony hands clutched at the pants to keep them from falling.

Horrified awe coated Jon. Ferdinan's suit looked as if a bolt of fabric was draped over the gent. Even buttoned, the collar hung down, revealing protruding bones and melted skin.

"It's huge..." *I'm never getting him to a healthy weight...*

Bright red, that skeletal face turned to the floor.

"Ah! You're ready," Leoniel jumped in, bright and smiley as always. "If you'll step back inside."

Shiny white shoes *clicked* over to the Tinkerer and colorful tuffs fluttered toward the dressing room.

Ferdinan's entire body cringed and he squeezed his eyes closed.

He always flinches when people touch him. But his reaction to Leoniel was more extreme. *Someone's been beating him...* But there was no one as colorful or comfortable with themselves as Leoniel. Neither did he look like anyone from the islands or Samultz family...

A soft sob drew his attention to Rinie. She excused herself, but not before her tear-filled eyes crushed Ferdinan with misery.

"Jon, dear, does any part of your suit need adjustment?"

It's amazing how easily he ignores and smooths over everything. I wish I had that talent. "Thank you, Kyo. It fits perfectly."

"Wonderful!" The indomitable man turned back to an incredibly pale Ferdinan, "Let's get you fitted properly."

Flinching, Ferdinan nodded – looking more miserable.

"Would you like Jon to join us?"

A small gasp left the gent, but the moment those blue crystals connected with chocolate brown, he looked down and shook his head. "No. Thank you, Kyo."

"I understand."

"Thank you..."

The door closed – leaving Jon wishing Ferdinan said "yes." *This is my break...so why...?*

Chapter 3

"That's a...generous...offer." The Duchess's eldest daughter studied Xhou's message. "Taking mouths away *and* providing food and various concessions... What are they getting in return?"

The lean, immaculately groomed Duchess nodded at her eldest's suspicion. "Unfortunately, we don't have much room for misgiving."

"You are right, but I still agree with Emelica."

A weary but pleased smile shaped the Duchess's lips. "And how would you advise your older sister, Kannani?"

"With the Duke...indisposed...and the only viable remedy to this blight being a multi-year operation..." Kannani sat back considering the choices. "'No' isn't an option, but we should leverage their own needs against them to test their sincerity."

"Agreed." Emelica nodded to her sister.

"How would you leverage their needs?" The Duchess prompted.

"If we secure the greatest percentage of transplants, we can sway ideological differences and finally establish a treatise with Azuté – opening our General to resources we've struggled for. Easing the generations-long strain would benefit us both as well."

"I was thinking the same." Emelica leaned forward, "But how do we obtain the highest percentage of transplants?"

"Research." Standing, the Duchess smiled at her daughters. "Kannani, consult with the Minister of Agricultural Resources. Determine the population we can sustain with Aguilla's projections."

"Yes, Ma'am."

"Emelica, contact Captain Tillelee. Figure out how many people East Azuté'll need to secure world food supplies and how many transplants other countries are likely to provide." Grabbing one of the little nutrition bars her household was living off of, she eyed it. The food substitute wasn't terrible, but she missed fresh produce. "I'll get what details and promises from the future Nu I can while you gather and analyze that information. We'll finalize our plan then."

The younger women nodded, stood, and bowed to their mother.

"Being weary of remarkably good offers is important, but always consider the other party's position. East Azuté's desperate. This offer is urgently needed for us, but how much more so for them? Neither was the future Nu groomed for these kinds of negotiations." Putting the bar down, she smiled. "Suspicion shouldn't drive our demands beyond what they can concede or both our peoples will suffer."

Again, the two younger women bowed, "Yes, Ma'am."

* * *

After the excruciating fitting, and turning down a haircut, they were finally done. It was late. Ferdinan's muscles begged to run, to fight, but they were hours from the Artimus estate. And... *This doesn't look familiar...* "Um... Where are we?"

Ozar smiled. "Leoniel Kyo invited us to dine at his estate."

All color drained from Ferdinan. *Dine...? How do I act? What do I do?* There were currently only three Kyo's in the world. Meeting one wasn't something Ferdinan was prepared for. How did he treat a person who earned a rank above "Master" and even "Lashi?" Someone who wasn't only the best at their craft, but used their success to enact positive change worldwide? Kyo's were what Ferdinan wished he was capable of being.

And this Kyo... Leoniel's effortless confidence and complete comfort with himself was beyond Ferdinan's experiences. It was admirable and amazing...and disconcerting. And it made this situation more overwhelming. *What's it like expressing such confidence? Joy? How am I not offensive to him?*

"You understand the honor due to a Kyo."

"Yes, sir." A massive hand mussed Ferdinan's messy hair.

"Don't call me 'sir,' little brother."

"I apologize, Hei-O." Ferdinan looked away when Ozar sighed.

Jon snuggled closer against the giant – pretending to sleep.

How does he do that? The display was normal for an Oueshian, but it disgusted Ferdinan. Feeling that way was wrong. But every time Jon was so affectionate... At least Samuel left early.

I'm a terrible person.

16

The road curved up to a gated bridge. And beyond that...

The entry to Leoniel's properties was as ostentatious as Berago's. And nearly as colorful. Every variety of flower covered lavish homes, growing in opulence as they neared the main estate buildings. Roads branched out behind the village - leading to beautiful orchards on one side and well-tended farm lands on the other.

The car continued uphill. Perfectly trimmed hedges joined an intricately cultivated gate of smooth vines and flowering fruits.

The main home was beyond description. Taken with everything leading to it Ferdinan couldn't help but wonder how this came to be. *He built all this from nothing...* Considering the man's title, he wouldn't be surprised if this lavish village was home to refugees and those needing sanctuary. *How many is he helping with this place?*

However, the excess was unnecessary. Providing safety and comfort was vital to human needs, but a few small changes could help countless more. Replacing flowering walls with producing ones. Transitioning excess rooms to green houses. Replacing exterior lighting with bioluminescent algae sculptures...

I've no right judging another by my standards.

But lean years were looming. His gut twisted. Ferdinan grabbed a pill from the top of his green tin - filling him and the compartment with mint.

Sitting up, Jon smoothed his vest, "Stomach still bothering you?"

"I'll be fine."

"Are you sure?" Ozar's deep voice reverberated through the car.

Ferdinan nodded - but they didn't believe him.

Leoniel greeted the brothers - respecting when Ferdinan stepped away. Rude or not, he never wanted to feel the Kyo's touch again.

Leoniel's welcome was spectacular. From the greeting to the decor to the meal, everything was exquisite - designed to cater to any possible guest. Lighting and colors. Walls, floors, paintings. Even the ceilings were constructed to elicit joy and a sense of familiarity. Both Ozar and Jon relaxed. But not Ferdinan. Compared to his sterile, uncluttered lab, this place was chaos. It felt...oppressive.

Even the dining ware's design matched the feel of the estate.

17

The first round was a cream soup. White with white lumps of something and specks of greens, yellows, and reds. His stomach complained. *Behave. Stay in control. Don't embarrass my country's strongest ally and inconvenience a Kyo.*

Ozar leaned over and whispered – interrupting his thoughts. "Your plates were prepared separately."

"That doesn't make it edible..." Red consumed Ferdinan's face. It was too creamy to be safe. But... *What do I do?*

Returning his attention to their host, Ozar chatted casually as if he said nothing. But moments later, the soup was replaced with a colorful bowl. Dozens of different vegetables lightly sprayed with lime were accompanied by a soft bread of unusual grain.

Ferdinan was left to massacre the bread and vegetables at his pace while the others enjoyed various dishes. What few bites he took were delicious. The rest was left torn or cut into countless pieces.

Dinner became an invitation to stay the night – one Ozar accepted gladly. Ferdinan smiled, but was horrified. Surviving a meal was difficult. Now he had to behave through breakfast.

Servants escorted him and Jon to a guestroom. Pajamas were laid out and travel clothes hung smartly for both of them. There were also a couple piles of folded fabric next to two new luggage bags.

What's this? "Can we...?"

A smile danced on Jon's lips as he inspected the piles of fabric waiting at the edge of the bed. "That stack's yours. Can we what?"

Mine? Ferdinan looked at the blue and gray pile of simple shirts. Behind it were a couple pairs of charcoal slacks and thrice as many button shirts neatly folded on top. *How long are we staying here?!*

"Ozar told him to make them loose since you don't like fitted clothing." Jon moved to the box on the side bench and opened it.

"I didn't ask for this."

Whatever was inside, his ally looked and returned the lid. "You needed clothes. Now you have them."

"I'm perfectly capable–"

Jon waved his hand dismissively. "That's beside the point."

Silence fell. Not wanting to argue, Ferdinan moved to the window and focused on the darkening sky.

"At Leoniel's shop..."

Ferdinan cringed. "I'm sorry. I didn't apologize to Ms. Rinie."

"What?"

"I hurt her...but couldn't find her to apologize..." Bony fingers picked at his frayed cuff. *I should've realized my skin was exposed... Why was I given consideration? Invited here? Presented with gifts? After hurting someone in his employ? Just existing I hurt people...*

Stinging needles enveloped his arm and he jerked away.

"You didn't hurt her."

"Yes, I did."

"Leoniel wouldn't have finished your fitting if you had." Jon moved closer – frustration twisting his face. "You didn't hurt her."

"I saw..." The horror...disgust... He was so revolting she ran.

"Ferdinan..." Jon grabbed his shoulders. "*You* were the one hurt. Knowing a child suffered like that was more than she could bare."

"I haven't suffered." *I've only caused suffering. You know that!* Ferdinan brushed away the stinging needles.

"Any mother would weep to see what you've been through. I can't imagine what your own mother will feel when she sees you."

Something hot and bitter burned inside him. "I'm tired."

Jaw set, Jon tried again. "Seeing any child with burned and twisted skin would hurt. You didn't hurt her. She hurt for you."

I caused her that pain. I hurt her.

* * *

"Haha! I win!" Pink eyes glowed in triumph as Yuyu demolished her father's power cell.

"Ah! Already?" Animated hands grabbed his head in defeat, but her dad's smile was proud. "My days of winning are over..."

She giggled – one hand playing with the little toy Herrard gave her. "You're at a natural disadvantage."

19

"True." He smiled and reset the game.

Yuyu took her dad's hand. Clouds enveloped her fingers – swirling up her arm to consume her. Dad's touch wasn't painful but disconcerting. It was like she never actually felt him, just a cool mist on her skin. It was nice not hurting, but she wished he felt substantial. Real... Smiling, they chatted until mom entered.

"Looks like my break's over. Beat your mom and I'll be impressed." He hugged his wife and left.

Mom offered a hand. Bracing herself, Yuyu took it. Unlike dad, mom felt like her. Like burning cold eating through your skin. It wasn't pleasant, but there was a twisted kind of comfort in it.

"What would you like to do?" Yuyu grimaced. Silence stretched on, but Yuyu was patient. Her mom would answer when ready.

"A walk?"

"I'd love that!" Yuyu guided her outside to a nearby lagoon.

They splashed their feet in the shallow pools. Yuyu rambled happily, stopping occasionally for her mother to speak. It was nice.

Û-ya'ïn behaved itself while they were there. Unlike with Elbie. It'd gladly tease her and chase them both up the beach. But her island brother never considered it strange. *Elbie... How many of his suitemate stayed? I should invite him to dinner with us.*

"Tomorrow..."

Yuyu turned pink eyes to her mother's identical ones and waited – smiling brightly.

"Project..."

"Really?! You've finished? I get to see it now?"

Her mother laughed and nodded.

"Thank you!" Yuyu spun the little ball and kicked at the water. In retaliation, Û-ya'ïn leapt into the wall of rocks - hitting them with a spray of mist. "Um... Can Elbie see too? I know he'd love it."

Yuyu waited for words to reach her mother's tongue. "Yes."

Chapter 4

A few more hours.

That was all.

Four days. And Zephyr only succeeded in wearing a path in the cabin's floorboards.

What do I do?

What do I do?

What do I do?

Those words circled around his mind – but no answer came. Dodging Aunt Tenalia concerning Ferdinan was manageable. But knowing what he was... How did he face his family? *Mom returned from the Grasslands...she'll be extra loving...* But he didn't deserve her love... And he didn't think he could handle it.

Knowing when to stay silent... This had to be it. Admitting his guilt would crush his mother – mothers – and strain their family more. But how did he keep the monster he was hidden? Now that he knew? Would his masked reflection fool them like before?

But...how could it? He didn't know before. The mask wasn't created to fool others. It was made to keep himself blind.

What do I do?

She might know... Zephyr shook his head. How broken was he? Turning to a figment of his imagination? But...

Laying down, he closed his eyes and walked the silver roads.

"You look troubled." The elf woman's annoying smirk greeted him when he stepped upon the twilight beach.

Golden hands moved desperately. "I'm almost home, but I don't know what to do."

"You came to me?"

"Yes." Pointing one golden finger forward, Zephyr brought his hand down.

"Why?" Leaning back, the elf readied herself to be entertained.

"I'm so ugly. I don't want them seeing my ugliness." A golden finger sliced across his face before pointing at his diaphragm.

"You're not ugly."

"How can you say that?"

"You *aren't* ugly, Zephyr." Sapphire eyes turned to the ink ocean. "Pain isn't ugly - it's simply hard to look at."

"You watched every memory! You saw what came out of the mirrors! We both know how ugly I am!" Sitting, Zephyr drew his legs to his chest, but his hands kept guiding his tongue. "I don't want my family seeing me - seeing how horrible I am."

Silence fell and settled in.

Both gazed at where the ink ocean met the starless sky. Though he needed a response, the silence was strangely comforting. And that comfort stayed for some time before the elf spoke.

"Reliving it taught you nothing? It brought no understanding? No realizations? No truth?"

"I don't understand." The Prince tapped his ring finger to his temple. "What truths?"

"I'll give you one. The others, I'll let you figure out."

"But if you know-"

"You need to learn to understand yourself. That won't happen if I give you the answers."

Use those truths to torment me! You'd be happy and it'd feel better than this... Placing a thumb to his forehead, Zephyr moved it forward while bowing his head. He then tapped his ear and cheek before pointing to her. "I'm sorry. I'm listening."

"You created the two who came out of the mirrors. You created them to protect your soul. They weren't originally there."

His hands portrayed the confusion he felt. "How? Why?"

"Humans are amazing creatures. When something's too painful - too overwhelming - you create a new existence where those things can't touch you." The elf smirked and laid back, "What else could you have done but created them? You were merely a toddler when he was born and still sleeping with your parents when you met him."

His hands flew. "I tried. For years I tried. I was older when I gave up. I was old enough to do something...to help." *I'm a disgrace. To my family, country, position. I gave up when I finally had the power to do something! I thought you understood that...*

"The anger you felt at...at what no one else saw... It was justified. Normal. Understandable. But that doesn't mean a child could handle it. Tearing it from yourself and hiding it away was how you protected yourself from things you couldn't understand or do anything about."

"There's no excuse for my sins!" His hands flew.

"Your pain from what happened – from being powerless to stop it – cut so deep you tore it away, blinded yourself to it. That part even renamed it so you still don't have to see it for what it is."

Palm down, Zephyr sliced away from his body. "No. That's–"

"And it got worse 'til you couldn't face any of it. So you tore another part of yourself away. That part lashed out in the only way you'd been taught to handle threats. *It* took care of the threat. *It* veiled your mind so you didn't have to remember."

"No. I let myself forget so I could feel like a good person."

"Those two parts were created to protect yourself – your soul – from something you couldn't do anything about."

"No! I made it all worse!" His hands pleaded for her to listen.

"And you're still powerless to help." Standing, the elf looked down at him. "Your mother taught you family's the most important. Family's the core and central to human existence. Your aunt taught you your duty was to serve and protect those in your care – everyone below you. But for your cousin, all you can do is watch the suffering."

"'Cause I caused it. *I* did all of it. It's unforgiveable..."

She knelt beside him. "Zephyr–"

"Nothing can change my sin!"

"True." A twisted grin marred the elf's face. "But what you choose from here can make amends. Even heal a couple souls."

His hands moved, but it took a moment for his mouth to catch up. "How can I change if they see these parts of me?"

"Now that you know they're there?"

23

Zephyr nodded. "Please."

"Those who know you. Care for you. Love you. They'll see the pain you now feel."

"What can I do?"

"Stop hurting."

"If it was that easy, I wouldn't be here!" Zephyr's whole body shouted his frustration with this conversation.

"You finally admit you're in pain."

This silenced the Prince. He had no right to hurt, but he did. Constantly his chest ached with an unappeasable tightness.

"How do you overcome pain and sorrow?"

Looking up, Zephyr locked on to sapphire eyes. That question was dead serious. *How?*

"Wake up and be happy to greet your loved ones." With a smirk, the elf waved a hand and Zephyr jolted awake.

* * *

Breakfast was delicious. Whoever Leoniel employed in his kitchen rivaled Jon's dad in skill and creativity.

Happiness radiated from every inch of the Kyo's estate. The brightness, colors, and intricate designs personified joy. Sitting there eating – Ozar and Leoniel reminiscing and teasing... This wasn't home, but it offered a needed break.

Until it ended...

I hope he's ready... They had a schedule to keep. Ferdinan was up and reading long before a servant came to wake them. But the gent insisted he wasn't well enough for breakfast. And Jon didn't press. *Should I have Ozar get him? I don't want to deal with him...*

Guilt conflicted with his need to escape the gent. *A few hours. A few hours and I'll get my real break.* Letting out a long, controlled breath, Jon opened the bedroom door.

The growing skeleton still sat by the window but was gazing out at the view. A few screens lay scattered on the small table and another sat in his lap. *What's he working on now?* Ferdinan was meticulous

24

about keeping his space clean and tidy – except while working – which always surprised Jon. It wasn't like the gent could do two things at once, so why have multiple screens scattered about?

And that wasn't the only strange thing. The mass of unruly hair Ferdinan refused to cut was tied back. A strip torn from an old shirt and folded into a makeshift tie held the top half of Ferdinan's hair. *Is he trying to look presentable to the Kyo?* Annoyance coated Jon. *Getting a haircut would've been easier.*

"Feeling well enough to leave?"

Surprised, Ferdinan turned, "We're leaving?"

"You don't want to?"

Blue crystals pleaded to escape, but Ferdinan's response was calm and controlled. "It seemed this was an extended visit."

"Leoniel's invitation was due to the late hour..."

Blushing, the skeleton walked over to the clothing gifted him. Boney hands carefully selected an undershirt, two long sleeved shirts, and a button up to add to the travel clothes already hanging.

Why does he wear so many shirts...?

Before undressing, Ferdinan grabbed tattered underwear and a pair of holey socks from his bag.

I didn't think of basic necessities... If the gent couldn't keep up a daily wardrobe... Chocolate brown eyes drifted to the worn shoes Ferdinan neatly stored next to the armoire. They were scratched and one of the sols was separating from the top because they were too small. The Thinker sighed. He ordered a couple new pairs. It was unlikely they'd find replacements for the gent before leaving. It never ended... *Why can't he take care of himself? He does everything else!*

All motion stopped as Ferdinan stared at the mirror – undershirt held loosely in skeletal fingers. Ribs splayed out far past the gent's sunken waist. Prominent hip bones barely kept up loose slacks.

Shaking his head, Jon took his vest from the hanger – startling the skeleton. Opening the box, he grabbed socks and a pair of shoes and handed them to Ferdinan.

"What...?"

"They're part of your new wardrobe."

Ferdinan paled and looked away.

Placing them on the chair beside the gent, Jon seized the old shoes. "I'm having these burned."

Surprisingly, Ferdinan didn't argue. He simply returned to his scarred and twisted reflection.

Jon preened while studying his ally. "What's wrong?"

Those nearly colorless crystals clouded over. The skeleton didn't respond. Just stood trapped in his own mind.

"Ferdinan?"

Clouded eyes drifted impossibly far away. Thin lips mouthed something.

"Why does Leoniel scare you?"

There was a small pause before Ferdinan answered robotically. "I wasn't prepared to meet a Kyo."

"You were terrified before you knew what he was."

Shaking, Ferdinan dressed.

One shirt after another was used to ignore Jon. "Does Leoniel remind you of someone?"

"He's unquestionably unique." Still standing, Ferdinan put on the new socks and shoes, kneeling to lace them. "I'll reimburse your family for the clothes."

That grated against Jon's nerves. "Would you reimburse the Duchess for getting you clothing?"

"Yes."

Flabbergasted... Jon blinked. "You're joking."

"No." Pushing past his ally, Ferdinan grabbed his screens and bag. "I apologize for making you wait."

"Ferdinan."

"What?!" Frustration burst out of the skeleton – then regret...

No. I'm tired of arguing. Something else. Anything else. The first words he found were unexpected. "Could Oya be a dual?"

"What...?"

Where did that come from...? It didn't really matter. They wouldn't argue about something completely ridiculous. An undocumented person with the mutation was unlikely enough. It wasn't possible for a dual to be lost. "Ya... She easily matches an Athlete for energy and physical prowess. But she also keeps people from noticing her. Gongie says Psychs can't do that. But maybe being a dual causes a Psych's abilities to express themselves differently."

"A dual...?" Tension eased out of Ferdinan as he gazed at the window.

* * *

Moving was difficult. It shouldn't be. This was her world, but Oya panted, hand trembling, as she pushed the needle through a middle-aged woman's chest. This was only her tenth collected this session...

Reaching behind the woman's back, Oya grabbed the needle. Every string fell and Oya claimed them – weaving her latest prize into the rest...

A defeated laugh left her. Wild green eyes turned to the orbs laying at her feet. Dim and unmoving.

"I pushed us too far?" Every day she worked until she couldn't. Then she played until she could work again. Plopping down, she gathered the orbs onto her lap. "I'm sorry."

They didn't scold her. They didn't do much but lay – exhausted.

"Don't let me drag you so far again."

Leaning back, Oya closed her eyes and sighed. *I'm so tired...* But there was one thing she needed to do before resting. Gently she returned the orbs to lay at her feet and stood. If she had the energy...

For a long time, Oya did nothing more than stare. It was undeniable. A number of connections directly linked to the woman were fading and new strings formed to another. A man.

Oya didn't know much about him. But he was there that day. The impression he left was simple – a well-schooled but generally forgettable man. Only his hair stood out. Most of the world's population had black hair. Brown wasn't common and blond was mostly unheard of. It was even considered demonic in some cultures. Which was fitting for the blond man. Despite the nearly extinct trait, he was fairly unremarkable.

Dismissing him was a mistake... Considering how strong the man's connection with the Kōjomà had grown, a separation wasn't likely. Unfortunate. Discontent among them would make her job easier.

Alien green eyes studied the braided cord securely wrapped around her hand. It wasn't getting any thicker tonight. *I need to stay ahead of that woman's infection.*

Setting her jaw, Oya stepped forward. She'd do what she could, then take a break.

Dark tendrils exploded into existence and grabbed her.

The grip was inescapable.

Every ounce of her soul stubbornly fought against them. But they enveloped her.

Squeezed the life from her.

Crushed her into oblivion.

Dragged her down an infinite void.

Chapter 5

The list of expectations kept going. *I'm not ready for young adulthood...* Herrard put down the screen and headed outside – wishing he could go back to being a child. But he was twenty now...

Salty air filled his lungs. Sunlight warmed him. And a gentle breeze played with his long hair. Removing the tie let it cascade down his back. Soon he'd be expected to keep it tied when he wasn't alone. Long fingers ran through soft strands. *A few months before...*

Shaking his head, Herrard breathed in deep. This was a perfect day in the most perfect place in the world. And he'd enjoy every second. Ahead was a flowered meadow separating the older boy's and girl's dormitories. *Hard to believe the Scientists planted this...*

Across all the islands, if any land seemed out of place, a Scientist planted it. *What concerned them when establishing this school?*

Removing his shoes was tempting as he strolled in. The soft grass and relaxing scent of wild flowers were hard to ignore...

Maybe next time.

Sitting, light brown eyes drifted lazily. Various dormitory windows were open – telling him who was there. Ilu must've finished morning training early. Tillia was mastering the spiritual rituals she needed to take over her mother's position. Herrard chuckled. *I bet she's counting the seconds 'til she can return to the dojos...*

Each open window hinted at what was happening beyond view. They were his family. Leaving them to be a stranger in another world hurt. It hurt deeply. But it was coming and there was no stopping it. So he let himself mourn before focusing on the open windows again.

Luyou's window... The Artist was gone for the break, but Oya was there. Alone. *I should check on her.*

Standing, he made his way to the girl's dormitory, signaled the chime, and waited. And waited.

And waited.

He signaled again, but no answer. Windows closed automatically when no one was inside and he didn't pass her in the stairwell.

This time he knocked. And when silence met him, he panicked. *Calm down. She's sleeping. That's all.* But...she was alone. *Why didn't the school put her with other girls over break?* It wasn't safe.

Chewing his lip, he knocked again. Oya was new to his island family, so he couldn't guess if she was ok. Cold rested in his gut, turning metallic. But she didn't answer. *Something has to be wrong.* And he promised to help with her...so he forced a medical override.

The door swung – hitting the stop harder than intended. "Oya?"

He waited. Wanting to hear her laugh. Or yell. Or tease him like she did Ilu and Xhou. But nothing. *Maybe the system glitched?*

Stepping across the threshold, the Healer made his way through to the common room. The small girl laid on the floor – eyes closed.

Relief sighed out of him. *She's sleeping....*

She is sleeping?

Herrard watched – waiting for her belly to rise. But it didn't.

Rushing forward, he dropped beside her. *She's not breathing? Why isn't she breathing?* She was young and healthy. There was no sign of injury. Placing a hand on her shoulder, he delved...

Or...tried to.

What is this? A shiver consumed him. He scanned her again, but it was the same. And...it wasn't possible... He needed to make her lungs work – make her heart beat – fix whatever was wrong!

Again, he forced a scan. But... Whatever he was touching wasn't a body. It was a picture book. One new Healers were taught from.

He wasn't touching a body... Just a book... A picture of what each part should look like. No cells came to his call – telling him vital information. No blood or warmth. Just a picture...

His eyes said she was a girl in need of help. But his ability said she was a book...

He didn't realize he was shaking her until she gasped.

Golden brown hands grabbed him, flipping him to his back. Strong legs pinned his arms and wild green saucers glowed with unearthly fury. She shouted something as a delicate hand grabbed his neck and the other lifted high – threatening. Death rang in his ears.

"It's me!" he screamed. "Oya! It's me! Herrard!"

"Hemi..." Green eyes clouded over, then sharpened. "Herrard?"

"Yah." The Healer focused on the fist ready to crush his face.

Slowly. Too slowly, she relaxed, lowering her arm and releasing his throat. Standing, she offered a hand, which he didn't want to take.

Giggles spilled out of her.

Giggles... *Why's she laughing?* Herrard wasn't sure what was going on, but he was fully unnerved.

Her wicked grin glowed. "What you did was dangerous and rude. But you didn't know it was unwise to wake me."

"You weren't breathing."

Plopping onto the couch, she rested her chin in her hand. "Are you familiar with the Monks of Washubae?"

Washubae...? That ancient monastery? "Vaguely..."

"Their meditation practices are intense." Again she stood and offered her hand. "You honor me with a surprise visit."

That startled Herrard. People didn't normally phrase greetings that way. And the use of "honor" was out of place. Unless she knew about some of Kidico's older traditions. "You're teasing me."

She giggled and pulled him to his feet. "Time to wear out the younger children again?"

What...? Was that real?

* * *

Today would be interesting – if this outfit was any indication.

Jon admired himself in the mirror. It didn't compared to the tux from yesterday, but he liked it. It made him smile. A genuine smile. Spinning in place – the jacket flared – revealing hidden colors. Ozar and Leoniel both clapped and laughed.

And the gent hid. "Show us how it looks, Ferdinan."

"I was *not* fitted for this."

"The tuxes are for later. That's for today." Silence followed. "I'm coming in."

31

Jon threw back the curtain and nearly laughed. The most colorful skeleton to ever exist stood aghast and bright red. A purple and green clad Kyo moved closer. As did Ozar, who looked like an ancient priest showered in yellow sequins.

"You look *adorable!*" *What would Oya say?* Jon ignored the gent's glare and spun - revealing the hidden colors. "I look cute too."

Utter horror twisted Ferdinan's face and stole Jon's joy. *I need mom. Get through today and she's all mine.* They promised him.

"What do you think, dear?"

"I look like a confetti bowl." Ferdinan growled but dropped his head, apologizing for his rudeness.

Jon snorted. It was the perfect description.

Leaning in, Ferdinan seethed under his breath. "You look like an ice cream swirl with too many sprinkles."

"I do." Jon preened. "Leoniel did a wonderful job."

Ring laden fingers offered a thin book to the skeleton. Inside were an assortment of simple pictures. "Evelyn drew these..."

"Obviously." Jon teased.

"No. Her way of drawing people is distinctive." The back of the first picture hosted a child's scrawl. "*Me and my big brother.*"

Seeing those characters made Jon smile... And feel a little bitter.

Handing the book back, Ferdinan bowed. "I apologize."

"No need. The Oza wanted to surprise you, so we obliged her." Leoniel's comment didn't help.

* * *

Fine, snow-white hair fluttered like a cape as Haoyu soared off. Elbie watched, giggling.

The flying disk Master Ferdinan made was magnificent. And tricky. Once each player's skills were assessed, the disk adjusted itself to make the game balanced and interesting.

When it flew toward him, it behaved as a normal flying disk. But when thrown for the Energist, it'd dash away - twisting and turning. Always out of reach - like an obnoxious bird teasing its predator.

It took a few tries, but Haoyu bested it. Spinning mid-air, the Energist flung it with all his strength toward Iilli. And it changed. Whenever it sensed the Athlete, it came in hard and fast – looking for a break in his defense. It never hurt his island brother, but Iilli insisted grappling his mentor was easier than catching the disk.

It bore full in, slipping between Iilli's arm and side, rounding back to zoom between his legs. Frustrated, the young Athlete lunged, but it darted to the side. Again, his suitemate dove. It swerved and flung back at his legs – tripping him. Growling, Iilli rolled to his feet and attacked again and again. The disk countered, relentlessly. Until he let an opening slip. The disk took it. A grin painted across Iilli's face. He leapt. And before the disk could counter, he tackled it.

Laughing, he stood and threw it to Veccidi – giving it a wicked spin...that didn't matter. By the time it reached the Artist, it'd slowed and all but hovered there for him to grab.

"Ah! That's unfair! I work so hard but it flies into Cidi's hands?!"

Veccidi threw it back to Elbie and it behaved like a normal disk again. Though laughing nearly caused him to drop it.

"If you didn't give everything you had when it assessed your skills, it wouldn't be so difficult this soon."

"It's still not fair!" Iilli complained, but was grinning.

"It's fairer than a normal disk." Veccidi grinned at the Athlete.

Haoyu's voice floated over from the distance. "I'm ready!"

"Ok!" Elbie chucked it toward his flying friend.

And the disk was a mischievous bird again. *How did Master Ferdinan do that? How would I...?* Giggles and cheers filled the air while Elbie considered how to build and program it. Simple drawings etched across his mind, morphing into blueprints. *What materials...?*

Cheers became shouts. Urgent shouts. *What?*

Mismatched eyes scanned the area. Haoyu sat on a rock protruding from the cliff's face holding his arm. Iilli was half-way to the Energist and Veccidi ran toward the multi-purpose building.

Elbie's feet moved. *Pay attention!* By the time he reached the cliff, Haoyu stood on the sand clutching his blood-soaked arm. Rocks crushed Elbie's hands as he gently rolled up the Energist's sleeve. "I'm sorry! I'm so sorry! I should've paid more attention."

A pained chuckle brushed off the apologies. "I got too close to the rocks – *I* should've been paying attention."

"Is it broken?" Iilli leaned in, careful not to touch Elbie.

"No. It just stings..."

Crushing rocks smashed his fingers while Elbie studied Haoyu's arm. There was so much blood. Like every other time. Most of the skin from the outer part of the Energist's arm was missing from just below the shoulder down to the forearm – where it bunched. *How does skin sluff off like this?* "I'm going to fix this one day."

It was a promise Elbie made the first time he saw it happen. But it'd be years before he learned enough to keep it.

"It's ok." Haoyu smiled to hide his grimace. "Energists are delicate flowers. I'll have to accept that...eventually."

Iilli snorted and Elbie smiled. But he let those rocks continue crushing him until the Healer arrived with Veccidi. She pulled off the torn skin and forced what was still attached to regrow. And it was fascinating. *Is that what happened to my skin? To Yuyu's?* Was it different with burned skin? His hands were fine... But Yuyu's burns were worse... *What did she look like...?* Fire raged through Elbie's mind. *No. It's over. There's no fire. I'm safe. We're both safe.*

"Joining us for dinner tonight? Or are you eating with Yuyu again?" Haoyu asked while the Healer worked.

"No. I told her to enjoy the evening with her parents. They'll be leaving next week." Stealing time from another's family felt wrong. And it hurt seeing them. "It's my turn to cook tonight, right?"

"The older students have planned dinner and a story night."

"How does that feel?" The Healer interrupted.

"Good, thank you." Haoyu moved – hoping to avoid a lecture.

It didn't work. They all stood through it – apologizing and promising to be more careful after it ended.

Chapter 6

Neither brother would tell Ferdinan what the outfits were for. Or what the extravagant building he was dragged into was.

Or why he and Jon were waiting in a small room.

Considering the outfits... Once Ozar closed the door, Ferdinan turned to the overly sprinkled ice cream swirl. "Well?"

"Well?" Jon parroted back.

"What's going on?"

Annoyance coated his ally. "Patience."

High-pitched squeals made Ferdinan's heart race erratically. A stampeding hoard screaming and bashing things was coming closer...

Stinging needles enveloped his shoulder egging his heart on faster. "Are you ok?"

"I'm fine."

"You're breathing hard and really pale."

Am I...? His chest hurt and his lungs struggled to move properly. Knocking away Jon's hand, Ferdinan forced himself to calm down.

The door flung open. Dozens of young, randomly costumed children stared at them – at Ferdinan – eyes wide and confused.

In the center, dressed as a fairytale wizard – complete with a dozen hip pouches, tome, and flowing cloak – was Evelyn.

Green-ringed black eyes stared. An excited scream left her and she charged her big brother. "*They told me you couldn't make it! They told me your boat was late!*"

Hearing her speak Yemeri startled the skeleton. Common was used at Jon's home when he was there. But it'd be different for her... Picking up the bundle of lightning, Ferdinan gave her his best smile. She was as tiny as the last time he saw her. "*Did they?*"

Mother Artimus walked forward – summoning a cheer of "*surprise!*" The Oza giggled and rang his neck with her little arms.

"*Lady Evelyn, may I ask what's going on?*" He smiled brighter as lightning lashed out at his forehead.

"*It's my birthday* party!" Evelyn shouted, impervious to how close she was to his face.

"*Party? Ah...*" *I guess she's still learning.* Ferdinan glared at Jon, but was met by a strange expression he couldn't interpret. *It's not his fault. I should've remembered...* Grandmother loved rambling about... The Tinkerer shook his head. He had no right thinking of her. He didn't deserve her memory. "*Happy birthday.*"

Jon's strange expression changed to a grin. He swiped his niece's tome and mussed her hair.

"*Ah! That's mine!*" she scolded. "*You aren't a wizard!*"

"*No...*" Something between pain and disappointment tainted Jon's smile. "No greeting for your youngest uncle?"

Giggles preceded him receiving both. Only then did he return the tome and pull the hood of her cloak up.

The birthday girl rambled to one person after another, but Ferdinan wasn't listening. Those shocked little eyes kept staring at him – unease turning to curiosity the longer Evelyn chattered.

Wiggling out of his arms, she opened her wizard's robe to show off a colorful swimsuit with a little ruffle at the waist. "*Yay! Now you can swim with me! Like on the little island in my dreams!*"

Swim....? His forced smile warped into a grimace. "*I'm sorry, I didn't know to bring a swimsuit.*"

"Leoniel made you one," Ozar spoke softly. "It's with Jon's. But swimming's later."

"Are you sure that's wise?" Ferdinan glanced at the guests.

"It's up to you. But the option's there nonetheless." Ozar tossed his niece into the air then gave her a hug. "*Happy birthday.*"

She shouted and giggled and begged to be tossed again which the giant obliged before putting her down.

Lightning coiled around his hand and dragged Ferdinan into a larger room filled with all manner of colorful toys and decorations.

"*Everyone! I told you!*" Evelyn's declaration grabbed their attention. "*This is my big brother!*"

Dozens of tiny bodies swarmed.

Dozens and dozens of tiny hands pressed in, each eager to greet him. Each bombarding him with different sensations. Ice and fire and knives and hammers! Peeled skin and crushing weight. Something tore the meat from his bones bit by bit and it felt his eyes were being pecked out. Swarms of wasps stung in waves across his body as sandpaper grated him raw. *Get away from me!*

He couldn't push them back; he'd hurt them and upset Evelyn. But...! *Stop touching me! Stop touching me!!*

His heart jumped erratically. Pathetic coughs shook out of him. Then stinging needles and an endless fall grabbed hold and pulled him from the onslaught.

"Don't touch me..." Ferdinan whimpered. "Please."

The impossibly long frame of Mother Artimus flowed down until she was kneeling beside him. "You're really pale."

"I'm fine." Boney fingers clutched at his chest. *What is this pain?*

"Are you sure?"

This doesn't feel right... But it faded. Slowly. *There's too much stimulation. That's all. Everything's fine. Everything-*

"*No! It's true! He's the best story teller!*" Evelyn's adorable voice cut through the room.

It took a while, but a little girl sheepishly stepped forward. "*I want to hear a story...*"

The little wizard turned to him - bright and filled with joy.

"If you don't feel well..."

Ferdinan shook his head at Mother Artimus's concern and walked over. Again they swarmed him, but he jumped back. His heart couldn't take another round of that. "*Sit down and don't move if you want a story.*"

Every child sat - save Evelyn who ran up and hugged him. Her lightning felt more intense after the barrage he'd survived. "*Thank* you! I told them all about the stories you told me at the hospital!"

"I need you to sit with your friends. Is that ok?"

Disappointment flashed across her adorable face, but she smiled and sat with them.

"What's the story about, Lady Evelyn?"

"Ooo! Ogres!"

That made Ferdinan smile. He wasn't sure where her fascination with ogres came from, but she usually requested a couple stories about them whenever he visited. Melancholy welled up, so he pushed those days from his mind. "What are the ogres doing?"

"Hunting! There's a great ogre hunt!" Cheers from the other children supported Evelyn's request.

Nodding, he weaved a tale for her. The other children might enjoy it, but the story was for Evelyn. It wasn't long, but it was silly – and inspired a game of Ogre Hunting when he finished. Playing with this many children was terrifying. But he kept out of their reach – running them all around the large and spacious building.

Each room led to a battle against a different group of beasts – kobolds, lava monsters, pixies... The children took turns picking a monster. The adults looked relieved for the break, so Ferdinan kept going until Xingho stopped them.

"It's time for lunch, young ogres." Xingho chuckled and turned to Ferdinan, "please lead them to that room, little brother."

Ferdinan motioned to the children. "Ready for lunch?"

But an argument between Evelyn and a little boy had their focus.

"You said he was your brother," the young child accused.

"He is!" Fists on her hips, Evelyn threw her shoulders back.

"Your dad called him 'brother,' so he's your uncle!"

"He was my brother before Xingho was my dad!"

The little boy crossed his arms. "That doesn't make sense!"

Such a silly argument turning to blood wasn't ideal. Neither was being in the middle of so many unrestrained children. But Ferdinan walked over and knelt between them. "*What's your name?*"

Defiance hardened the little boy's face. "*Lotiér.*"

"*Ah, Lotiér Sul, it's true. Lady Evelyn claimed me as her brother before the Artimuses claimed her as their daughter.*"

"*You can claim a brother?*" Amazement filled Lotiér.

Xingho laughed. "*Of course! We claimed Ferdinan the moment we saw him!*"

"*Can you be my big brother too?*" All the innocence of a five-year-old shone at Ferdinan – moving uncomfortably close.

"*You already have a brother!*" Another child objected.

"*But he doesn't play with me!*"

Standing, Ferdinan jogged to the door lunch was being served behind, "*Oh no! A wyvern escaped!*"

The children charged after, leaving Xingho alone chuckling.

~

The table and chairs were too small, so Ferdinan knelt on the floor next to Evelyn. Guests young and old enjoyed the feast while he nibbled at the vegetable medley prepared for him.

It was enjoyable. Until dessert came.

The wet, chocolatey cake held everyone's attention. Cheers and prosperous wishes were given before slicing up the chocolate death. It smelled bitter and sweet – but not as sweet as he expected.

Anticipation grew as everyone watched Evelyn take the first bite.

A giant smile and rosy glow brightened her face. "*Yummy!*"

Everyone joined her. Save Ferdinan. Kneeling by her side, he averted his eyes from the guests greedily munching the monstrosity.

"*Where's yours?*"

"Hm?" Ferdinan forced a natural smile – answering in Common to avoid attention. "I'm full. But thank you."

39

"But Pa-papa said he made it so you could eat it." Evelyn looked up. "I don't know what that meant, but it tastes as yummy as Papa's."

Evelyn's papa... Ferdinan hated his last memory of Liramarc. It was Evelyn's too. But she didn't look sad... *Has her family faded from her already?* It wouldn't be surprising. She was four when shipped across the world to be a test subject. Now she was six.

"Big brother!" Evelyn sounded like she'd called him a few times.

"Sorry... I was distracted..."

She smiled and lifted a spoon full of the chocolate monstrosity. "Try it! It's my favorite!"

He fought the cringe crumpling his body. *It smells sweet, but also bitter... Is it bitter enough?*

Blue crystals stared as the offered bite moved closer. Children and adults alike ate greedily – enjoying the treat immensely. *It's her favorite...and well received...*

If Father Artimus made it so I could eat it... But no one else would enjoy it if that was true. But it was Evelyn's birthday...

Swallowing hard, Ferdinan allowed it into his mouth.

Every nerve in his face exploded.

Pain.

Searing pain.

His teeth vibrated. And his gums crawled. The sugar...it went to work rotting his mouth on contact.

Swallowing would end the torture, but Ferdinan couldn't chew. Every cell screamed to spit it out. Trapped in a crowded room, dying from a decade's worth of sugar, and trying not to offend the one who always called him "big brother," the skeleton fought back gags.

"See?! It's really, really good!"

Every eye glared at him – agreeing with her. All watched – waiting for him to ruin it.

An eternity passed unable to breathe, unable to chew. When his stomach twisted, he grabbed a napkin and spit the sugar saturated cake into it. Water did nothing to rinse away the repulsive sweetness.

"You...you don't like it?"

Everyone's staring at me... Why did I leave the islands....?

"I'm sorry...it's too sweet for me." When her lip quivered, Ferdinan bowed, "But...would you enjoy it for both of us?"

"I'm sorry, I didn't know..."

"This is your birthday, not mine." Mussing her hair, he stood, "Please excuse me; I'll be back."

"Ok..." Pure determination lit up her green-ringed eyes. "I'll enjoy it for both of us!"

"Thank you, little sister." A grateful smile tugged at thin lips and Ferdinan left to scour out his mouth before he was sick.

~

No amount of scalding water stopped his teeth from vibrating.

"Are you ok?" Ozar's deep voice resonated impressively.

"Yeah..."

"I'm sorry, I thought you saw me gesture to not eat it. Dad altered the recipe when Evelyn insisted on surprising you, but that was the mildest we could make it and it still turn out."

Ferdinan bowed, "I apologize for not paying attention."

"Bitter tea?" The glass Ozar offered looked comically small in his giant hand. "It's hot."

"Thank you... I'm sorry..." Hot bitterness ate up the sweetness.

Sorrow and disappointment clouded the Hei-O's face. "They're giving presents. After will be swimming."

Ferdinan cringed.

"You don't have to, but the suit Leoniel made you comes with a long-sleeved top that covers up to your neck."

The Kyo provided every consideration... "She wants me to."

"Evelyn designed a surprise for you." A light chuckle left the man. "Thought you'd appreciate knowing so you're prepared."

"Thank you." Ferdinan bowed to his ally again. "Um..."

41

"Yes?"

"This... Are we going to your estate after?" Escaping the Artimuses for a day or two was easy, but a Kyo...? Impossible.

"Yes." Ozar smiled. When Ferdinan didn't speak, he prodded, "what do you need?"

"I'm supposed to meet a local engineer in a few days. And...I..."

"I'll have a car arranged for you."

"I can do that. You don't need to bother."

Ozar mussed his hair, but the Hei-O didn't say more.

They returned to the dining area and the fortress of presents Evelyn was working through. Each one left her as thrilled as the last. As if it were impossible to disappoint her.

When the pile was conquered, each of her uncles presented her with a gift. Toys. Instruments. Various artistic mediums. She loved them all.

Her parents were next. But they gave Children's Day ceremonial robes with her new family's crest. Evelyn was their child now...

Those robes... They made her being an Artimus too real. And...Ferdinan wasn't sure how he felt about it.

Father Artimus's gift made her squeal in delight. Her first set of kitchen tools. Sadness warped the skeleton's forced smile. Even as a toddler she loved helping her grandmother and father in the kitchen, though she was mostly underfoot. *I'm glad she hasn't lost that joy...*

Last was Mother Artimus. The impossibly tall, beautiful woman knelt before her first grandchild with a gift Ferdinan knew she'd been waiting to give since Xhingho and Raonie claimed Evelyn. It was a gift given by the family's highest matriarch on a child's fifth birthday or a year after being claimed – depending on the situation.

Bright with excitement, Evelyn opened the long, flat box. A smile glowed on her adorable face. Tears filled the room. Joyful tears.

But Ferdinan couldn't share in the collective emotion.

Inside was a bamboo sash. It looked simple. But Ferdinan knew the embroidery was exquisite and as elaborate as the Kyo's properties.

Each stitch held meaning. A recounting of the child's journey to their place in the family hierarchy. For a child like Evelyn, that journey was longer and more painful than most. But she bounced and twirled – delighted with the sash.

And Ferdinan's heart twisted.

For everyone here, this was sweet. The moment a child starts creating their purpose in the family. But all Ferdinan saw was a beloved little girl who lost everything because of him.

And now...

How much of her grandmother and father does she remember? How long 'til she doesn't remember them at all? 'Cause I wasn't fast enough. I wasn't good enough...

The room blurred. He blinked fast to block the tears. *Why did she put her trust in me? Anyone else would've saved her...*

Carefully, tiny hands returned the sash to the box. It'd be properly displayed at the estate come morning. The first in a new row... The next generation of the family.

And that was the end.

Everyone, young and old, had presented her with a gift. Except him. Birthdays didn't matter. For his own culture, the only one of importance was a child's day of birth. There were a few who's seventh' was important due to inheritance rights. But...

Green ringed black eyes widened and flew toward him. Excited chittering spilled out of her as she recounted the gifts and how kind everyone was. *"You got to see them, right?"*

"Yes. They were wonderful. I'm happy you like them."

The children rushed over – talking excitedly about all the things Evelyn received. Some talked about Children's Day and how much fun she'll have. Others asked questions, like which was a favorite.

But one question made Ferdinan cringe, *"What gift did your big brother bring? I didn't see him present anything."*

Evelyn stood taken aback. Folding her arms, she schooled the child. *"My big brother doesn't celebrate birthday anniversaries.*

43

And he's given me lots of presents all the time, so he doesn't need to give me one today."

Relief and surprise hit. *She remembered... How much did Grandmother teach her about my culture...?* Ferdinan forced his mind to stop. He didn't want to think about her. He didn't deserve to think about her.

"Who's ready to swim?" Cheers followed Evelyn's question. Tossing her wizards robe on a chair, she waved to her dad – begging permission to start the part she'd been waiting for.

Chapter 7

It was a heroic fight.

Sandwiched between Ozar and Bastian, Jon chuckled as his niece struggled for freedom from the water obstacle course to greet Ferdinan. The suit Leoniel made eliminated any excuse his ally had not to swim. And it looked better than he expected. *Ozar's amazing...*

It was nice. This break.

Knowing his family was taking care of things was a relief. If only the party would end – he really needed to talk to mom. There was so much to tell her. So much to say.

Evelyn grabbed Ferdinan's hand and dragged him to the pool – unfazed by the gent's disgustingly thin body. *"Ready to play?!"*

She speaks Yemeri better than me. His home. His language!

While she was enjoying love and codling, hearing Yemeri daily, he was on the islands...half a world away...

Jon was the only student listed as knowing it, so there was no one to practice with. But apparently there was. Something hot and metal settled in Jon's gut and twisted his face. The skeleton was fluent but never used it around him! They could've–! But they rarely interacted before South Chūzo.

Still... *The five Ferdinan reported, Yuchio, Oya's Oŭndo, and now Yemeri...* Eight languages was impressive... *Why would he hide that? And when did he learn?*

Boney fingers tugged nervously at a cuff while Evelyn pointed at the obstacle course saying something Jon couldn't understand.

Bitterness aside... The Thinker studied his ally. Ferdinan stood timidly. Something he hadn't seen in a while. *His jaw's trembling.* Jon shook his head. His family could figure it out while he relaxed and cuddled with his brothers. This was his break. The one he'd needed since South Chūzo. The one the gent kept stealing from him.

And! And with all the trouble his ally caused for a year now! He was vindicated in letting the skeleton squirm...

Jon growled out a soft sigh. That wasn't true. Or right.

Evelyn cheered – catching the younger childrens' attentions – and dragged Ferdinan to the start of the course.

Even covered neck to knees, the skeleton's grotesqueness was obvious. The gruesome child followed unsteadily toward an odd collection of slides and water traps.

Blue crystals studied the random compilation. It was hilariously haphazard. A random, chaotic challenge impossible for all who tried. Even with his ability to figure things out, Jon couldn't find a solution to the course – not for a normal human. It'd challenge Athletes.

But...

Something flashed in those nearly colorless crystals.

"*??...dad can...?...it! I...??...that...?...!*" Evelyn was bragging, but Jon couldn't piece together what she said.

Thin lips tugged upward.

That smile... It was genuine... Something discomforting tugged at the back of his mind. The last time Ferdinan gave an expression like that... *How close is he to regressing again?*

Scared and exhausted, Jon took Ozar's and Bastian's hands. Together they watched. Ferdinan stepped onto the platform with feigned confidence. Impossible blue eyes scoured the challenge. And overgrown, shaggy hair bobbed to a tune no one could hear.

Then...

The skeleton ran.

Leaping.

Spinning.

Dodging.

Jon leaned forward. *How's he moving like that?*

This...couldn't be Ferdinan. With each obstacle cleared, Jon's disbelief grew. He held his breath and squeezed his brother's hands. Some were close, but his ally managed each faster than expected. Until a random burst of water blasted the gent off a stepping stone.

"That was impressive..."

Jon looked up at Bastian – thinking the same thing.

Giggles filled the room. Giggles from dozens of mesmerized children. Instead of getting out, Ferdinan held onto the pool's edge – studying the rest of the course.

A grin split that gaunt face. *He's figured it out...*

Ferdinan called to Evelyn.

"*Yes!!*" She jumped up and down – sparking the rest of the children to join – all chattering excitedly.

This is worse than Ferdinan and Oya excluding me with Oŭndo.

Diving under, Ferdinan shot toward the start – too graceful for a Scientist who never swam...

Evelyn's cheers were adorable beyond description.

Beat, rhythm, Ferdinan listened... *What's he hearing that I don't?* This gathered more attention. Only two made it halfway – a guest's older sister and Ferdinan. Finding...something, the gent ran, keeping his speed and movements in time to a beat Jon almost saw.

Leaping, climbing, swinging, the pale skeleton flew.

His ally dodged the cannons' random water shots. Slides' and logs' and contraptions' attempts to take the gent out came to no avail.

Slowing, Ferdinan sprang off the last wobbling mushroom and caught the swinging vine. Grip tight, he swung high, releasing before the apex. Landing in a crouch, he stayed low until sliding to a stop.

The cheers were deafening.

Jon was speechless.

Delight and joy in the form of a six-year-old girl ran over and leapt off the pool's edge and into Ferdinan's arms. The skeleton flinched as she nearly strangled him – screaming with excitement.

Did I really see that?

A sickly child who spends his days in a lab...did that? Jon glanced at his brothers. They were surprised too.

Children screamed for Ferdinan to do it again as parents moved in on the course. But Jon was shocked. *There's no way...*

Bastian squeezed his hand. "Sorry, baby brother, there's a message I've been waiting for. I'll be back in a minute."

"It's ok. I need to talk to mom." Hugging both his big brothers, Jon left. He didn't want to learn anything new about the gent.

Outside the pool area, his mom greeted guests, but went to him immediately. That beautiful smile and her warm embrace... Jon felt the year's burdens and irritations melt away. "Can I talk to you now? I know I said I'd wait 'til we were home. But I really need to."

Squeezing him again, she dismissed everyone and sent security to prepare a room. They walked to the other side of the huge building. Eeriness lined the empty halls – reminding him of the hospital in South Chūzo, the secluded lab they worked in. Mom secured the office door while Jon arranged a comfortable place for them to sit.

"I'm sorry you had to wait this long." Mom hugged him again, then sat down.

"I... I'm sorry, but I...I need a break." Shaky hands clasped together. "I'm starting to resent him. Without a break...I'll hate him."

His words visibly broke her heart. But a year struggling alone... He couldn't anymore... There was no love lost between him and Ferdinan, but Jon didn't want to hate someone his family loved. Or feel ungracious toward a sick child. But he did.

"I'm sorry for not realizing the position I put you in."

Jon took her hand – soaking in her warmth. "I don't blame you. I'm just tired. If I can have this break away from him, I'll be ok."

Mother nodded. "I'm listening for as long as you need."

"Thank you." He laid out everything. Everything. All of it.

The unexpected was the most troubling in retrospect. Jon braced for trouble after Rura's death, but... Instead of claiming responsibility, his ally seemingly forgot about her. Then the gent's behavior became bizarre. Conversations felt like Ferdinan wasn't talking to him. Shouting and reacting to nothing. Losing interest in everything – sleeping all the time.

And...the night he found Ferdinan – heart stopped... Telling a mother their child nearly died... They were both crying.

"He agreed things had to change." Jon clasped his hands to steady their shaking. "And they did! It stopped. His mood improved; his appetite increased. He was an entirely different person..."

All that happened in one block? And there was still more...

"Then what?"

"He...he lost control. He'd be calm or happy and in the same breath would yell. He couldn't be still and became easily angered. He got so hungry I had to take food away from him so he wouldn't make himself sick. It all...it spiraled out of control. Each day was worse. Then..." This was the most frustrating part. The gent regained control. *Just in time to make me a liar.* "...he stopped. The change wasn't as abrupt...he still overreacts, but he doesn't fly into a rage..."

"A rage?" Mother squeezed Jon's hand.

"Ya... The Superintendent summoned him to discuss his attendance. According to Master Dæya, Ferdinan knocked over furniture and was screaming. He asked me to stay close incase Ferdinan 'reacted badly' again."

Mother hugged him.

"I'm tired mom. I'm so tired." Jon hoped he could finish before tears took over completely. "It's killing me...watching all this...seeing it...being powerless to do anything. I can't... I can't-"

"You're a wonderful son and a loving brother." Mother rocked him while he sobbed. "I'm sorry. I never thought it'd be like this. I never wanted you in such a position. You've done a wonderful job. I won't ask any more."

Jon shook his head - face pressed into his mother's shoulder. "...it's not enough... Nothing...is enough..."

"I know it feels that way."

Pushing himself back, he faced her. "It doesn't feel that way...it *is* that way."

"If it is, then there's no hope." Mother dried his tears. "I have to believe there's happiness for him."

The weight of her words where too horrible to bear. *...I can't stop...* But he couldn't keep going either. Weakness shrank his insides. He'd reached his limit. But how did you tell your mom that?

How did you tell her you can't stand the idea of helping her child?
"I'm sorry..."

"We're here now. You don't have to do anything you don't want
to. You don't have to worry anymore."

"I'm sorry..." Those words squeaked out high, betraying how
conflicted he was.

"I'm sorry. I asked too much. I won't ask anything more."

"I'm sorry..." He cuddled up in his mom's arms and soaked in
her comfort. Until he was ready. "It's probably time to end the party.
And I'd like to get into my normal clothes."

Taking her hand, they walked back to their guests. Evelyn and
her parents lined up to thank everyone while his brothers gathered
presents.

Not long after Jon snuck away to the dressing rooms, Ferdinan
entered. The gent looked relieved to find regular clothing waiting for
him.

Tense silence filled the room. Unable to take it, Jon said the first
thing that came to mind. "How did you do that?"

"Do what?" Ferdinan kept his back turned while drying off.

"Beat the course. That wasn't possible."

Boney shoulders disfigured from the fire and an odd build of
muscles shrugged. "It was all math and timing."

If that were true, why couldn't I figure out a possible route? But
arguing wasn't worth it. Putting on his travel clothes, Jon found his
mom and begged to ride home with her.

Chapter 8

Smoke bombs flew, unleashing a caustic vapor. This wasn't the Duchess's preferred method, but dissidents raiding or destroying the food reserves was unacceptable.

Civilians fell. Corralling troublemakers into a safe area was simple for the masked soldiers. There she let silence crush them.

Once most were trembling, she spoke. "*Hurting yourselves is your prerogative. But harming your fellow citizens through your selfishness is unacceptable.*"

"*How dare you live lavishly off our backs!*" A man bellowed.

Those with him cried out their anger, but the Duchess waited for silence – carefully considering her reply. Denying his accusation was pointless. They wouldn't believe her. And it was her responsibility to assure all citizens were clothed and fed. Only children ate without regard to rank. After that, it was as it should be. First, the General. Second, the King. Third, the citizens. Next, came the soldiers, save in times of contention. And last, the lesser nobles.

The unforgivable indulgence of Lords like Orthan gave them every right to their anger. And how many needed one to hate to last the day? To face their hungry families? But her duty was to the majority's welfare. *I've taken all the time I can. My next conversation with the Zi I'll start negotiations in earnest.* There hadn't been enough time to create much leverage, but she'd do what she could.

As she told her spoiled cousin, when playing the villain, do so with a purpose. She had a purpose. A goal. One as vital to her country as the terms she coaxed from the Zi. "*It isn't your place to question how I use my lands. I've cared for you and your children. Provided you with shelter. Seen to it no one has starved. All the care and rights have been provided. And in turn you attack the silos sustaining your countrymen?*"

Injured bodies required more nourishment and resources... This made punishing them all inadvisable. But she shouldn't need to. In her hand was a coin and at her hip – an urumi. She held both high for the crowd to see. "*Crown, you watch. Throne, you learn. All those who learn will learn. No healer will touch you save one I approve.*

All who watch will have their rations cut ten percent to pay back what was lost today. If you're found stealing from your children or fellowmen, a much harsher punishment will be dealt."

Murmurs waved through the crowd.

"*Lieutenant.*" The Duchess instructed the platoon leader to bring them one by one. Each offender was given the coin to determined their fate. Those who got "crown" were thoroughly documented and their information changed to reflect the punishment.

Those who got "throne" were forced to remove their shirt and kneel before her. Not a single ounce of pity showed on the Duchess's face as she flicked the metal whip. Once. Twice. Thrice.

Every "throne" was taken away torn and bloodied.

* * *

Tiny hands squeezed a stuffed, knitted monstrosity while Xingho held his new daughter steady on his shoulders.

When did she get that thing? Jon studied it while she and his brothers stared through the crack in the window's curtain. "Evelyn, what are you holding?"

Green-ringed black eyes beamed. "It's my stuffed ogre! I get one like this every year. And this year, I got him!"

"Every year?"

"Yah! My first was a dragon! Then I got a crow and a wizard...and..." Evelyn looked up thinking hard. "Oh! A wizard, a tree guardian, and a pixie. Now I have an ogre too!"

"Where are the others?"

"Ma-mama said they'd wait for me at home." Her smile faded and she turned back to the window. "What's he doing?"

Regret soured Jon's insides. "He's making...something."

Whatever the gent was up to, Ferdinan requested the music room to himself for a few hours. It was an odd request for the gent. Which made them curious. So curious, they dragged Jon away from being lazy to watch from outside.

"Ya, but what?" Rigel smushed him to get a better look through the crack in the window's curtain.

"I couldn't guess." Jon stood to leave but was stopped by Evelyn.

"Why's he hitting them with sticks?"

Jon studied the arrangement of drums Ferdinan was assaulting. *What's he doing? He'd never purposely damage another's property.*

In the last hour, the skeleton played the same song on three instruments. *When did he become interested in music?* Learning one instrument to proficiency was part of their curriculum, but afterward they didn't have to bother with it any more.

Drums...stolen from the soldier's training huts. Piano. Harp. Plus the violin and mandolin Jon already knew about... *How long has he studied music? I thought he considered it a nuisance...*

Once the gent stopped assailing the drums, he grabbed a screen and secured it at face level.

A tap and the gent started singing.

Those words felt familiar but Jon didn't understand them.

"I didn't know he spoke that," Ozar mumbled.

Ozar only speaks one ancient language and it's not one Ferdinan knows... Nine? That's not possible... Is it? How much does he know? The lovely sounding music warped Ozar's face into unpleasant expressions. How could a song sound beautiful, but trouble his brother? Jon wanted to ask, but was too slow.

"What's he saying?" Xingho shifted his daughter to one shoulder, preparing for when she'd want down.

"Um..." Ozar swallowed hard. "It's a song about wild flowers."

His older brothers exchanged strained looks. Xingho nodded and squeezed Evelyn's hand. "Time's almost up. Ready to get him?"

Evelyn giggled and nodded excitedly.

* * *

Chūzo's Master summoning Aunt Tenalia solved one problem. The next was one Zephyr needed his second father's help to fix. The Prince stood in the doorway to Rutoric's office. Emphasizing his submission, he tapped his temple with his middle finger and dropped his head - hand falling to his side. "Captain Rutoric, sir."

The Captain gave Zephyr his full attention – double tapping his sternum with a finger. The motion allowed the ringed birthmark to peek out from his collar.

Why? The golden Prince knew why, but not how to answer. After a moment, his hands moved. "May I speak confidentially?"

Offering the Prince a chair, Rutoric locked the door. Strong, golden hands danced.

"The young woman I scared before returning to school..."

Rutoric bumped one hand with two raised fingers against a closed fist – lowering one finger on the first hand and raising one on the second, only to point away.

No wonder I can't find her... That tightness in his chest grew until his heart couldn't move. He needed to apologize. Not sure what to say, Zephyr drew his thumb from the corner of his mouth to his chin.

Rutoric's hands moved and stopped over and over. When they found the words, despair coated his movements.

"I was wrong." Neither the Prince's tongue nor hands moved farther. What things should he admit to? What should he hold back? If only he could bury them all. Zephyr almost heard the elf laugh.

Rutoric tapped the side of his hand over his heart and turned it palm up.

"She didn't do anything wrong. I need to apologize."

Sighing, the Captain sat back looking troubled.

"I'm sorry."

Shaking his head, Rutoric gave a firm answer.

"I should apologize," Zephyr insisted, flinging his hands open.

The captain expanded on his answer.

And it was hard to take. *I did that to a Ragnian Camp survivor...?* "How do I make this right?"

Rutoric shook his head – tapping one finger to his forehead only to point two upward. Surprise was evident on Rutoric's face.

I'm a fool. Again, Zephyr drew his thumb from the corner of his mouth to his chin. "I will. Starting with what I've missed."

Standing, Rutoric pressed the flat of his hand against his chest then pointed at Zephyr - eyes expecting an answer.

I wanted to apologize...to make things right... But if an apology could erase his past, he wouldn't be a monster. Brushing two fingers over his shoulder, Zephyr nodded.

Pointing forward, Rutoric slashed his hand down - repeating Zephyr's gesture.

But it didn't matter how passionately the man disagreed. Since the Prince couldn't do anything...

A strong hand rotated, finger and thumb parallel to each other. The other grabbed a screen.

A man I've always trusted... No. Disappointing Rutoric...he couldn't face that. "There's nothing else bothering me."

When Zephyr tried leaving, Rutoric stopped him. He should turn around, but he couldn't lie to the man's face. Rutoric would know. His second father always knew when he lied. "Everything's fine. I promise. I won't falter again."

* * *

"Look! There it is!" Evelyn pressed a finger against the window.

It's huge... This is a normal school? Ferdinan shook his head in amazement. Lightning seized his hand and pulled him closer to the window. "I see! It looks fun."

It was colorful with multiple plots of outdoor equipment. And children. *Lots* of children near Evelyn's age. Seeing them running around screaming... Lead soured his stomach. Being surrounded by the dozens at the party was too much. There were hundreds here.

Once parked, lightning wrapped around his arm, trying to rip it from its socket. Until a massive hand came down gently on her head.

"I know you're excited, but classes start soon and Ferdinan has a meeting." Jingjing's deep voice reverberated through the car.

Ferdinan sighed.

"I know! But! Just to the front doors. Please?"

Bastian looked to Ferdinan – giving him the choice.

Bony fingers unlatched their restraints and opened the door. A shout of joy and lightning wrapped around him again. Jumping out, Evelyn waved, calling to the other children. By the time Ferdinan stood beside her, they lined the fence – shouting and waving back.

Until they looked at him. All of them stared. In awe or fear.

Closing his eyes, Ferdinan let out a slow, controlled breath. *"To the door."*

Evelyn pouted but didn't object. The adults gave him the same looks as the children. But Ferdinan trained his eyes on Evelyn until she was inside.

Worse than the staring was the brothers' pity when he returned to the car. "I apologize for the inconvenience."

"It's not an inconvenience. We're curious about your work and want to meet the man who's earned your respect," Bastian smiled.

Liar. You are being forced to attend me. What did Jon tell them? He couldn't slip away once – they were always watching.

It was an hour's drive to Master Fulason's warehouse. An hour with two of Jon's brothers...without the Thinker... It was awkward. Had he ever been with an Artimus without Jon there?

Seeing the magnificent buildings and bald man waiting for them was a relief. Getting out of the car, Ferdinan bowed. *He's so small...*

The man was surprised to – and a little concerned at the extra foot Ferdinan had on him. Master Fulason returned the bow then properly greeted the brothers. "I'm honored, Dintas. We've prepared an area for you to relax while we work."

Jingjing laughed and Bastian held up his hands. "We were hoping to see two master engineers at work. Unless it's distracting."

"I'm honored. Don't feel pressed to stay if you're uninterested."

Master Fulason escorted them to an assembly building. Inside, a giant machine awaited. The majesty of it was awe inspiring. Blue crystals searched every inch of the beast laying before him.

"If you like the mama, come check out the pup," Fulason stood next to a significantly smaller version about the length and breadth of a dining table – and as tall as the master engineer.

Joy filled Ferdinan's soul. It'd been two years since he last played with such a magnificent machine.

Fulason plopped a bag of tools into boney hands – careful not to touch the boy. "Impress me."

"Yes, sir."

Disassembling the pup was wonderful.

The world melted away. Everything disappeared. It was just him and this beautiful, intricate machine. Each piece's purpose and placement were memorized before removing it. Exploring a machine he hadn't designed was a joy. Learning. Discovering new ways to build and design layouts... But once it was over...

Standing, Ferdinan accepted the cloth Fulason offered – wiping his face and hands. "What do you make with the model?"

"Nothing currently. It can easily be fitted to make simple parts." The man patted it like a well-behaved puppy. "Ready for the mama?"

"I think so..."

"I'd be grateful." Fulason grabbed a small screen from his back pocket. "Your standard fee? Or will this take more?"

"Standard fee?" Bastian turned to the skeleton.

Red, Ferdinan cringed and focused on the full-scale machine. *Don't mention that with them here...* "What'll you do with the pup?"

"It'll probably sit in storage 'til an intern decides to play with it."

Hesitating, Ferdinan bowed. "I'll take the pup in leu of the fee."

"You already have an idea for it?!" the man laughed. "You can *have* the pup. The fee's still yours."

"Unnecessary." Ferdinan turned back to the beautiful beast.

"Master Ferdinan–"

"I promise, sir, it's more than fair recompense."

"That's not what I'm trying to say."

Turning back, Ferdinan gave his full attention. "I apologize, sir."

Master Fulason handed him a screen. On it was a generous list and a message congratulating employees on the successful fundraiser for East Azuté. Those supplies... *I can set up an extra village with this...* Turning his back to the Artimus brothers, Ferdinan placed his thumbprint to authorize the transfer to the account Grandpa Huey managed for him. "I'll show them how many they helped."

Returning the screen, Ferdinan ignored Bastian's and Jingjing's exchange of glances – and Master Fulason's fussing about.

I'll be alone inside... Alone... Solitude. He hadn't truly been alone since South Chūzo... Ferdinan pushed those thoughts away.

Slipping into the access hatch was...awkward. And tight. He had to shift his shoulders at an odd angle to get through. And his too tall body was bent and hunched inside. Long limbs tested the limits of mobility within the small space. But Ferdinan smiled and set to work.

Sounded like the problem was among a communications pathway. Some were firing at the wrong time. Some not at all. Starting at the terminal, Ferdinan traced each path. Testing. Taking notes. Fixing misconnected lines. Getting into a rhythm didn't take long. From there the world faded away and it was just him and this amazing creation. All alone in this tiny space. *If I don't stop growing, I won't fit next time...* That thought was too distressing. He never should've been this tall. A little taller than Zephyr maybe, but not like this...

Pushing those thoughts away, he went back to work.

Going over each line again was tempting, but he promised Evelyn they'd play after school. Sighing, he patted the interior wall, "Thank you for the reprieve."

Turning in the tight space was a feat, but Ferdinan managed and crawled out of the beast's belly. Master Fulason was doing something on a screen – paperwork or design. The Artimus brothers were dozing on a comically large couch set that'd been brought in.

"Got it."

"Got what?" Jingjing yawned and shook Bastian.

Fulason jumped up from the work table. "Wonderful! What was the problem?"

Handing over his notes, Ferdinan summarized them and offered suggestions to avoid the same problem in the future. The oversights surprised Fulason, but he nodded and took notes of his own.

"Thank you. I'll see it's corrected." Fulason raised an arm to the brothers, inviting them over. "Is everything closed?"

"Yes, sir."

The machine roared to life then softened to an inviting purr as soft clinks chimed inside. Its life sounded exactly as Ferdinan imagined. Reaching out, he touched it – soaking in the soft vibrations of its *hum* – the light tingle of electricity giving it life. If only people felt like this...

Fulason smiled approvingly. "You never cease to impress me."

"It was a simple problem..." Ferdinan almost added, "*if you are small enough to reach it.*"

Smiling became difficult.

* * *

It was beautiful. Jon loved home in the summer. It was warm but not hot like the islands year-round – making the transition less jarring than winter break. Lying around outside was relaxing. And there was no better place than the orchards when everyone was busy. Shade from trees and the wonderful scent of ripe fruit... It was glorious.

Jon dozed in and out. Sometimes he read a story from his screen. Sometimes he laid back and watched the bees. It was nice. An eternity like this... Except add a couple brothers to smoosh.

An idea sprouted to life. Sitting up, Jon grabbed the screen and outlined a program idea usable for his final project next year. As he did so, a call request chimed.

"Gongie!" Warmth filled Jon's chest and a smile sprang on his lips.

"Jon! How're things going? How're you doing?"

"I'm taking full advantage of my opportunity to be lazy."

Gongie smiled brightly. "Enjoy it."

"What're you gents doing?" A small pang hit Jon's heart. "I'm glad you're there for Marcus. I'm sorry I haven't helped much."

"Things haven't been easy for you either." Gongie scratched the back of his head. "We're having fun. Oya's not pestering Ilu as much. And Marcus has good days and bad. The younger children are wreaking havoc though."

Thank you, Xhou, for keeping her entertained. "The younger children?"

"There's this strange flying disc they've been playing with. It's led to a number of minor injuries." Gongie's dark eyes looked distant for a moment. "My last pair of shoes got ruined chasing after the thing."

Jon chuckled. "How did that happen?"

"It flew too close to Yuyu and I just ran to stop it...right into the lagoon – in a less than graceful fashion..."

A hand stifled Jon's laugh. "Are you ok?"

"Yah...nothing the Healer couldn't fix." Gongie looked away sheepishly. "Shoes didn't make it though. Tore some grand holes in my clothes too... I hope you don't mind, I pilfered a pair you said didn't fit right anymore. And a couple shirts you put aside for the clothing exchange."

Jon smiled brightly. "You're welcome to anything I left behind."

"Thank you!" Gongie smiled – dark eyes gleaming with a masterful plan. "If I sent my measurements, would you pick some shoes and outfits out for me? Mine are getting too small. And these are the most comfortable things I've ever worn. I can see why you like clothing so much."

I love you, Gongie. His island brother knew how much he enjoyed Berago's. And it'd be nice shopping without Ferdinan there. Worrying about the gent ruined his last visit.

"I trust you to pick what'll look great on me." The Psych tapped the screen and a new message appeared on Jon's end. "Your sense of style is better than mine anyway."

Jon checked to see he had all the information. "Thanks for the excuse to go shopping."

"Thank you for taking it."

Chapter 9

Evelyn, Naizu, and Rigel were at school. Jingjing and Bastian were with Ferdinan. Xingho and Samuel accompanied mom to some meeting. Dad wouldn't be back from the main capital for a while. And his three in-laws were caring for their provinces.

This left Ozar – who was working...

Jon dragged an overstuffed sac into the Hei-O's study and laid it against his brother's chair. Curling up, he scooted until he felt the warmth of Ozar's leg. Security and comfort filled him, easing his heart. If he could do this all year...

Jon felt Ozar smile. Soft tapping danced in the quiet room. Laying there. Feigning sleep while his brother worked was wonderful.

Then Ozar had the audacity to move.

"No..." Jon murmured.

Deep chuckles warmed the room. Slipping off his chair, the Hei-O sat on the floor. "It's been a while since we talked."

Talking to his family. Being with them. That's all he wanted. But he told mom everything. Saying that again... His heart twisted. But he wanted to listen to his brother's voice. To hear something that made him happy. "What do you want to talk about?"

"Read any good stories lately?" Ozar hugged his baby brother.

Shaky relief sighed out of him. *I never want to leave home again.*

* * *

"Again!" Zephyr picked himself off the ground and charged.

There was no strategy. And Captain Rutoric didn't stop him – just kept knocking him down. Which he deserved. Zephyr wanted a beating. He needed it.

That goo filling his lungs... Denila's blade was better, but Captain Rutoric's strikes still brought relief. And he needed more. More pain! Until it was all gone! He wanted that goo gone!

He needed it gone...

Blow after blow - he'd take them all day to free his lungs...for his heart to beat unobstructed. For his skin not to feel tight.

Except... Rutoric stopped. A strong, golden hand grabbed him and threw him to the ground, holding him in place.

Rutoric sliced his hand downward - face stern.

"I'm not finished." *Please don't stop.*

Rutoric lifted Zephyr. A golden hand pointed at him before resting atop the other.

The Prince's hands moved - searching for an excuse. "No... I have to train or I won't be ready to step up as General."

Disappointment filled Rutoric's face - he didn't believe the lie. Those strong hands moved again.

Ice filled Zephyr, stopping his hands and filling his chest to bursting. His ears rang and the world blurred. He didn't want to hear that - see that... He knew... And it was wrong... But he needed this!

Rutoric snapped his fingers an inch from Zephyr's onyx eyes - forcing him to focus again. Those hands demanded an answer.

I can't... "If we're done, I have other things to attend to." Before Zephyr could turn away, the Captain grabbed his wrist - holding it in a vice grip. Dark eyes pleaded for him to talk. "Release me, please."

Pressing a thumb against his heart and lips before extending toward Zephyr, Rutoric let go.

"There's no reason for concern. I'm doing what I need to."

Worry clouded Rutoric's face and he repeated the gesture.

Closing his eyes for a moment, Zephyr thought. *What do I do?* "I have reports to read."

The man wasn't happy. Neither was Zephyr. He needed relief. But he'd been too obvious and now he was stuck.

Once in his room, the Prince grabbed his screen and flopped on his couch. One report after another - none of them positive... Those things weren't his fault - but it felt like they were. He was gone most of the year. But... He was too vile to not be the cause of his country's ills. It didn't make sense. But it felt right.

Heaving a sigh, Zephyr put the screen down. Golden fingers rubbed his tight chest as he considered everything he read.

Crop failures are getting worse... The citizens weren't happy with the Duchess's efforts. But no one was starving. Neither could anyone else do half as well under the circumstances. Still...he was worried for her. Her actions with the extremists in particular. He agreed. No matter how unhappy they were, taking actions that'd hurt their fellow countrymen was unacceptable. And rebellion was starting in the north now, how did he keep that from turning violent as well?

His mom was called back to the Grasslands. Aunt Tenalia was still with Chūzo's Master. And the Duchess and her older daughters were handling various issues. This presented him with an unexpected opportunity for his age: addressing citizen's concerns directly.

A year ago he would've been thrilled. But now... He should be imprisoned or banished for his sins.

But...that strange girl's words circled around his mind.

"Being General isn't about me..." Zephyr looked over the reports.

Placing both hands on his knees, he focused all his energy into breathing deep. It was only getting worse. *School work's next.* Pulling out a different screen, Zephyr stared at it, but couldn't concentrate. How could he when it felt his chest would explode? Nothing was wrong with him. The Healers would've noticed anything after being stabbed. And those little disks confirmed it. But...

He clawed at his chest. Why did it feel so tight!?

Think about something else. But that led to thoughts of Ferdinan and how much he couldn't bare facing his cousin's soul.

Denila's blade... When it pierced his chest, the goo leaked out. All this suffocating goo... When the metal – pain – forced it out.

It went away for a while...

Onyx eyes flew open wide. What was he thinking? No matter how uncomfortable – he couldn't stab his chest! He couldn't...

Golden hands clawed again – as if tearing open his skin would allow the goo to escape. *Does it have to be the chest?*

The elf's words floated around his mind. *"How do you overcome pain and sorrow?"*

Jaw set, Zephyr walked to the weapons rack decorating his room.

Most of the blades were too large.

But there was one.

A small blade Denila gave for his Right of Ascension Ceremony. The width was that of a standard hunting knife, but it was barely two inches long. She joked, "*Once you beat me, you'll earn a real blade.*"

The stub-nosed knife was only useful for the cherished memory.

Until now.

Removing the blade from its perch, he unsheathed it and stared into the reflective surface.

My eyes are dull. Filled with pain he didn't want to acknowledge.

I'll do what I must.

Locking the bathroom door, he retreated to the shower. Sitting on the tub's edge, he rolled up a pant leg. And his heart quickened.

Please work.

This was wrong.

I need to breathe.

No one could know...

Lifting the precious gift high, with all his might he brought it down into his thigh. White hot pain shot through him... Warmth bubbled out – red and glistening. And the goo... It leaked out with the red – letting him inhale.

Finally...

Each deep, steady breath came easier than the one before.

"Whatever it takes. I'll do whatever it takes, obnoxious elf."

* * *

"Up there! I see one up there!!" Evelyn squealed, pointing to the top of a large apple tree. "I see a yellow one!"

Smiling brightly, Ferdinan climbed to retrieve the "mystical yellow Wombrie fruit" – the last item she needed for her potion.

64

This wasn't the same as running on his island or fighting with Oya, but his muscles appreciated the mild exertion.

Giggles followed him up the trunk. Suspense radiated from her as he inched across the limb below the fruit.

"Oh! You almost have it!"

Anyone else would worry he'd fall or the branch would break, but Evelyn had complete confidence in him. The fruit snapped off easily. Safely tucked inside his top shirt, Ferdinan shimmied down. Cheers and bouncing feet greeted him.

"My big brother can do anything! Rura didn't believe me! Said only her brother could do anything. But she's wrong! I wish she was here now so she can see!"

Hand outstretched, Ferdinan froze. *Rura? Oh... Xhou's little sister... She's being hosted here...* "Is she visiting another family?"

"Nope!" Jumping up, Evelyn grabbed the apple and plopped it into her bag of "magical ingredients." "She went home!"

"Already?" A small ache started near his temples and confusion set in. But what was he confused about?

"After playing at your school, Uncle Samuel rode home with her. It wasn't fair! I didn't get to see your school! Or say goodbye to her either." Evelyn pouted. "It was fun having a sister too."

"She didn't come back here?"

"No." Shiny black hair swayed. "She left with Uncle Samuel and Uncle Ozar, but went home without saying 'goodbye.'"

"Oh..." The ache grew to a light throbbing. *But... East Azuté isn't safe enough... Unnecessarily returning a young child there was irresponsible.* Boney hands rubbed at the symmetrical pounding. "I'm sorry, Lady Evelyn, can we go inside?"

She looked at him, worried. "Did you hurt your head climbing?"

"No. I'm feeling ill. Will you play with your uncles for a while?"

A frown quivered on her lip and her eyes glistened. "I'm sorry. I played with you too much."

Swallowing hard and forcing a smile, Ferdinan offered his hand. "No. Headaches just happen. Let me rest and we'll play later. Ok?"

Determination curved her lips upward and she grasped his fingers with electric enthusiasm. "Ok! Let's go back!"

Evelyn announcing his condition to everyone they passed was embarrassing. The Artimuses' unwanted concern made it worse. By the time they stopped fussing over him, the headache had spread and intensified, making sleep impossible.

Evelyn's words circled around his mind.

And circled.

And the confusion surged... *What am I so confused about?*

Part of him insisted he knew. Like a voice scratching at the back of his head. Grabbing a screen, he hacked the school's travel records and looked through the manifests following Family Week. As Evelyn said...

Rura didn't return here. Samuel traveled directly to East Azuté...

Rura's name wasn't listed. But... The cargo list...

One box of human remains delivered to East Azuté's capital...

Acid climbed up this throat.

Searching the school's records confirmed the fire was the only incident that week.

Nothing else happened.

Horrible words danced passed his eyes.

Parts of conversations he didn't remember jumped to the forefront of his mind. "*She was dead before you got there, there was no way to save her.*"

Flying debris from the explosion crushed her skull – killing her instantly. "*You saved us. Xhou understands Rura couldn't be.*"

She was there and he never knew.

"*When you lifted the beam, I saw her. She was under Yuyu–*"

"*Ngh...*" Two conversations he never had twisted around inside his head until they exploded.

Dizziness hit. His heart raced. *When did I talk to them?*

Those conversations settled loosely in his mind.

He was on his way to class. Elbie was sick...

He ran to hide in his lab, but Oya could get in anywhere...

Grabbing at his chest didn't ease the sharp pains. His jaw hurt from being clutched so tightly. Lunch left him.

Two walls offered a corner to huddle in. Two to hide him. To hide him from this. From that...

I left a child behind... I stole another life.

* * *

"This is interesting." The man in a floppy fisherman's hat looked around the void Oya created for the Kōjomǎ's minions.

"It fits the job." Unnatural green eyes looked over the grand task that'd become complicated. Every soul she found was there, but only a quarter were collected. Gathering connections took too much energy...too much of herself to work faster. "Tell me what you see."

The Fisherman studied the scene. "Two groups are forming."

Delicate hands tugged at her steel locket. "I'll need a permanent connection between the Kōjomǎ and her second to track them both."

"Do you have enough to establish and maintain it?"

Oya grimaced. The cord of woven lighted strands felt heavy. Her arm and shoulder ached. Putting it down for a moment... *No. If I let go, I'll have to start over again.* "I don't know."

"Your escorts are stretched thin."

"I know." A sad grin turned to the orbs always in her peripheral. "Are there more?"

"Yes, but not many."

"Take a message to Kumi for me?"

Straightening, the Fisherman nodded.

"Tell him about the two groups. And to put eyes on the man. If I don't know what he's doing, I'll fail." Sighing, Oya turned to all those standing in the void she created. Was this a waste of time?

If she could cry...

* * *

Ferdinan knew mother was watching over him. Heard her voice when she spoke. Fell endlessly when she took his hand.

But he was torn from the world.

Inside... Something rattled. Something wanting purchase it couldn't find. Something holding him hostage until he provided it...

Boney hands cradled his head because only his hands existed.

And when the rattling stopped, memories he didn't want rushed in. *No... I want to forget.* He wanted the rattling to return.

And it did.

And he remembered wanting to forget, wanting it gone. But he couldn't remember what "it" was. Nothing felt real. Everything was wrong. *I'm asleep. I'm sleeping... How do I wake up?*

A whisper left thin lips. But he didn't know what he said – didn't remember saying anything.

"What is it, my child?" Mother's soft voice lingered gently.

"No one told me." *That's what I said? In this dream? This place with the rattling? I don't like it here. I need to leave. Leave forever...*

"About what?" Taking his hand, she squeezed it.

Again he fell, endlessly. Forever...forever... "Rura Za..."

The rattling stopped. Unwanted memories drowned him. *After Elbie told me, I ran. Oya was there with my violin. Then everything stopped. Stop! I need to leave! To wake up! I need it to stop!*

And the rattling obliged. *What was I...?*

"Ferdinan, please answer me."

Answer what? "I'm sorry..." *That covers everything, right?*

"My child, please tell me what's happening right now."

Is that what she asked? "I don't know...I don't feel well..."

"Ferdinan?"

I know, I'll sleep so... Sleep so I... Can wake up! I'll sleep so I can wake up...

Chapter 10

Random assignment wouldn't work. Not with those two.

It wasn't unusual for Dæya to be displeased with the results, but he had to do something this time. Zephyr returning late left the Superintendent with one less option for seeing to Ferdinan's health.

If Oya wasn't there, he'd put Jon and Ferdinan in the same group. But that wasn't fair either. They'd put too much on the Thinker for too long. If there was another choice... Except Jon received pressure from home to care for the skeleton as well.

Jon needs a break. Ferdinan's needs are more extreme than students should be asked to handle...

Then there was Oya.

I know she'd gladly stay with Ferdinan - watch over him. But Dæya suspected she enabled some of his self-destructive behaviors and wouldn't report when they became dangerous.

No, putting her with Ferdinan isn't wise. Since she came to the islands, the boy skipped more classes than he attended and never returned to his suite. *What other influences does she have on him?*

But placing Oya in a group who didn't know how to handle her was worse. Having her in a group with children younger or less forceful than herself... The ensuing chaos...

That left Jon. With Zephyr no longer an option, he needed Jon to stay with his ally. But the Thinker desperately needed a break.

All three together is unfair to the last person in the group... Scratching at his bald, tattooed head, Dæya returned to Ferdinan.

The location was planned before the plague. And the continent needed every extra hand. *Sending him to Azuté... Seeing the devastation will be traumatic. I could keep him on the islands...*

But he couldn't. The fieldtrip was the only event Ferdinan enjoyed - one message to the Duchess and she'd override him.

Dæya could hear her, *"Let him do as he pleases."* As she did every time he tried intervening to Ferdinan's benefit.

Ferdinan and Oya... Part of him wanted those two in the same group. Keeping them separated felt cruel. Their friendship wasn't healthy. But they were friends. The first he'd ever seen the Tinkerer accept. Thirteen years and the boy finally had a chance to experience a major event with a friend... And Dæya couldn't allow it...

Hematite eyes returned to the results.

Placing Oya in a larger group with strong willed people... That'd work better. But the only person competent at handling her besides Ferdinan was Jon. Though Jon needed a break from Ferdinan, the boy would benefit with a break from both of them. But...

No. Jon and Oya together is the best option. As long as I place someone who'll help Jon. But Ferdinan...? He was difficult.

There weren't many students going who were both older and been at school longer. Ferdinan would be more subservient and cooperative if he considered himself the lowest ranking student.

"How do I want to do this?"

* * *

Bastian read aloud while mussing Jon's hair. Jon relaxed, legs propped over Rigel's belly and head in Bastian's lap with one arm rested against Naizu's shoulder. It felt like an eternity since he last got to cuddle like this. Even with his island brothers...

If only all his brothers were here...

Bastian's deep baritone rolled gently through the room. It felt like a thick blanket. Soft and comfortable and heavy. Jon stopped listening to the story some time ago, but he wrapped his brother's voice around him - laying contented.

Until it stopped.

"No..."

"I love you too, baby brother, but my throat's getting tired."

Giving an exaggerated pout, Jon's freehand reached up and rested on Bastian's forearm.

"Rigel and I were thinking of going to Tillippii's Garden. You want to join us?"

"Sounds fun." Jon smiled - laying still until Naizu moved.

* * *

I wonder what's happening...

It took two weeks to finally hear from her dear friend. Oya hovered over Û-ya'în. All she could see in any direction was ocean and sky. One hand held a screen with Ferdinan's message – wrapped around the other was a lighted cord that might be useless. Collecting more connections was pointless until she knew. But letting go was just as wasteful. *I'm tired.* Not as tired as the glowing orbs drooping in her peripheral. But tired all the same.

Closing her eyes, she let out a slow steady breath. And hovered. Her friend was safely with the family of Giants. Yuyu and Zephyr were fine for now. Herrard was doing better – though uncertain of her after pulling her from the land of dreams.

And she could do nothing. So she hovered – hovered over her oldest friend and beyond Humawit's animosity. And she thought. There weren't many options. But each needed her full consideration.

Because that was all she could do.

Think. And rewatched the beautiful gift her dear friend sent her.

* * *

How do I make him comfortable? Whenever Ozar moved or spoke, his little brother tensed – apologizing over nothing. Yet there was no indication Ferdinan remembered anything from last night. The skeleton behaved exactly as usual.

And this wasn't the first time, but last night was different – more extreme. Coupled with Jon's report... *How many meetings have we held with them? How many times have we begged them?*

There'd be another meeting in a couple days. Seeing the Duchess's oldest daughters wouldn't be good for Ferdinan. And Jon needed a break. But was this the best choice? Ozar felt helpless. After South Chūzo everything changed for his youngest brothers. It terrified him. But he'd find a way to return Ferdinan's futures to him.

Oya's similar... But... The Hei-O shook his head. Right now, he had his family to care for.

"Before we arrive." Ozar winced at Ferdinan's full body cringe. "Leoniel invited us to lunch before picking up our tuxes."

"Those weren't a ploy?" Ferdinan paled. "I apologize."

Ozar laughed, but it only made his little brother flinch. *How do we help him?* "Evelyn requested them for family pictures."

"...then—" Clenching his mouth shut, Ferdinan nodded.

When the car stopped in front of Berago's, his little brother paled magnificently. "Then?"

Red tinged Ferdinan's cheeks and he looked away.

"You've always been our family." Ozar's heart twisted. Those words pained Ferdinan every time he heard them. *We never should've agreed with the Duke and Duchess.*

Leoniel greeted them at the entrance – sweet and bubbly and energetic as always. Unsurprisingly, Ferdinan hid behind Ozar. *Why's he so averse to love and affection?* Nothing they did helped.

"Feeling shy, dear?" Giggles drifted in the air. "I hope you don't mind the simple fair I serve."

Ozar brought a hand down on his old friend's head. Today the Kyo was best described as "shiny." Rich purple and gray sequins and gems reflected light in every direction. *Only he could manage such extreme fashion.* And Leoniel did every day since primary school. It became a game of sorts. "*What would Leoniel come up with next?*"

Finishing school was just as interesting. Ozar smiled. They didn't attend the same one, but Leoniel visited regularly, making sure there was plenty of fun and joy – and that his wardrobe always fit. Together they conquered childhood and young adulthood. And when he stepped up as Hei-O, Leoniel built this place to fund his projects and maintain the eccentricities of their youth. And because the Kyo loved the challenge of clothing a family of giants.

"What surprise is there today?"

"Peak of the season, of course!" Skipping, Leoniel led them to a spacious balcony. "Summer's for eating outside."

"Agreed." Ozar stifled laughter as Leoniel and Ferdinan danced around who should sit last. A gesture to his friend convinced the man to give up. The boy could never sit before a Kyo.

Soon food arrived. Ozar expected Ferdinan to shy away. But the boy studied the chilled vegetable stew instead. *That's unexpected...*

Before Ozar's eyes, Ferdinan relaxed.

His little brother actually relaxed... Briefly.

Boney hands snatched the spoon. Then put it down. A strange look took over that gaunt face and Ferdinan forced his hands to his lap. Ozar saw him salivating, but he sat there – every muscle tense as if only willpower kept him from attacking the bowl.

And Leoniel watched silently, taking in everything.

Before his old friend could find a course of action, Ozar took the first bite. It was light. Notes of each vegetable danced on his tongue. Despite little seasoning, the flavors were exquisite. *He always outdoes himself.* But caring for guests' needs was where the man excelled. "This is amazing. I'll have to steal the recipe."

"Of course!" Dozens of thin, silvery rings reflected the sun's light as Leoniel waved a hand around. "Eat up before it gets warm!"

Ferdinan jolted forward, but stopped himself – blue crystals locked onto the bowl. Staring it down. Knowing this was only the beginning of the strange eating rituals the boy engaged in, Ozar signaled his friend to start. It took a few minutes, but boney fingers finally grabbed the spoon and scooped up a piece of summer squash.

Instead of eating it, his little brother taunted himself with it. Taking a tiny bite. And another. And a third.

Every time Leoniel stared – fascinated by the oddity – Ozar shot a warning glance and shook his head. If Ferdinan noticed the Kyo studying him, he'd stop eating.

A couple more tiny bites of the same piece of squash and the boy allowed the rest into his mouth. His little brother spent as long chewing as he did teasing himself.

Then the process repeated.

The entire process was confusing and nonsensical. But it was fairly standard for Ferdinan – though more elaborate than normal. *Jon understated how bad he's gotten.* Those strange eating behaviors started eight years ago. They were frustrating. But when Ferdinan's health declined, Ozar stopped caring what bizarre rituals his little brother adhered to, so long as he ate.

Even eating slowly, the men finished long before Ferdinan. So they enjoyed a nice conversation until the boy pushed his half-full bowl aside.

An employee arrived to gather the dishes – handing Leoniel a screen. Reading it, the Kyo nodded and thanked them.

This probably wasn't the best plan, but Ferdinan's sisters arrived tomorrow evening and would stay a few days. They needed a safe place for his little brother until it was over. Being present while mom discussed the sensitive things Jon reported would destroy the boy. And they'd lose what little trust they'd earned.

"Ozar, considering your meeting with the Ulie won't end 'til late, I've arranged rooms for you and Lord Ferdinan." Leoniel stood – sparking Ferdinan to jump to his feet. "Dear, your suit's not quite ready. You wouldn't mind coming back for a final fitting?"

Ferdinan stood, uncertain how to respond.

Smile bright and warm, Leoniel gave an apologetic bow. "I apologize for the rushed work on the birthday outfit. I'll make sure these are perfect!"

Bright red and squirming, Ferdinan glued his eyes on the ground and bowed deeply. "I apologize for the inconvenience."

"Not at all!" Silver ringed fingers dance through the air. "Anything for the darling Oza."

Ozar smiled at their mismatched communication styles.

And he worried.

Chapter 11

Xhou stretched. Three hours and he hadn't made any progress on his graduation project. *Home's more important than school work.*

Running fingers through his thick black hair, Xhou sighed. To keep helping mom, he had to get it done. As well as the break's supplemental lessons... *Ugh...* At least his graduation project would be useful when complete. He hoped. The next few months would determine if it was needed or useless.

Combing through code, he searched for the issue. Overworked eyes blurred until his screen *beeped* - giving him an excuse to stop for a moment.

That was unexpectedly fast... A message and a call request? How would the Duchess weasel information out of him this time? *But... She wants to talk and there isn't much time to waste.*

Xhou braced himself and accepted the request. No practiced negotiators survived. Only his mom had experience and she had a million other responsibilities. *This was my idea; I'll see it to the end.*

There wasn't enough time to read over the message before the regal woman appeared - strict and firm. Xhou inclined his head to her. "Duchess Samultz. I apologize, I'm still reading what you sent."

"Understandable. Thank you for speedily accepting my request."

"Unnecessary delays hurt us both." Xhou's response brought a strange kind of joy to the Duchess's eyes - making him uneasy. Scanning over the proposed contract and various sheets of data, he started with the biggest issue. "I can't guarantee harvest yield."

"I'm aware. But that's what's needed to make this work."

Xhou studied the proposal again. The numbers were outrageous. *But she looks perfectly confident. What am I missing?* Untrained or not, he wouldn't complain or run away. Her confidence was unnerving though. "The best I can agree to is a percentage."

"Yes. That's something we'll need to address." Shrewd eyes glanced down at a small screen she held. "What you are asking for is insufficient. Short and long term."

Xhou choked as words jumbled on his tongue. His best advisor ran the numbers. He double checked them. That should be enough to get his country back to its previous functioning within ten years. *What does she know?* "I'm sorry, but that's all I can negotiate with."

The Duchess stretched her neck to the side and put down the small screen. "You misunderstand me."

Despite the high neck of her shirt, Xhou saw every contour accentuated beyond healthy. Blue-black eyes studied her closer. The shirt covered her skin, but its light fabric didn't hide the unpadded bones underneath. *She's thinner...* "Please, correct me."

"Four percent of your population survived and recovered well enough to work. Three percent are permanently disabled beyond the ability of the strenuous physical labor needed to reclaim farmland and get it producing efficiently. The rest left."

"Yes, ma'am." Facing the reality of those numbers was painful.

"Neither have you fully considered the feasibility of your request. Kidico's populations are small and there's little incentive for them to migrate. It's unlikely you'll get a third of what you hope. Oueshian countries were hit hardest after yours – limiting the generosity they can provide. North Oueshi will manage a sizable portion of your request. The Grasslands will turn you down, though they'll take in any hand speakers." The Duchess used both her words and hands when speaking about the Grasslands. "South Oueshi's struggling with their own labor shortage – shoring up yours is beyond them."

"I concede concerning South Oueshi and the Grasslands, but we have strong ties with Kidico..." A sharp, raised brow cut through Xhou, causing him to trail off.

"If you'll allow me to finish, Zi."

"My apologies." Guilt forced his eyes down before he realized it. *Wait...why am I apologizing?* Yet, the rest slipped off his tongue. "Please forgive my rudeness."

"Yes. As you've said, Kidico and Azuté have always been closely tied, but they have the smallest countries. They don't have the population needed no matter how much they want to help or how much pressure you could manage." Those sharp eyes stared at him an extra beat, solidifying her authority. "Mundan is unreachable."

"What?" That wasn't information he'd been given. "I apologize."

"I'm not surprised you're uninformed. Even we are only starting to get the full scope of their isolating." The Duchess bowed her head slightly, emphasizing the free intel she graciously offered. "No one can get in or out. Not since the plague."

Lacking such vital information! *I'm incompetent...* Mundan oscillated in their extremes, but... Closing off once the plague was raging explained why he didn't know. "That leave's Chūzo's countries. Have I underestimated them as well?"

"Some." The Duchess listed the countries he assessed well then detailed the rest. "Self-sufficiency isn't attainable with your plan as is – even before we discuss how sorely you've underestimated the number of people you'll need working off the farms."

Xhou frowned and thought over the reports he'd read.

"Even with your offered concessions, there isn't enough incentive to us for the cost. Yes, we'll have a few fewer mouths to feed – but the number's marginal. Keeping those hands will guarantee higher food production once they're properly placed."

He couldn't argue. A few thousand hands working mass production farms would produce more food than that many fewer mouths would save. *I'm not failing my first negotiation. I refuse.*

The Duchess' brown eyes turned cold. Detached. They were truly terrifying. "But we can make this equally beneficial."

If that proposal wouldn't help his country or benefit her enough to send hands... *The next largest countries focus on military and technology...* He needed people with agricultural knowledge, so they'd be less helpful. North Chūzo kept the world's plates full – they were his best bet for covering basic needs until his country stabilized.

However, mentioning an *equally* beneficial agreement made him want to listen. *The Duchess doesn't lie...not directly.* Like Ferdinan, she wasn't always upfront and would gladly let others make assumptions if it benefited her. But stating that directly... "Please."

"My scientists have run projections. You'll need at least ten percent of our population to become self-sufficient."

This time when Xhou choked, he started coughing.

"Are you unwell, Zi?"

"No! No. I apologize, my throat's dry." Swallowing a few times, he replayed her last statement over in his mind. "Did you say ten?"

"Yes. The third file contains the projections and needs you'll be facing the next few years." She focused on the small screen– giving him time to study the file. "Please verify the data at your leisure."

"Thank you, I will."

"Ten percent will allow you to reach self-sustainability within a year if done efficiently. However..."

Xhou's mind sifted through his knowledge of North Chūzo, but the ten percent was distracting him. "Yes?"

"I'm willing to provide thirty percent of our population."

Xhou simply stared... "Thirty? You said we needed ten."

"You need ten to become self-sufficient. If that's your goal, you are missing the opportunity to secure a more beneficial position for your country – globally speaking."

"How so?" *Thirty...? Thirty percent of North Chuzo's population...what is that? How much more is it than what we had?*

"Frankly, Azuté doesn't utilize its land efficiently due to its small population." The Duchess tapped her screen – sending him another file. "Overall, only two percent of the world's population was lost. Yet food production decreased disproportionately worldwide. Though our own lack will soon hurt other countries."

Xhou nodded. North Chūzo was the largest country both in size and population with the most fertile lands. Which allowed their odd eccentricities to perpetuate. *Why would she use her declining power as a negotiation point?* Azuté's lands weren't failing. They were sitting feral. They weren't as fertile as Chūzo's western most countries, but they yielded well. *She's offering me a power spot for worldwide trade in exchange for taking in a third of her population... How badly are they hurting...and why would she let that show so easily?*

But the offer... Being able to place his country in such an important position... Rebuilding East Azuté with more global weight wasn't something he could turn down easily. "You're willing to send nearly a third of your population to another country?"

"'Til things stabilize. Note my dual citizenship proposal. This'll guarantee those sent may return once they've fulfilled their contract."

"Yes...but..." *A temporary influx 'til we've become a prominent fixture on the world stage wouldn't strain North Chūzo long-run?*

"There'll be concessions on your part." An approving smile glowed at him. "If you'll note the third paragraph of the second file."

Blue-black eyes scanned the document. Frowning, Xhou shook his head. "Children can be managed; we'd never separate them from their parents. But we don't have resources to accept more infirm."

"Everyone sent will be capable of earning their keep." That cold detachment returned to her gaze. "Few people are incapable of some level of work. Whether they run numbers, care for children, prepare meals, label boxes, or ambassador for agricultural collations and the nearby towns and cities. Everyone I send will be capable of something you need. They just won't all be abled bodied."

* * *

Famine brought disgruntled citizens. Poor conditions lead to complaints, then to anger. Hungry people had every right to make demands. But destruction was unfounded. And self-sabotaging.

Why are they putting themselves above their fellow citizens?

On the far west side of the city was an old church where local leaders waited for him. His aunt's domestic platoon was securing the surrounding buildings and a small force protected each silo.

At the signal, Zephyr limped to the church. It was the first building constructed here. Countless expansions and repairs made it feel like a mash of mismatched patches surrounding a grand, awe-inspiring center. It suited Qualilla. *If gods exist, Qualilla blessed and protected this city consistently...until now.*

Like the church, the city was expanded and repaired countless times. Patchwork neighborhoods nestled against well planned ones. Some grand, some less. But all were enough.

The Goddess of Plenty provided well for this city. Not excess. Not want. But enough for them and to give afterward.

Last time the Prince was here, both the people's visage and pockets were comfortably full. A few short years later...

A golden hand reached into his pocket and jabbed the wound he'd inflicted this morning. Irritating it kept the goo away. Kept him in line. The first stab worked for a while. The second and third ones as well. Once one healed, he created a new source of relief.

Readying his sword to draw, he swung the door open. Ahead was the worship hall and a much larger gathering than expected.

All were ready for a fight. Or a dance.

The sword's length was ridiculous considering Zephyr's height, but he laid it on the ground. "I won't shed my citizens' blood."

A middle-aged man walked up and copied the gesture with a less ornamental sword. "The Duchess won't take our lands after stealing our food. Without our lands to glean from, we'd all have starved."

"So, she left you with sufficient?" The Prince's question garnered the expected reaction – irritation, anger, dismay. "'Cause of the Duchess, there's still food in this country despite the famine."

"What concerns us is feeding our children." Deep eyes held a stark distrust.

Turning, Zephyr gestured for the two soldiers behind him to close the doors.

"We can't do that, my Prince."

"To assure my safety, wait outside." At their hesitation, he added, "That's not a request."

The doors closed and Zephyr grabbed two of the many benches stored along the walls. One he placed before the older gentleman and the second facing the first. As a show of respect and a symbol of openness, Zephyr gestured for the man to sit before doing the same. "What's your name, sir?"

"Ermhet Yujalim, my Prince."

"Mr. Yujalim, I wish to listen. Speak your mind; I won't interrupt. And you'll return the courtesy when I respond."

Uncertainty filled the man's face.

"I'm the General's heir before I'm a child."

The man sized him up for a moment before nodding.

* * *

Xhou's head spun. There was so much information...so much he never considered... *My incompetence will destroy my country...*

"It'll take three waves. First, skilled agriculturalists will go into the existing farms and orchards. Based on your annual yield and last fall's..." The Duchess stopped and corrected herself. "My apologies, it'd be your spring. Since last spring's crops were never harvested, they can gather what grew on its own to sustain you while the second wave tames unused land. Efficiently managed, the farms can provide for both waves. The last group will be expert mass food producers. They'll set up greenhouse plantations for year-round production."

And the Duchess kept going. *She's put more thought and planning into this than I have...* Nothing sounded amiss, but there wasn't time to absorb her words. She gave more detail than he knew what to do with. But every part of her plan made sense.

The scope of this was enormous! How naïve was he? Thinking he could manage something so vital? But she laid out a thorough plan broken into easy bites. One that'd benefit them both.

The more she spoke, the more he felt her concern for his citizens. The urgency of everything was troubling. If they didn't start quickly, they'd miss a crucial harvest. So much was lost already. He didn't want his people waiting any longer to find a normal life again.

When she finally placed her small screen down and looked at him, Xhou was awed.

"That's quite generous. You're right, we should-" A frantic knock interrupted him - startling them both. "My apologies. If you'll give me a moment."

* * *

Evening training was done. It wasn't difficult or as exhausting as the last block, but Herrard was tired nonetheless. Yawning, the Healer entered his passcode and opened the door. Light from the window bathed the common room in a gentle glow.

One more block and this won't be home anymore...

There was something indescribably sad about that thought. For fourteen years... He returned to his country - his palace - most

81

breaks for training. But...this was home since he was five. The Kalj couldn't name his siblings. But he knew everyone here.

His home.

His family.

His life.

I don't want to lose them. But one block and he'd have to. The first requirement he faced was choosing a spouse so his father could retire. *How does courting work, anyway?* Then he'd be assigned a wife from each of Kidico's major families and forced to give them as many children as they wanted. *Will I know their names? Or need to be reminded before visits like father? Will I forget the lesser children once an heir and surrogate are selected?* Aside from the one spouse of his choosing, would he be alone? Surrounded by countless advisors and flatterers and ambassadors – but always alone...

A sad chuckle left him. Here. This was temporary. Pretend. He knew that. His father made it clear every chance... No matter how much this felt like home, it never would be. Not for him.

Blinking back tears, he forced his mind to Nammie. She'd be an amazing Lead. Despite him. Because of him. Or something else entirely. She was going to be amazing.

I'm tired...

Part way to his room, he heard a voice he couldn't ignore.

It was as shrewd and convincing as his advisors warned. And his island brother was talking to her alone. *You idiot!*

Still, Herrard learned much. Foremost being why they sent only their most skilled negotiators when dealing with the Duchess. Every time it sounded like Xhou might get some footing, she knocked him further off balance. And by the end...

"That's quite generous."

No! No! Don't agree to that!

"You're right, we should–"

Rude or not, he had to stop this. The way Xhou's mind worked was weak against how the Duchess operated. Given time, the Thinker would see everything wrong with what she was saying. But she wasn't giving him time. She convinced him there wasn't any. Raising a fist, he pounded on the door hard and urgent.

"My apologies. If you'll give me a moment." Xhou appeared, first frightened. Then confused.

Loud enough to be overheard, Herrard blurted out the first thought that came to him. "One of the Science students...something's happened."

The Thinker paled considerably. "Who?"

Overtly as he could, Herrard glanced past his island brother to the screen with an unperturbed Duchess listening closely. "Shina."

Xhou leapt back to the screen. "My apologies, but there's an emergency I need to attend to. I'll get back to you as soon as I can."

"Don't apologize." The woman's smile was sweet, but knowing. "Attending to charges without delay is vital."

"Thank you." Xhou fumbled, but got the screen turned off and was about to plow through Herrard.

"Stop."

"Shina...!" Xhou blinked – breath slowing. "You lied to me? Do you know how important that meeting was?"

"Yes. I heard. You're an idiot. *Never* deal with her alone." Herrard sighed. "Stop and think. What did you almost agree to?"

"I..." Blue-black eyes darted around as the Thinker processed the onslaught that'd nearly drown him. "I'm sorry...I'm not sure..."

Brilliance in science doesn't translate to high stakes negotiations. What were you thinking? "Never go into negotiations with her alone."

"It wasn't...we were discussing options..." Xhou paled. "'Til we weren't... Thanks..."

"We have a team and a front man who deal with her. I'll message them. We'll go over this together." Dropping a hand on Xhou's shoulder, Herrard shook his head. "If you asked, I would've been here."

"It wasn't a planned meeting..." Xhou turned back to the blank screen hovering above his graduation project. "Thank you."

Chapter 12

Û-ya'în jumped and splashed - eager to play. *Next break I'll get to go home.* Playing in the orchards and meadows with dad! Working on projects with mom! She missed it, but was glad her parents could visit for a short while. *It'll be difficult playing with Û-ya'în at home...*

Spending this time with Elbie was also fun. But...it made her worry. *Why did he seem sad?*

Elbie waited on the pier - bare feet slowly swinging and mismatched eyes glued to his hands.

How lonely is he each break? His island brothers stayed this time, but how often will they leave in the future? How many breaks will Elbie spend alone? And he never talked about his family. Was never excited to leave the islands.

Û-ya'în splashed against the pier - spraying Elbie with mist.

Don't worry, little one. I'll see that he's never alone.

Thank you.

Pulling out the little toy, she ran up to him. Mismatched eyes turned and smiled at her.

"Ready for the cookout?" She slid to a stop.

It took a moment, but he shook his head and stood. "I found a cute spot not far from Master Ferdinan's lab. Want to see it first?"

Nodding, Yuyu chased after as Elbie guided her there.

Hidden in the thickest part of the forest was a small clearing.

Tiny flowering bushes formed a little maze with a path just wide enough for one person to walk. At the center was a rock big enough for one person to sit. Pink eyes brightened at the cuteness. "Who do you think made this?"

* * *

It'd been blissfully uneventful the last few days. Jon missed Ozar, but he'd forgotten how calm life was without Ferdinan.

And boring.

Taking his older brother's hand, Jon looked up and up and up. Jingjing was the tallest and still growing. Being near him, feeling small, was comforting. "Let's go to Berago's."

The mountain of a man smiled. "Sounds fun."

"Gongie needs some clothes, I volunteered," Jon chuckled.

A massive boulder gently mussed his hair. "Let's go."

The car ride was spent studying Berago's catalogs – discussing what'd look best on the Telepath. Soon the ostentatious sign came into view. Then bright colors and upbeat energy greeted them.

Berago's was safe and happy. And fun.

Leoniel didn't appear, but a dozen employees doted on them for hours. Two dozen outfits were picked – and five pairs of shoes. Standing, Jon stretched. Gongie would lecture him if he didn't scale back. "I'm going to walk around while I decide which to keep."

Jingjing laughed. "I'm going to pick a couple outfits for myself."

"Show me when I get back!"

Bright colors. Joyful lights. Exciting patterns and textures. This was a better paradise than the islands. Looking over every piece, Jon roamed...until he heard Ozar's voice. It came from a private room. *He's here without me?* Cracking open the door, he saw Leoniel and Ozar waiting patiently. The pale, panicked skeleton was barely visible through a part in the curtains.

A too small tux restricted that grotesque frame. Boney fingers attacked the buttons, but couldn't get them latched. Green tinged the skeleton's lips. The gent grabbed his chest – eyes closed and panting.

"Ferdinan?" Regret glowed in his older brother's eyes.

"Is everything ok, dear?"

Ozar approached the curtain. "Ferdinan, are you ok?"

"I..." The skeleton forced one steady breath after another. "I'm sorry. It doesn't fit."

"I'll refit it!" Leoniel's voice was as bright as his fashion.

"It...it...it's too small..."

"That's wonderful, dear!" Silver rings waived around.

"I told you to leave a little growing room, didn't I?" Ozar chuckled – though it didn't extend past his lips.

Glimmer and flare attacked with a measuring tape. Sweat beaded on translucent skin and Ferdinan screamed in silent horror. Colorless crystals searched every inch of his reflection. Again. And again.

Part of Jon wanted to help. But he turned and walked away. Ozar and Leoniel were there now. If he stepped in, his break would end and he wouldn't make it through the next block.

* * *

"You didn't forget me." A sly grin greeted the too perfect man.

The Fisherman removed his floppy hat and looked at the starless twilight sky and its unnaturally large moon. "They aren't splitting."

"They're working separately toward the same goal?"

"Testing different theories simultaneously."

Delicate fingers tugged at her steel locket. "How far along?"

"The woman's put something into motion in Chūzo." The Fisherman studied Oya. "The man's seeking research passes in East Kidico, North Mundan, and North Oueshi."

"Two of those are troubling."

"Yes."

"I'll warn the remaining camp and villages."

"Kumi'll keep watching the man."

"Thank you." She studied the braided cord of lighted strands. *It wasn't in vain. Guess I should end my game now...*

Oya closed her eyes and opened them to the beautiful view of her old friend. Activating her cuffs, she flew until she spotted him. Black hair shone and lightly tanned skin soaked up the sun. When those dark eyes saw her, his face twisted in panic and despair.

It's been fun Ilu, but I'm out of time and energy. Reaching out to his soul, she drew him to her. Though conflicted, he couldn't resist. The Healer's hands rubbed his face and combed through his thick black hair. Worry coated him as he approached.

Oya grinned.

"Are you ok?"

"I'm sorry, Ilu. It's been fun...for me at least."

"What?"

She giggled and looked at the dimming sky. "No stars yet."

"What?" Confused, Ilu studied her.

Her wicked grin softened. Touching his forehead, she eased him to sleep. Wild green eyes studied the Healer's chest. There were so many connections, but she only needed the two richest royal blue.

Taking them, she offered a memory they'd never question. One too normal to not be real. The three latched onto it with great relief. Then she aged it – making the details fuzzy but the broad picture undeniably clear. One last look and Oya released those blue strings.

What do I do about that man? This new situation? Looking up, she saw a face frozen in a strange kind of horror. It was the same face from the day Humawit stole her climbing holds.

Hesitantly, the boy approached. "What're you doing to my island brother?"

"Tucking him in," she giggled

Horror intensified his angular features and he turned green. "Stop. Please. Leave us alone. We can't take the stress anymore."

"Ok."

"What?" Startled, he stepped back.

"I've no reason to be difficult anymore."

Confusion glazed his dark eyes before horror returned. "Please."

Cuffs activated, she grinned and soared away. High over Û-ya'īn and out to the smallest piece of rock she could still climb. There she played the gift her dear friend gave her. The first time she watched it was an unexpected joy. The second...she loved it all the more.

Music danced and morphed to the transformation of a butterfly. An odd choice. But it suited her best. The message at the end...

The first time it caught her off guard. The second...left her contemplating. And now, she laughed.

"Happy possibly late or early birthday."

What day is it? There were no seasons on the islands. None she noticed. Tapping one random thing after another, she found a calendar. *The 25ᵗʰ day of the 10ᵗʰ month...*

Can I change that as well? She'd contemplated this for five days. *I castoff my past when I cut my hair... Why hold onto that?*

Tapping on the box, she pressed the button to record.

"How did you know the twentieth was my birthday? Thank you very much for the beautiful gift! You're an amazing friend!" Winking, she stopped the recording. Lighted orbs swayed in her peripheral and delicate fingers played with the small steel locket. Grasping it tightly, she looked to the evening sky. *"But I can't give myself everything..."*

* * *

Every meal was arduous. *Is stress driving his eating behaviors?* Every day the rituals became more intense. But Ozar kept quiet – his little brother was getting *some* food in him.

The two men finished and Leoniel leaned back and spread his arms wide. This last ploy would keep them to the end of break.

"Before we retire, I want to thank you for so graciously accepting my request for assistance in preparing for Jon's party."

Surprise flashed across Ferdinan's face.

"Are you ok?" Ozar searched again for any future for Ferdinan.

"Um..."

Guilt hit hard. But Ferdinan's health was deteriorating quickly. *I wish he'd choose to stay...*

Colorless crystals dulled and drifted to the massacred plate. "I apologize. I'm not feeling well. May I be excused?"

"Of course, dear." A heavily ringed hand waved an attendant over. "Feel better. Don't hesitate to ask for anything."

The skeleton bowed and followed the attendant.

"He took that better than I was expecting."

Ozar shook his head. "That's what worries me."

"What do you mean?" The Kyo leaned forward.

There was no one more trustworthy than Leoniel, he'd proved this countless times. Earned his title because of it. But everything with Ferdinan was complicated.

"It's why you requested sanctuary for him."

"You know the Duchess and her daughters..." Ozar exhaled. "We invited them to discuss Ferdinan's health. If he knew, it'd drive him away from us and isolate him from the Samultz' family."

"Are they unaware?"

"It's impossible to miss his physical health..."

The normally energetic man sat calmly, considering his next words. "It's his mind you're worried about."

Ozar looked down. "In strict confidence?"

"Always."

"Our little brother..." Ozar paused – figuring out how to phrase this. "Separating him and Jon was also important. Ferdinan's needs crushed our baby brother before we realized it'd gotten this bad."

"That doesn't sound like you."

"Jon wasn't comfortable discussing things over a screen. And Ferdinan habitually suppresses pain 'til he doesn't feel it – doesn't recognize it... 'Til he forgets. By the time we can get him home it's hard to assess..." Strong hands rubbed his face. Ozar was betraying his little brother. But if things didn't go well, he'd have to call on Leoniel for another favor. "He had an incident at school – and another right before I called you. Among other things..."

"And the Duchess hasn't helped him?"

"She insists he gets the care he needs." His next thought...Ozar hated thinking it about anyone. "It feels like they're making it worse."

"He's the fifth child. Why not claim him?"

Ozar laughed – but it wasn't funny, just terrible. "We have. He won't accept it. Neither will the Duchess acknowledge our claim. Forcing the matter would destroy him."

Chapter 13

Everyone was tense.

Everyone.

And all they could do was wait.

No stories held Jon's attention. Xingho and Raonie kept Evelyn busy. And Ferdinan was somewhere with Ozar. He was too nervous to lounge with his brothers. Even his neglected piano was too much.

Minutes crawled to hours. The day faded away.

And they held their breath.

What's going on? Why's it taking so long? The Samultz never stayed longer than necessary. Everything they approached was with brutal efficiency. So why was it taking so long?

Jon rubbed his face. This was his break – his chance to relax with his family and not worry about the gent. But...what happened in mom's office determined his future.

He roamed the halls. Wandered around outside. And nervously picked at his food. *I can't take it anymore.* Quietly, he snuck down the hall and pressed an ear against the door. His hands shook and his heart raced. What was taking so long?

"Repeating yourself doesn't change anything. He's merely eccentric, like any *special* child. Like the Duke." The emphasis of "special" indicated the word tasted of sewage.

"He isn't eccentric. Your brother's ill and needs proper care."

"We've provided sufficient. Neither his schooling nor fulfilment of responsibilities have suffered. He's even gained world recognition for a number of his inventions. There's no such concern."

Silence hit the room hard. *I know mom told them everything. So how can they say that? Believe that?* What else had they said? How much had they broken his mom's heart with such coldness?

"Very well." The pure fire in Mother's voice burned through the tension. "Since you refuse to listen, I'll deal with *my* child the way I see fit. Objections will be met swiftly and publicly."

Mom's fiery words vanished in the sister's frozen response. "We've no objections. While he's in your home, he's expected to behave. Troubling you is failing this expectation."

What a backhanded remark... Breathing hard, Jon clutched his jaw – chest burning. In one breath they both didn't claim their only brother and denied his mom's claim. And... *They blamed Ferdinan... The fear of failing. It's made everything worse his whole life.*

"He's never troubled me. And regardless of where he is, he's *my* child." A chair scooted and Jon pictured his mom towering three heads over Ferdinan's sisters, cloaked in pure fury. "You'll accept my claim or we'll bring it before the world."

"You'll do well to remember our agreement." More chairs scooted across the floor. "Adhere to that and you can do whatever you please with it...him. He's not our concern at the moment."

Fire flared across Jon's chest. *"It?"*

Ice settled in his gut. *What agreement?*

Bile rose in his throat. *Did...they just throw him away...?*

Tears blurred the world. A hand stifled a sob as he pushed away from the door and into Samuel's arms. Jon didn't resist his older brother guiding him to an empty room.

"That's not a conversation you should've heard."

* * *

The Kyo insisted Ferdinan try the hot springs. Even assured he'd have the natural baths to himself – every day until the skeleton gave in. He'd never done this before, but he knew the proper etiquette.

Fully washed, he made his way to the prized baths.

It was hotter near the springs than by the gardens out back. The warmth was nice – but the floating steam was disconcerting... Still, insulting a Kyo was unacceptable. Removing his robe, he stepped into the water.

Heat enveloped him.

His heart raced. Spots faded in and out. Heat and steam – smoke choked his lungs... Gasping he stood. He needed to get away. *Run!* He needed to escape! *Run faster! Get there first!*

A fiery beam fell on his shoulder. Crying out, he jumped away. A voice stopped him. Spots danced faster – obscuring his surroundings. And sound echoed. It echoed... Fire encased him.

"Ferdinan? Are you ok?" Ozar's voice broke through.

Blue crystals searched for an escape. "Yes! Yes, I'm fine."

"What's wrong?"

"I'm sorry. I'm sorry..." Ferdinan forced himself to straighten – ignoring the black spots. "I'm tired."

Ozar sighed. "What's wrong, little brother?"

"I'm sorry..." Ferdinan bowed and slipped into his room.

The air was cool but smelled of smoke...

Grabbing his green mint tin, Ferdinan sat on the bed and stared at the wall. *There's enough...* A bitter laugh strangled out of him. That'd hurt Jon more. He hurt everyone... *A couple days.* Then they'd return to the islands. Putting the tin away Ferdinan laid down.

And when he closed his eyes, searing heat bit into his shoulder.

Skin and muscle melted. Digging deeper and deeper. The weight was impossible but he had to keep it off of them! His trembling hand offered a shirt. "Save them! Both of them! Don't leave her behind!"

"*When you lifted the beam, I saw her. She was under Yuyu–*" Oya's green eyes loomed, face dark and serious.

His heart skipped. "*I know! Save them both! Please!*"

"*She was already gone.*" Reaching down, Oya lifted Yuyu.

No one else was there.

She's here. I know she's here! Running through the building – staying on Oya's heels – they reached their last chance for escape and bolted. But he needed to reach the window first.

"Why're you leaving me behind?"

Fire swirled, attacking from all directions, eating his skin. Pain choked him. *No! I couldn't find you! I tried! You weren't there!*

"I'm right here." Amidst the raging flames stood a small figure – flesh melted and bones blackened. "I'm right here. Don't leave me."

93

* * *

Various kinds of snoring filled the air.

All of them slept together in the common room for Jon. His parents, brothers, in-laws, and Evelyn were piled together, sleeping peacefully. But that conversation haunted him.

They threw him away. How could you do that to family? To a child? A sick child...

What did he do now that he knew? All those years being told Ferdinan was a brother – to befriend the gent... It was annoying! Frustrating! And he didn't understand. No one told him.

So many things made sense now...

Guilt tripled. He tried being a brother, a friend. Tried for years despite Ferdinan's rudeness, verbal abuse, and stealing his family's time and attention. Tried until he couldn't anymore. Things finally became tolerable after he started treating Ferdinan as an ally. *But his health declined rapidly...*

No one should be alone. No child should be abandoned. But Jon almost did...because he didn't realize...

He knew now.

Only... How could he be a brother or a friend to Ferdinan? The gent was impossible. *Nothing works...*

Samuel mussed his hair and whispered, "why're you still awake?"

"Can we talk?"

Carefully, they disentangled themselves from the pile and moved to the hallway. But Jon's bare feet didn't stop. They kept going to the front door and out into the star filled night. It was warm and the grass felt nice between his toes. "How do you be a brother to someone who doesn't want you?"

Samuel hugged him. "I'm sorry we pressured you. We'll continue from here – you don't have to worry anymore."

"But I do. Maybe a few weeks a year he'll come here. The rest of the time he's on the islands or traveling alone." Jon wasn't ready to end his break, but he wanted a plan before leaving. "How do you be a brother to someone who hates you?"

"He doesn't hate you. He...doesn't know how to accept you. Any of us." Samuel gazed at the sliver moon. "He never learned how."

"I tried for years and nothing worked." Shame forced his eyes away. "If I'd known...I wouldn't have given up."

"But could you've kept it from him?" Samuel offered his hand. "How would he have reacted when he saw? There's a reason only the three oldest of us know. And if we hadn't been there, I doubt we would've been informed."

"That doesn't help me know what to do."

"Love him like you love us. That's all you can do."

* * *

Jerking away, Ferdinan choked on smoke filled air. The charred and disfigured girl reached out to him – the unquenchable fire...

His stomach turned. *I need to get us out!*

The window... I have to reach it! I have to get out!

Staggering. Searching. Flames surrounded him. He should be hot. His skin should be melting, blistering. But it felt cool.

Elbie.

Yuyu.

Unforgiving fire reared up – surrounding him. He needed to reach the window, but if he opened it, the flames would attack him... Attack all of them...

But he didn't have a choice. Stomach twisting harder, he dashed forward. But the half-melted girl grabbed him. "Don't leave me behind!"

Metal coated his tongue and filled his lungs – becoming solid. He couldn't breathe. Clawing his throat and chest, dizziness set in and he sunk to his knees. The floor...the blazing table he leaned against...were cold. *Why is it cold?*

Holding on tight, she pleaded, "I'm right here. Don't leave me."

Thick blood held his lungs – keeping him from answering her. *I'm sorry...I tried...you weren't there...*

* * *

Jon loved Samuel, but that advice wasn't useful.

He could learn to see Ferdinan as a brother – could learn to love the gent. But how did he *be* a brother to the skeleton? Sighing, Jon looked at the star filled sky. Whatever it took, he knew he couldn't do it alone. For years his efforts only made things worse – until he rejected the gent. And his family wouldn't be there to help him. But his island brothers would.

"I'm going to get a screen and sit out here and read."

"Would you like company? I've got plenty of reading as well." Samuel gave one last squeeze and step back.

"No. No." Jon took in a deep breath. "I need to think for a bit."

* * *

Leoniel looked over the weekly reports while Ozar snored softly in the armchair. *A new guest?* It always broke his heart when a child needed sanctuary, but a month was plenty of time to prepare for their needs. After reaching out to contacts and ordering supplies, Leoniel watched over his sleeping friend. *How can I give Ozar a break and keep Ferdinan busy?* He'd never met anyone so resistant to rest.

The boy's quite unusual. Even compared to Leoniel's more unique guests. He didn't see the level of distress Ozar claimed, but the child was definitely unhappy. *How can I make him smile?*

A startled gasp broke through the door separating his suite from Ferdinan's – interrupting Leoniel's thoughts. Approaching... *Should I wake Ozar?* But his stressed friend finally fell asleep...

Cracking the door open, dark eyes peeked inside. It was eerie seeing the sickly child stagger around. Those nearly colorless eyes reminded him of the dead. If not for the terror twisting the boy's face Leoniel would've thought he stumbled upon a corpse.

Is he sleepwalking? Or confused? Those eyes stayed in one place instead of jumping all around, the hypervigilance Ferdinan portrayed before now was gone, and the child staggered as if blind. *He has to be asleep.*

Planning the safest route to guide the boy back to bed, Leoniel entered. But Ferdinan stumbled into the bathroom. The skeletal child desperately turned side to side. Keeping a respectful distance, the Kyo watched for an opportunity to intervene.

But Ferdinan kept searching. Something Leoniel couldn't see caught the boy's attention. Then he charged the window.

Miraculously, the Kyo reached him before the child leapt through. Stick thin limbs thrashed and fought! Nails reached out. *How is he so fast? And strong?* "Ferdinan, wake up."

The struggling stopped and lifeless eyes filled with tears and horror. Boney fingers turned to claw at his throat and chest.

Leoniel almost lost his grip as Ferdinan sank to the floor – lips turning blue. "Ferdinan. This is Leoniel. You need to wake up."

Painful retching sparked Leoniel to lift the boy and turn him in time to throw up in the tub instead of on the floor.

"Ozar! Ozar, get in here now!"

There was a rustling of blankets and stumbling feet as the half-awake giant made his way through the rooms. "What's wrong?!"

"I don't know." Leoniel restrained Ferdinan's arms when the child returned to clawing at his throat.

Blinking, Ozar's eyes doubled in size. "Let go of him!"

Immediately Leoniel obeyed – falling backward.

Gasps and whimpers and more vomiting followed. Pathetic moans left Ferdinan and he mumbled things like "I'm sorry, I tried to save you" and "I looked, you weren't there."

Ozar knelt on the other side of the boy – careful not to touch him. "You should've woken me immediately."

"I apologize. I've never had a sleepwalker react like that."

"When he's like this, touching him his dangerous."

Leoniel looked between the boy and his old friend. "I'm sorry for not believing he was as sick as you said."

"Don't mention this come morning. If you do and he doesn't remember, it'll make things worse."

"Of course. Tell me what to do and I'll do it."

* * *

Jon didn't read. He called his most trusted island brother. It didn't take long for Gongie to respond. But where did he start?

"It's pretty late there." Gongie sat back. "Is something wrong?"

"I got the outfits you asked for." Jon's voice broke and he had to blinked back tears.

"I'm listening."

"How do you be a brother?"

Confusion lined the Telepath's face. "You'd know better than me. You're the best brother of us all."

"I don't know how to be a brother to Ferdinan."

"I thought this was your break from him." Gongie leaned forward, giving his full attention.

"It is." Jon shook his head. "The break's almost over."

Worry lined Gongie's brow. "Why now? Your family's always insisted he's a brother. Why's it important now?"

"Some things have happened." Jon brushed away falling tears. The idea of being thrown away like that... "I have to figure it out. But I need help. And my family...they won't be on the islands. We will. Will you help me?"

"It'll be difficult. I'm a Psych and Ilu's a Healer." Pain filled Gongie when Jon cried harder. "But we'll figure out how to help. We'll figure this out."

Chapter 14

"*Ferdinan!*"

"*Hi… I'm sorry…*" The view behind Oya caught Ferdinan's attention. "*Where are you?*"

Exotic green eyes beamed. "*Climbing! I found a new cliff!*"

The screen rotated, showing him how high she was.

"*Why are you juggling a screen halfway up a cliff?!*"

A golden-brown wrist showed off the cuff she pilfered. "*No place could prevent me from answering your call.*"

His face lit on fire. "*Please don't die.*"

"*I'll not die today!*"

That's…not comforting.

"*Isn't this view amazing?*" She moved the screen to show the purple sky blending into the water.

I should've checked the time. "*You shouldn't have answered. And climbing after dark is dangerous.*" Ferdinan almost closed out the box but stopped. "*I'm sorry you were alone on your birthday.*"

Giggles jumped out of the screen. "*I wasn't. Your message was sweet and my present, beautiful! It's the best birthday I've had in a while. I look forward to playing when you return.*"

Bright red, Ferdinan looked away. "*Me too. Good night. Be safe.*"

She winked and the box went black. The conversation was too short. He'd replied to all his messages. Both the Kyo and Ozar had nothing for him to do. And there was no lab to borrow.

Lifting the screen with Oya's histories, he chose a random story. It was cute – as much as he understood. On a smaller screen, he recorded every word and phrase he couldn't find translations for. Deciphering them from context left him lost. *Would Oya know?*

These were her histories…but the sheer volume of information was more than one could hope to glance, let alone memorize.

Finishing the chapter, his mind turned to unpleasant thoughts.

Family pictures were today. His stomach churned. Swallowing hard, Ferdinan stood and paced the room. *What if it doesn't fit again?* He already caused enough trouble. Was too out of control...

Forcing out a breath, Ferdinan pushed those thoughts away. *If I knew how Oya goes unnoticed. I'd run...* Run. Through the woods and across the countryside. How far could he go before passing out?

It wouldn't be the same. Without Oya ready to throw a punch, to start a battle... It'd just be him running... Under-exercised muscles demanded to move. But he couldn't. Not here. There was nowhere secluded, nowhere to hide... *I wish I was on the islands with her...*

Pacing faster and faster...

Where does she come from? What culture creates someone like her? Guilt hit hard. All this time and he hadn't earned any of these answers... *It's been a year...nearly...* He wanted to know more about her, but he couldn't even figure out where she was from.

His body moved faster – making full use of the small room.

The strange things she said. The oddities she considered normal. Her eccentricities and conflicting parts... The only normal thing was her admitting how much she missed her family. She'd been perfectly sincere in that moment. But it wasn't useful. Every culture had close ties with family – even if definitions of family varied.

There was only one other thing shared by all cultures. The celebration of a person's birth. It was the first show of respect. But... Bony fingers scratched at his head. She said she liked her gift. But did she really? He wasn't good with these things.

Even surrounded by those who considered the yearly celebration important...he never understood. They were already born. Their life was in motion. It was the birth itself that mattered. Why keep celebrating their infancy? Even the Ascension Ceremony on an heir's seventh year was about recognizing them as capable of eventually taking over that role – not reliving the day they were born.

That's why he gave Yuyu and Elbie a gift when they turned seven. To let them know he celebrated their birth and show them they'd easily surpass him when they were ready.

But Oya... What was the right thing for her?

He didn't deserve her, but she was his first friend. And each day he was more grateful she'd been born. But... *Am I being a coward?*

Forcing out another breath, he dropped to the floor for pushups. His thoughts were jumbled and useless. Sweat beaded on his brow. He was about to switch to crunches when the chime sounded.

Opening the door... *Jon? What do I do? What do I say? What can I say?* Ozar obviously separated them for Jon's sake. So why?

His ally couldn't look at him – so Ferdinan lowered his head.

Stinging needles pushed a tux against his chest. "Pictures are in half an hour."

Bile climbed up Ferdinan's throat. The Duchess's fury filled his mind. Had he gained more? Would it fit?

"They're normal. Not like the ones for Evelyn's party." Jon frowned when Ferdinan didn't take it.

"I know..." *What do I do if it doesn't fit? I couldn't keep myself under control. I failed. I've gained more. I've gained too much...!*

"We better hurry." Letting out a sigh, Jon stepped over the threshold. "Need help with anything?"

Taking the tux, Ferdinan retreated to the bathroom. The giant mirror loomed. He didn't want to look. But he had to. One shirt at a time fell to the floor until he faced his scarred and warped skin.

Twisting and turning, he examined every inch of his body. Pinching and pulling... *Will it fit?* The mirror said he gained more.

His heart raced. Faster and faster. Twisting and jumping. The more he pinched... The more he pulled... The more he looked... *How much have I gained? I need to get myself under control!* His mind drifted to the green mint tin in his bag. *Is it 'cause of them?* They increased appetite. Made it hard to ignore...

But living with that voice again... *What do I do?*

Knocking danced around the bathroom. "Ferdinan?"

What should he do? He failed miserably... What if it didn't fit?

"Ferdinan, is everything ok?" Jon's voice came through louder.

Grabbing the suit, Ferdinan forced it on – heart pounding.

"Are you Ok?" Jon's shouted.

It fit.

Relief hit hard. But his heart kept pounding – leaving him dizzy. He sat on the edge of the tub. *Ok...ok...I can do this.*

"Ferdinan! Answer me! Are you ok?"

The first few times he tried responding, his face twisted and his throat closed up. But he eventually forced out an apology.

* * *

Centering himself, Gongie forced everyone's voice to the back of his mind and entered the common room. But he said nothing.

"What's wrong?" Ilu gestured to an open seat.

"Jon wants to try again."

The room's collective mood plummeted.

Gongie understood. Years of effort and nothing improved until Jon stopped. Whatever happened in South Chūzo pulled him back into that toxic situation – leaving them struggling to keep him sane.

It was harder for Gongie. He wasn't allowed near Ferdinan. And he didn't want to be. The things that child felt and thought... And the Tinkerer's mind was so loud! Always screaming! Saturated in agony... And when the skeleton saw him, equations, blueprints, and countless words he didn't know exploded in his mind.

Ilu was rightly afraid of Ferdinan. He was there that day. And Gongie suffered through those nightmares alongside the Healer.

But knowing it wasn't Ferdinan's fault and not being allowed to say anything... As a child, what could he say? What could he do?

That last question he'd considered for days.

"Why?" Ilu clasped tanned hands together to hide their shaking. "Why? He should return to how they were before South Chūzo."

"He didn't tell me." Gongie scratched the back of his head, "I doubt he can talk about what happened."

Tuel floated down and placed his screen on the side table. "What does Jon need?"

"Our support? Ideas? I don't know. But he wouldn't..." How did Gongie answer without saying too much? "He wouldn't...keep putting himself through the frustration of the last year if it wasn't important."

Silence filled the room, magnifying Marcus's muffled tears. Deep sorrow was stifled by the veil Gongie held in place. The mid-day shadow lowered to the couch and wrapped an arm around the Artist.

"Where do we start?" Ilu shook his head. "We know nothing of what's happening inside the Tinkerer...nothing useful. We have no starting point for someone who doesn't want anyone in their life."

"People need people." Tuel pushed Marcus's long braids aside to rub his back. "And... Ferdinan accepted Oya. Maybe she'll help."

Ilu cringed. They all did. Especially Gongie. He didn't know who or what Oya was, but she wasn't real. Every time he saw her... If so many people didn't have memories of her, he would've sworn she was a hallucination of Jon's mind...and Ferdinan's.

The few times he saw her... A shiver consumed his spine. *Could a trickster god truly exist?* Shivering again, he pushed those memories away. Despite how uneasy she made them, it wasn't a bad suggestion.

A tsunami of sorrow broke through Gongie's mental veil. Tears slid faster down Marcus's face. Thoughts and emotions cluttered together. So many his island brother was struggling with...

"I'm sorry." It took Gongie a bit to force the wave back.

A strangled laugh left Marcus. "I can't."

"It's ok," Tuel squeezed the Artist's shoulder.

Marcus gazed at his hands. "I can't...I can't get close to someone who could die with their next breath. I can't lose anymore... I can't."

"I understand. We won't put you in that position." The tsunami doubled in size – forcing out Gongie's tears. "And we don't have to decide anything now. But..."

"Herrard insists she's a nice person." Ilu squeezed Marcus's hand. "I'll ask him the best way to approach her."

"I'll come with you." Wiping his face dry, Gongie moved to offer Marcus comfort as well.

* * *

The pictures went well, but smiling was difficult.

How do I be a brother to him? What kind of brother does he need? Jon had no idea, but trying was the first step. He delivered the tuxes. Made sure Evelyn spent as much time with the gent as possible. And now...

Stepping outside, Jon made his way to the little gazebo. Quiet, peaceful, and surrounded by flowers – finding the skeleton there wasn't surprising. *This place was made for Ferdinan.*

Looking at the gent wasn't easy. Taking out his screen, he sat on the covered benches to read over the message he got every year. He felt the perturbed look his ally...brother gave him, but kept reading.

Every year for his birthday he got a blank message with an attached recipe in an ancient language.

Attempts at tracing these messages were always unsuccessful. But he knew it was one of his brothers. Considering a different dead language was used each year, it was probably from all of them. Or maybe they took turns.

Opening a new box on the screen, Jon went to work translating the recipe, hoping to find something to say before his ally...brother got annoyed and walked away. Surprisingly, Ferdinan didn't move – just continued reading. *Why isn't he leaving?*

This year's recipe was enthralling. Deciphering the extinct characters was a reasonable challenge, but one ingredient gave him trouble. There was no common equivalent he could find. And the systems he had access to didn't recognize it.

Jon growled out a sigh – catching the Tinkerer's attention.

"Is something wrong?"

"I can't figure out this word." *It has to exist...*

When the skeleton leaned over, Jon showed his ally – brother – the screen.

Blue crystals looked over the ancient script before studying the characters Jon pointed to. "Ba-na-anī."

What? "That's how it's pronounced?"

"Yeah."

"You know what it is?"

"It's a fruit. It went extinct millennia ago. I doubt there's an equivalent or you'd have found it."

How does he know such a random thing? "Then how do you know what it is?"

"Most ancient languages have a similar word for that fruit." Looking over the rest of the recipe, Ferdinan's face scrunched up.

"What?" *This isn't one of the languages he knows...is it?*

"Too sweet."

"You know this language?"

Ferdinan shrugged.

"They've never sent an impossible recipe before." *That would be...? Ten? What is he?* "I've replicated all of them. How do I replace an unknown fruit?"

"Is it the texture or flavor required for the dish?"

Jon sat stunned. *He's helping me with something food related?* "How would I figure that out?"

"I'm sorry." Again, Ferdinan shrugged. "Trial and error. Research."

That answer wasn't useful, but Jon relaxed and offered a smile. *We aren't arguing...* "An excuse to play in the kitchen."

"You should enjoy that." Ferdinan scooted away and returned to his own screen.

Jon followed suit, but couldn't focus. *How bad is it if mom would publicly claim him? It'd destroy him. And his sisters wouldn't care... Unless it interfered with whatever "agreement" they had.*

But why throw him away? That'd hurt them politically. The Queen Mother claiming their sick brother could cost North Chūzo allies and treaties. A public claim would hurt Ferdinan and lessen North Chūzo's world power. *If mom says Ferdinan's been abused and neglected... Worse, if she announced they had years to fix things and it only got worse...* One look at the gent and no one would doubt her.

But she didn't for him... And she should've for him... What's mom been struggling with?

Jon didn't realize he was staring until the skeleton pointedly looked away. Awkward silence separated them until his brothers floated out of the building – full of life and energy. Standing, he walked over and hugged them – only to be snatched up.

Then he was crashing through toasty water. Evelyn splashed over and her small arms wrapped around his neck. Water attacked his eyes. And there was light and color and joy everywhere. Dad returned from his summons and was sitting on the hot spring's edge next to mom – tiny beside her. Seeing them was always odd. But he loved it. Even sitting, mom was two heads taller. His brothers and in-laws splashed around him.

Colorful swimsuits slipped under the water and reappeared elsewhere. Evelyn tossed a water toy over his head – starting a game of keep-away.

Losing the toy frog was easier than keeping it – especially against the giants he was battling. Evelyn squealed and cheered! Laughing he jumped to snatch up the toy but it slipped through his fingers. He turned to grab it before Bastian...but saw Nigel kneeling next to the skeleton huddled in the corner.

Sorrow and guilt hit. Seeing Ferdinan alone, clutching a blanket tightly around himself... All Jon could think of were the gent's sisters throwing him away. Who did that to family? Their brother? A child?

"That's not how you win, Jon!" Bastian's deep voice called him back to the game.

Turning, Jon was met with a wall of water to the face. He laughed! But felt hollow.

He'd be happier if he accepted us.

Chocolate eyes drifted back to the skeleton and Nigel.

I won't abandon someone thrown away by their family.

Chapter 15

Impatience poured out of Oya.

Evening colors stain the sky brilliantly by the time the ship arrived. Once the plank was down, she ran up. Waiting was simple enough. But roaming the ship sounded more enjoyable. Besides, no matter where they were, she'd always find her friends.

Bare feet ran full bore over the deck before following Evelyn's yellow string to their cabin door. Neither boy noticed her slip inside.

Ferdinan sat with his back to her - arms folded while Jon crammed scattered items into a bag. A smirk played in his voice. "If I'm lectured for being slow, I'm blaming you."

"It'd be accurate." Concern and annoyance puckered Jon's face.

"You're both slow."

Jon jumped. But Ferdinan turned and smiled at her - relief washing over him. And Oya giggled.

"*I'm sorry for making you wait.*" Ferdinan stood and bowed.

"*What did you bring to make up for it?*" She teased.

"*Nothing... but Evelyn did.*"

Jon threw his arms out, "I'm here."

"Really? What is it?" Bouncing, Oya gave Jon a smirk.

Ferdinan grabbed something large and lumpy wrapped in a beautiful orange cloth dotted with purple and blue butterflies. "Evelyn says 'happy birthday.'"

"You're lucky having such a sweet sister." Nimble fingers conquered the knot and laughter filled the small cabin.

Jon grinned and shook his head.

"It's wonderful!" She violently hugged the giant stuffed animal. Its body was as tall as her and the tentacles double that. Soft and squishy. Enormous and orange. And cartoony. It was the perfect squid. She never had something so...whatever it was.

Oya hoisted it to her shoulders – securing floppy legs with folded arms. "I love it! Almost as much as the song from my dear friend! Next time you talk to Evelyn, let me thank her."

"Gladly." Ferdinan smiled at her childish joy.

Grabbing the silk sheet, Oya tied it around her waist. "Even the packaging is awesome."

"Jon picked it."

"Thank you very much!" She spun before attacking them with a hug. Jon relaxed, but Ferdinan stiffened uncomfortably, so she released them. "Three gifts from three friends, how loved am I?"

The two boys smiled pensively – exchanging uncertain looks.

* * *

"You do this every break?" Yuyu smiled – spinning the little toy.

"Yah..." Mismatched eyes watched students disembark. Even before starting classes, Elbie watched when the boats returned. It was an odd ritual. But he had to be there.

"Why?"

"I don't know... I guess..." *What can I say?* The first time he failed to watch, his mentor didn't return. "It was fascinating. Then it became habit. Now..."

"Now?" Yuyu prompted.

"Now... I don't know... It's... It's like I'm watching to see if I still have a mentor..."

"I'm sorry."

Elbie shook his head – watching Oya run on board. "She asked about my project. Asked me to explain it to her. And listened without interruption even though I could tell she didn't understand..."

"Who?" Pink eyes turned her full attention to Elbie.

"Oya. It was strange..." Elbie wasn't sure where he was going, he was just talking and Oya was the first thought to pop into his head. "She's a confusing person."

"I don't think I've talked to her. Even when she helped us with the show..." Yuyu trailed off and returned her gaze to the boat.

Warm ocean air tugged at their hair and the evening colors grew more intense. Reds. Oranges. Swallowing hard, he forced his mind to stay calm and his eyes on the groups of students disembarking. But it wasn't until the sky's intensity had faded that Oya reappeared.

"What's she carrying?" Yuyu leaned forward - perplexed.

Whatever it was, it was as big as the unusual girl. Long danglies flared to the side when she spun. The two tall boys behind her were harder to tell apart than expected. They were the same height and their shoulders similarly broad. From this distance, it was impossible to see those nearly colorless eyes and Ferdinan's loose clothing made him appear larger. *I never realized how similar they look...*

* * *

"*A couple birthdays kept you busy for three weeks?*" Oya teased - coated in sweat and sprawled on the grass. Her head rested above his shoulder - ear nearly touching his.

"*Also some business meetings and Evelyn.*" Her warm presence eased every tension. This was paradise after a month of agony. Just laying here talking. "*I think they were purposely keeping me busy.*"

"*Not much of a break?*"

"*No. But your histories were a nice distraction.*"

"*What interesting things did you find in them?*"

"*There were some words that didn't make sense... Maybe slang or metaphor of some kind. And some phrases. But I couldn't find anything like them in the language databases.*"

Giggles filled the small space between Oya and her dear friend. "*What's the most interesting?*"

"*There were a number.*" Ferdinan rambled off a few. Most Oya didn't know, but some she did. One lit up her face.

"*How about: Jack-of-all-trades...? I couldn't decipher anything from the context. It was only used once. Each part of the phrase didn't make sense together – there were no records of it...*"

"*Jack-of-all-trades... Jack-of-all-trades? Dad loved that one.*" Reaching up, she played with his unruly hair.

Ferdinan gave his full attention.

"*It isn't uncommon for the Mwã-tonô or Tonō to be proficient at most things.*" Exotic green eyes studied the stars overhead. "*That's what it means. Someone who's good at almost everything.*"

"*That's quite the feat.*"

"*How did that phrase go?*" Oya played with his hair again. "*A jack-of-all-trades but master of none...*"

"*Ah...*"

"*There's more.*" Her fingers moved vigorously through his thick locks. "*Ah! Though often better than a master of one!*"

"*That...makes sense.*" The only thing he was good at still killed millions of people. "*Um... What did you do during the break?*"

The very essence of life radiated from her. "*Haha! I played with Ilu and Elbie and Xhou! And I made a new friend!*"

He smiled at her enthusiasm. *I'm glad she had fun.* "*Who?*"

"*Herrard!*"

"*Kalj Herrard?*" His smile faded and he paled considerably.

"*Yah?*"

"*Why aren't you making friends with girls?*" Ferdinan blurted – flustered by the Kalj's name. "*Sorry... that was rude, I apologize.*"

Scooting so she could roll to her side and face him, she grinned. "*Boys are more fun to play with.*"

"*I don't know what to do with some of the things you say.*"

A wicked grin curled her lips.

He wanted to stay like this all night. Stay like this forever.

* * *

"Little Samuel! I apologize for the delay." General Tenalia smiled at her old friend. "You're needing some information?"

Samuel's face tensed. "This is difficult, so please don't interrupt."

"What is it?" The General leaned forward, coated in concern.

110

"Is there any family history of mood or emotional difficulties?"

"Excuse me?" The buff woman bristled – fire in her eyes.

"Deep sadness, unfounded anxiousness, undue energy, worrying excessively...or other *difficult* problems."

Jaw clenched, eyes hard, Tenalia moved to close out the box.

"Wait! I mean no offence; I'm trying to help my little brother."

"Ferdinan?" Her fury gave way to worry. "There's no history of such difficulties. And Ferdinan isn't defective. He's just...sensitive."

"He needs help."

"What's happening with my nephew?"

Samuel considered his words. *How do I get her to take this seriously without offending her? And not betray what little trust Ferdinan's given?* "He suffered...extreme sleep disturbances."

"Like Zephyr?"

"No. Sleepwalking. Leoniel Kyo grabbed him before he jumped through a window. Also terrible nightmares. Waking nightmares."

"What do nightmares have to do with your earlier question?"

"Often such things are linked."

"There's no unsavory history." Tenalia's jaw twitched. "This stays between us. I won't let either of my nephews face hardships 'cause of a little sleep difficulty as children."

Samuel frowned. There were more questions. But if he alienated their strongest ally, they'd lose Ferdinan completely. *I'll have to figure out something else.* "I apologize for troubling you."

* * *

The five of them piled together in the common room. An eternity had passed since Jon relaxed with his island brothers.

If only the strain would go away.

He cooked for them and they loved it. After, they laid around the common room as some part of Jon smooshed each of them. They told him what happened on the islands and he described Evelyn's party and being lazy the entire break.

But the tension was still there.

"I know I'm asking a lot." Silence made the strain more oppressive. What could he say? How could he make them understand without...? Those cruel words played through his mind. The memory of that day. Forcing it to stop so Gongie wouldn't hear... It played again. And again. And when he gave up, the whole thing jumped around repeating the worst parts.

The Psych took his hand and squeezed it – pain twisting his face.

"Why?" Ilu looked down. "Why go through that again?"

"'Cause this time I want to."

"Your family isn't making you?"

"No. They said I don't have to try anymore. It's not a duty." Jon sighed and that terrible conversation played through his head again. "I truly want to be his brother this time."

"Ok." Tuel spoke up when silence fell. "We considered where to start and... And Oya...she's the only one he's accepted. But we couldn't find her."

"Months of torment, then she disappears the moment I finally classify her."

Jon sat up and looked directly at Ilu. "You classified her?"

He nodded. "Finally. I don't know why they assigned her to me."

"What is she?" Jon waited, but Ilu's eyes went distant and Gongie squirmed. "Ilu?"

"I never would've guessed it either."

"Never would've guessed what?" Jon's question surprised Ilu.

Marcus sat up. "You didn't say what she was."

Ilu looked around confused.

And Gongie's face twisted. "He didn't 'cause he couldn't."

What does that mean?

Chapter 16

The Superintendent summoning him before classes started didn't bode well. *How much trouble am I in?*

Cruel truths scratched at the back of his mind – that voice's laugh was almost audible. Shivering, Ferdinan retrieved his green tin, grabbed a capsule, and slipped it onto his tongue. *The lower dose is too low...I can feel it. How high can I increase it and keep myself in control? How long 'til the voice comes back if I don't?*

Swallowing hard, he entered Ms. Radery's reception area and was immediately ushered into the man's office and directed to the sofa set where he screamed at Dæya over a month ago. *What's he going to say? I don't want to talk about that.*

"Have a seat, Lord Ferdinan." The Superintendent's frustrated expression suggested he'd repeated himself more than once.

"I'll stand, thank you."

Dæya's jaw twitched. "You're aware the fieldtrip's this block."

"Yes, sir." Cold chilled Ferdinan's spine. Of the three regular events at the school, only the fieldtrip was enjoyable. It didn't matter where they went, getting away to focus on serving was paradise. Considering the trouble he caused... Blue crystals slowly drifted to the floor. *He wouldn't punish me like that, right?*

"Please consider staying on the islands this year."

Fire flared up white hot. "I'm always useful on fieldtrips."

"Considering your health and the other difficulties, it's not–"

"I want to go." The force Ferdinan used pushed the Mind Talker back. "My health's fine. There's no reason to keep me here."

"There is." Dæya waited for the boy's full attention. "The location was chosen before the plague hit."

"East Azuté?" That's where he *needed* to go. If Jon's family would stop summoning him... He needed to see what to prepare. "I have a duty to fix what I destroyed. You won't deny me that."

"You feeling this way proves you shouldn't go."

Ferdinan's breath quickened and his chest burned. His jaw clenched so tight it hurt. "I'm taking responsibility for my actions! You've no idea how much was destroyed 'cause of me!"

Dæya spoke before Ferdinan could continue. "Exactly my point. It wasn't your fault. There wouldn't be a country left to assist if not for you. There wouldn't be a world."

Fists clenched, Ferdinan fought for calm. "I know exactly what is and isn't my fault. Regardless, it has no bearing on whether I go." *You've no right denying me this!*

"Ferdinan. You're worrying me further."

Swallowing hard, he closed his eyes and pictured himself running along the beach. Muscles screamed to make the daydream reality. He wanted to run with Oya, to fight. "You are welcome to convince the Duchess to forbid my involvement with your unfounded concerns."

Defeat sighed out of the Superintendent. "I'm not forbidding you; I'm encouraging you not to. This won't be good for you."

Ferdinan drew back his shoulders. "I'm going."

Dæya's eyes widened, uncertain of the tall, broad skeleton. "Stay and devote that time to your apprentice. His project you endorsed is fascinating. You'd have a month undisturbed to help him with it – to do whatever you wanted with full access to all your resources."

"I'm going." Ferdinan gave a curt nod and left.

* * *

"Are you ready?" Herrard held up a screen with everything Kidico's "Duchess team" sent.

"Yah..." Xhou pushed his graduation project away – looking in desperate need of a break. "Thank you for helping me."

If only you'd accept all the help you need... Herrard motioned his island brother to the common room. "Why're you working on that here instead of your lab?"

Pink tinged Xhou's cheeks. "Fewer distractions."

"Ah." Herrard offered the screen. "The Duchess wasn't lying. Azuté will benefit long-term."

"But it won't really be my country anymore."

114

Herrard leaned forward. "We're sure that's what's driving her. Otherwise offering an inexperienced negotiator a prominent trade position – lessening her own country's power – doesn't make sense."

"Yah... But I don't think it's as sinister as you do."

"She wants to flood your country with her citizens – making it a branch of North Chūzo. That's not threatening?"

"It is...but..." Xhou's blue-black eyes wandered around the room. "How well do you understand that culture?"

Herrard snorted, "Only people born into it understand it."

"Agreed. But look at their governmental structure."

That gave Herrard pause. Only the General and King or Queen were above the citizens. Other nobles would be replaced by a capable citizen for incompetence or greed. Ensuring a region's daily needs and negotiating with other provinces were considered base duties. Even the Duchess would be stripped of her position if she stopped benefiting the population. The Kalj conceded, "I haven't considered how strongly that'd reflect on their international priorities."

"I don't know why she'd send a third of her population..."

"Their farms are failing." Herrard summarized the important parts. "To feed the world, the Duchess has deprived her dukedom."

"What?"

"We don't know how bad, but our spies learned that much."

Xhou nodded. "She isn't giving up power, she's losing it."

"By securing your country with her people, she'll stabilize North Chūzo while maintaining a strong hold on the food production."

"And guarantee treaties that've never happened before."

Herrard's next thought vanished, "What would that matter?"

"I don't know, it's just a feeling..."

"No!" Herrard swiped a finger at the Thinker. "Don't ever go on feeling. She's logical and calculated. Emotions don't play into this."

Shaking his head, Xhou tapped on the screen and offered it. "I've done my own research. Despite poor relations and no strategic benefit, Ferdinan's spent most breaks in East Azuté... 'Til the plague.

He does everything his mother tells him to...so they've been setting something up for a while."

"But how would treaties benefit them now?" Herrard returned the screen. "And...he hasn't been back since. Wouldn't that indicate she's lost interest or their plan failed?"

"Maybe. But he's been in Oueshi instead of Azuté."

"Oueshi..." *...if their fields are failing... They're strengthening the Grasslands to boost the food supply...* "And the Grasslands."

Xhou nodded.

"But it doesn't benefit her."

"But it does." Xhou looked at the notes the Kalj's negotiation team provided. "If she can't decrease her population and increase the world's food supply, her people will starve. And it's not just food..."

"A strained food supply will destabilize the world. How close to their limits do you think the Grasslands are?"

"Depends on how long this has been happening."

"There's been no noticeable difference outside North Chūzo..." Taking a breath, Herrard looked at the numbers. "You can't handle sixty-five million people. Well over that once Mundite refugees learn they can leave camps for a permanent home. So what can you handle while still taking full advantage of the Duchess's offer of power?"

"And still making it worth her while." Xhou added, "I'm sure she has another plan if we can't come to an arrangement. I don't want to lose an opportunity like this."

"Didn't you design a program useful for projections like these?"

"Yah..." Xhou stood but Herrard stopped him.

"There're more than numbers."

"What?"

The Kalj's face hardened. "You'll benefit. As will North Chūzo. But regardless of intentions, I can't ignore the Duchess's aggression."

"What do you mean?"

"Kidico has checks to keep the larger countries from weakening us. And West Azuté will side with us."

Xhou stood looking shocked.

"I'm sorry. You're my island brother. I love you. But I have three countries to protect." Herrard stood.

"Herrard..."

"Things will change in East Azuté...all of Azuté really. Politically. Culturally. Power balance. There's no stopping it. But I have to ensure that change doesn't hurt my people. Doesn't change them." Saying this was hard. The Kalj didn't want to oppose his friend, but he wouldn't let North Chūzo's influence reach farther than he had to. "I'm helping you. But I've my own concerns I'll fight for first."

"Are...are you an ally or a foe?"

"An ally – but my people come first." Herrard let out a slow breath. "Other countries will oppose this. So let's figure out how to address possible concerns. If not, things will destabilize anyway."

* * *

They were back in the oversized auditorium. Only this time, half the chairs were replaced by small booths. "What's going on?"

"The assembly to announce fieldtrip groups and required goals," Jon answered the awed redhead.

"Today's for those fifteen and older. The two younger groups will meet later," Ferdinan sat, arms folded and shivering.

Wild green eyes danced around the room. "What's going to happen?"

"Random assignment." Jon waited for Oya to sit. "They keep groups small. Usually four or five students."

"Ah." A smirk grew on her lips. *How long would he stand there?* Testing this was tempting, but Oya sat so the growing giant could.

Soon the boss-man started proceedings. An unnecessary speech dragged on before Dæya read off the groups. *The random assignment was earlier? What's the point of the assembly?*

Ferdinan was in the third group called, along with other names she didn't recognize. She and Jon were announced in the fifth group with three others. Oya didn't know them but Jon rolled his eyes.

Everyone moved to the booth their group was assigned.

117

"Is there something wrong?" She asked the growing giant.

"Tillia's the leader of Bob's platoon."

"An unbalanced power dynamic? And the other one?"

"Gongie's my suitemate and a Telepath. Be nice to him, please."

Giggles spilled out of her. "An interesting party."

A boy with reddish skin and angular features waved to Jon. *The one who gives me strange looks... This'll be fun.*

"You're the new girl." Tillia studied her. "What's your ability?"

Green eyes widened – glowing bright. Slowly Oya circled. Slowly. Which Tillia didn't appreciate. "I do what I need to."

Jon stepped between them. "What's our assignment?"

"East Azuté's southern regions." Tillia kept her eyes on Oya. "Use our strengths to help the 'individuals of a group or company.'"

Uncertainty creased Jon's brow as he eyed Oya.

"Sounds easy enough," alien green eyes didn't waver from Tillia's gaze.

"Does she understand the purpose of the fieldtrip?"

"Why're you asking Jon? I'm right here." Oya held the Thinker's tongue hostage.

Determined lips twitched and sharp eyes glared at Oya – continuing the contest of wills. "Do you?"

This girl was entertaining. Oya would have fun. "Find a place which needs two Fighters, a growing giant, a sensitive boy, and me."

Tillia blinked.

The intensity of Oya's grin increased. *I won.*

"Where do we want to start?" Jon redirected them.

Oya's eyes widened and her grin turned Cheshire. The full force of her personality consumed Tillia's soul. "I know a place."

Though the Fighter didn't back down, she looked to Bob uncertainly.

Jon hung his head.

Gongie stared. Terrified. Horrified.

And Oya smirked. *You're the same as the woman at the hospital. She gave me that look too.*

The girl threw back her shoulders and stepped closer to Oya. "We need to know your ability so we can find a suitable place."

"No worries." Oya smiled when her dear friend headed over. "I'll do whatever's needed of me."

Tillia frowned and shook her head. "You think you can do everything?"

An unexpected voice whispered just loud enough for Oya to hear, "*a jack of all trades and master of none.*"

She gave a giant grin. "*Though often better than a master of one.*"

Pale sunken cheeks reddened and Ferdinan took a step away.

Turning her attention back to Tillia, "how long 'til we leave?"

"We have two weeks to contact possible locations and receive permission to work with them."

Perfect. *I need to visit Azuté anyway.* "Consider it done."

◊

"Um..." *Will I be able to do this?* Jon was prepared to deal with Ferdinan, not a power struggle between the crazed redhead and an Athlete. Or Oya in general. Distracting her now and then was fine. But constantly for a month? If anything happened to her...

Why wasn't Ferdinan assigned to my group? Jon's stomach sank. Two weeks wasn't enough time to build a foundation with the gent. *How bad will he get in a month?* "Let's search individually and discuss what we've found in a couple days. We'll decide from there."

Tillia nodded, "Tell me your availability; I'll plan the meeting."

"Thank you." Jon bowed to the tiny girl. Once she and Bob left, he addressed his island brother's odd behavior. The entire time Gongie stared at Oya – looking truly horrified. Long fingers tapped the Telepath's shoulder breaking his suitemate's gaze.

Oya's domineering smirk turned to them and softened to a more pleasant grin. "Call me Oya, you're Gongie, correct?"

Confused eyes blinked a few times. "Um...yes...I'm Ari Gongie. It's nice meeting you, Miss Oya."

She gave him a stern look – making him tremble. "*Oya*. My name's not 'Miss.'"

"My apologies, Mi...Oya."

"Thank you."

Gongie stared again – thoroughly amusing Oya.

What's going on? Clearing his voice, Jon tapped the Telepath's shoulder again. "Is there something you want to say?"

"Oh...um." Gongie's eyes dropped to the floor. "I'm sorry..."

Oya giggled and walked away with Ferdinan.

It was odd seeing her actually leave. "Is everything ok?"

"Ilu can't remember what he classified her as." Gongie rung his hands. "Has she shown any Psychic abilities around you?"

Ice filled Jon's chest – making them both uncomfortable. *Oya? A Psych?* That terrifying idea made sense. "I don't know. But... What makes you think she might be?"

"I..." Gongie stared at his hands. "I couldn't feel anything from her. Like... Like..."

Jon watched his suitemate pale considerably. "Like?"

"Like I was looking at a doll."

"A doll? She blocked all thoughts and feelings?"

"No. I couldn't sense anything. If I hadn't been looking at her, I wouldn't have known she was there." Gongie shivered. "I should've sensed something when she egged Tillia, but there was nothing..."

Jon watched Ferdinan and Oya leave. *Nothing? How can one with so much presence be invisible to Gongie?* "And that means?"

"I don't know. Psychs can cut off their minds so other Psychs can't hear thoughts or feel emotion from them. Superintendent Dæya does it often. But I still feel their presence. I don't know how, but to me she doesn't exist."

Chapter 17

"You haven't returned to school?" The elf smirked.

Zephyr smirked back. "I'm finishing negotiations with my citizens."

"Haven't appeased your people yet?"

Golden hands danced, "What they want, I can't offer."

"Oh?"

"North Chūzo's lands belong to the General. It's rented to individuals via contract. Send a certain amount of food to the capital for distribution and they keep the land."

"They've stopped farming?"

"No." Zephyr hesitated though his hands moved. "The lands are sick. The Duchess allowed farmers to stay despite failing harvests. 'Til production fell too low. She had to take...unpopular action."

"'Unpopular?'" The elf found herself leaning in – fully curious.

"Some wouldn't leave, so she seized the land to prepare for treatments. Non-farming plots were claimed and converted for mass food production. To keep the population...the world...from panicking, the lands' condition is kept secret."

"Dying lands...?" Sapphire eyes drifted far away.

"Yes. And the people are terrified the Duchess will steal their farms and homes." Golden palm faceup, Zephyr tapped the center and sliced his hand away. "But the lands aren't theirs. And if their production continues declining..."

"And it's your duty to assuage their fears while preparing them to lose their homes – all without hating their future ruler." The elf gave a sympathetic nod. "And without causing panic."

"Yeah." Onyx eyes turned to the giant moon overhead. "And how to feed my people, the world, for two more years with severely compromised food production."

"You aren't the only country with farming lands."

"Other countries can't produce like we do...used to. There's a reason North Chūzo's the world's largest country. And that comes with responsibilities."

The elf considered that. "The Duchess can simply suppress dissidents after seizing the lands."

Golden hands moved, accentuating Zephyr's annoyance. "That's not who she is."

"It isn't?"

"The Duchess always puts her citizens first." Zephyr sighed and rubbed his face. "Her duty is protecting the well-being of our people. She takes it seriously."

"Which is why you're there instead of her."

"She's working on securing the world food supply. She doesn't have time for pettiness from misinformed citizens."

"But you do." Sapphire eyes cut through him. A knowing smirk followed. "Strange they'd let pettiness interrupt their future heir's schooling."

Heat flushed Zephyr's cheeks. *Of course she knows...* "I don't want to see him."

"It's hard looking at a soul as damaged as your own."

"I'm a monster, not damaged."

"Wounds are commonplace. Most heal – leaving nothing more than a scar. Some stay fresh for years. And some, like you and your cousin, are ignored 'til they weep with infection." A huge yawn and stretch took over the elf. "Humans connect too deeply to not be wounded. Not connecting...creates different kinds of wounds."

"Can I fix what I've done? Don't say 'become a great General.' That only keeps him from being forced into the role."

The grin on her face turned eerily Cheshire. "You aren't ready."

"I'll do anything." Squaring his shoulders, Zephyr prepared for whatever abuse she'd give.

"When you're ready."

"I *am* ready."

Her grin sharpened. A long finger pointed to where he stabbed himself. "You need better self-control to handle my medicine."

"I am."

"Your control's an illusion." Clapping her hands together, she changed directions. "Good luck, Zephyr. Time to wake up."

Blinking was a mistake.

Instead of on the twilight beach, he was in an unfamiliar bed with a dozen soldiers scattered around the room. Guilt sunk in. The elf was right. He was delaying – making this more difficult than needed so he wouldn't have to face his cousin. Face what he'd done.

* * *

Cover removed, Ferdinan marveled at his pupil's work. "This is impressive! And you accomplished more than I expected."

"Thank you, sir." Elbie fidgeted.

Ferdinan examined the carbon reservoir. "We'll focus on circuitry so you can keep working while I'm gone."

Elbie beamed. "Thank you very much!"

"Once I return from the fieldtrip..." Ferdinan slowly put down the box – his smile fading. "We'll finish what you need to complete your apprenticeship."

Uncertain what to say, Elbie nodded. "Any changes I should make before our next session?"

"Hmmm..." Ferdinan looked over the cube again. "You've welded it perfectly. The circuit boards platforms look to specs. Mechanics should work well once complete. But look inside."

"What do you mean?" Elbie eyed the case as Ferdinan had.

"Why would I suggest a double layered wall?"

"Huh?" Elbie considered the question. "To make it sturdier?"

"Yes. Why else?"

It took a little longer, but confidence carried Elbie's next answer. "To minimize contamination and regulate temperature."

Ferdinan nodded in approval.

"I'll make the changes. Thank you, Master Ferdinan."

A gentle smile floated across thin lips. The simple pleasure of watching someone learn...he missed it. Though he owed Evelyn more than he could repay, he would've preferred helping Elbie over break. "How will you minimize contaminants while building it?"

"By sterilizing the pieces and assembling them in a vacuum."

"Wonderful. Show me what you know about working with the vacuum chambers."

Pure excitement shone in those mismatched eyes.

* * *

"And that's Táqua's story." Muulam concluded – lightning fading from the twilight sky.

"Wow..." Yuyu sat stunned. "I love your stories. But... If humans built a glass orb around the earth, there'd be evidence of it."

Grinning deepened the lines around Muulam's eyes. "Humans have lost many things over the millennia."

"It's a fascinating idea..."

Gnarled hands slowly pushed Muulam from her chair. "I'm glad you liked the story – even if you're missing the joy of believing it."

"You're looking tired." Yuyu finished helping Muulam up.

"That I am. I'll see you soon, young one."

The Tinkerer faded – leaving Oya alone on her twilight beach. Reaching out, she called the Fisherman.

"Impressive what you've accomplished in a few days." That too perfect face smiled at her.

Oya let Muulam's façade fade away. "You'll be here?"

"If this is were you wish me to be."

"Watch over Yuyu and Û-ya'ïn for me."

"Of course." The Fisherman removed his floppy hat and looked at the strange fire. "Are you sure it's safe?"

Oya stared at the starless twilight sky. "I've implanted securities to protect the last camp."

124

A deep frown marred the Fisherman's face. "At what cost?"

"Hopefully none." Oya shrugged and opened the door to the silver roads. "The unease of four people is of little consequence..."

* * *

Instead of figuring out what to do about Ferdinan, Jon and Gongie focused on ways to keep Oya from annoying Tillia too much. *How do I keep a trickster god entertained in an unknown environment doing unknown work?*

Gongie snorted, but kept working – bringing his island brother's confession to the front of his mind.

How does a living person feel like a doll? Do other Psychs experience her the same?

"I'm afraid to ask." Gongie gave an apologetic smile. "Sorry, you're too loud to ignore."

"You know I don't mind. But I'm sorry..."

An amused smile brightened Gongie's face. "Do you believe there're such things as gods?"

If the thought wasn't so terrifying Jon might've laughed. "Women are the closest things to gods I know of. I don't think..."

Gongie's eyes doubled. "You're seeing her less as a girl."

Jon blushed. He knew better and he hated himself for it. Why was it so easy to disrespect her? "I guess... She's nothing like any girl I've known. And when I try showing her the respect she deserves – respect she's earned – she doesn't let me. But she loves when I'm rude and sarcastic..."

"Your idea of rude is more polite than other's idea of politeness."

Except for Ferdinan...

Gongie laughed. "Regardless, how do we keep her entertained?"

"If we knew where..."

Both boys stared at nothing for a while.

"What were we talking about?" Gongie looked around for clues.

"Packing for the fieldtrip." This didn't seem right...but it did.

* * *

Grass flattened under the clear screen as Ferdinan fought back chuckles. "**Lollipop flowers?**"

Wild green eyes lifted from the yellow blossom Oya was admiring. "*She was the one talking about* **apple tart trees**. *I thought it was genius myself.*"

"*You're a unique genius.*" Red coated the skeleton and guilt set in. He ignored her over break. Soon they'd be separated for another month. At least she was in Jon's group; the Thinker would protect her. Or would she be keeping his ally safe...? *Oya's amazing...* "*Um...do...how...uh, your group...how do you like it?*"

She giggled. "*They'll be interesting. But not as much fun as you.*"

"*It would've been enjoyable.*" Red darkened to magenta and the skeleton looked away. Blue crystals studied the diamond encrusted sky and uncertainty set in. He wanted to go. He needed to go. But how could he fix what he destroyed?

"*Ready for a month with your group?*" Her grin out shown the stars overhead.

Ferdinan frowned. No Healers. No Psychs. No Jon. And he was the youngest by four years. They were easy-going – and loyal to the Superintendent. *I can't trust them. What's that man's plan?* "*I want to help Azuté as soon as I can.*"

She gave him a knowing look, but leaned back and admired the stars with him – delicate fingers tugging at the steel chain she always wore.

It wasn't until Evelyn was running toward him – surrounded by bright colors and pure joy – Ferdinan realized he'd fallen asleep.

Chapter 18

Jon spent the four-day trip running between his ally...brother and his group. And Oya didn't help. Except she did...

The more Jon watched her, the more uncertain he was. *Is Oya making things better or worse?* Long fingers scratched at brown hair. *No. Focus on lunch.* Due to Ferdinan's health, Jon was allowed in the ship's galley - and it was a much-needed break. Wrapping the meals, he placed them in a carrying cloth and returned to the cabin.

The two sat at the table chatting in Oŭndo. Being denied the comfort of your first language was terrible. But using it to ignore him was rude... *Are they ignoring me? Or am I being discourteous?*

Was this how Ferdinan usually felt? Outside, only able to watch?

But it didn't make excluding him acceptable. These conflicting emotions made Jon feel like a little child again. And he felt guilty for feeling them. *I should learn Oŭndo. I have the program.*

Oya chattered excitedly, grinning her crazed grin. While his ally - brother smiled, matching the conversation. Watching them... *Is there anyone else he enjoys talking to? Anyone he's happy being with?*

Ferdinan went bright red and Oya looked too pleased with herself. But they laughed. And it made Jon jealous. Laughing, talking and relaxing with his suitemates would be wonderful...

No. I'll figure out how to be his brother. "What're you talking about?"

"Yay! Food." Golden brown hands snatched the bundle and laid it out on the table.

Once she finished and was sitting comfortably, Jon joined them. They didn't answer his question. But barging in on a conversation was rude. "Are you ready? I've heard it's still rough there."

* * *

I'm a coward.

A golden finger pressed into his freshest wound. The sharp pain - the minor relief from that goo - was comforting... It was the only thing Zephyr controlled. That and arriving late. He could've returned for the fieldtrip – but seeing his cousin, what he'd done... Not again.

Chewing on his lip, he tightened his grip on the bag. *How long can I avoid him?*

I'm a coward.

Hiding behind his citizens' discontent... Dragging his heels to arrive at school late... Standing there searching desperately for a reason – an excuse – to continue evading his cousin a month from now...until one of them died.

The stub-nosed knife tripled in weight. *Can I close my eyes so I never see him again?*

I'm a coward.

* * *

"Have you seen Oya?" Jon asked the three eating breakfast. "I can't find her."

Unconcerned heads shook.

She was capable. And mischievous. And loved roaming. Which was fine on the islands. But here? With her penchant for mischief, Oya vanishing troubled Jon. Rubbing his face, he sighed. *She isn't well traveled...* Naïveté and mischievousness wouldn't serve her. *If something happens to her, Ferdinan...* Jon Shook his head.

Oya was a girl and should be respected. He should worry about her, be concerned about *her* safety and happiness... But he wasn't. Not really. Oya could take care of Oya. But if something happened, no one could care for Ferdinan. The gent couldn't even go home. But... Was the Duchess's estate ever home to Ferdinan?

"Sit down and eat," Tillia commanded.

"She knows about the meeting with our site. She'll show up before it's time to leave," Bob offered.

Jon nodded, but something didn't feel right. He didn't know why. But there was something... Them being here, that meeting...it felt surreal. He tried recalling the name...

Gongie's uneasy smile encouraged him to sit.

But Oya didn't appear.

After finishing breakfast, Jon cleaned the dishes. They got ready to go...somewhere...somewhere he knew but couldn't recall...

Still, Oya didn't appear.

Fidgeting and pacing... Multiple times he stopped himself from calling out for her. Talking to the possibly invisible girl when he was alone was one thing – but here?

Unable to take it anymore, Jon barged into her room. It was empty. Save for a map on the desk. A secluded area surrounded by forest was circled with the message: "I'll meet you here."

Unhappy, Tillia griped. "We're here to work, *not* play games."

The spot was in the middle of nowhere and just barely inside East Azuté. *Why? ...when she knows we have a meeting...?* That surreal feeling intensified. "We should follow her instructions."

Tillia was ready to argue. For a moment. Her sharp eyes glazed over and when they focused again, she agreed. As did everyone else.

Uncertainty hounded Jon. *This doesn't feel right or make sense.* But it did. Everything was exactly as it should be. Somehow.

The drive was long and the road ended before arriving. This was expected. It shouldn't have been – why would any location be beyond the roads? But it was. *We need to get there soon.*

Lush canopies provided cover from the sun, shelter from the breeze, and relief from the mid-spring heat. There wasn't a trail. But they knew the way – where the easiest path was. How long had they walked? Five miles? Ten? Twenty...? He doubted more than twenty.

Complaints ended abruptly and were quickly forgotten. Poor Gongie struggled to keep pace with the Athlete, Fighter, and significantly taller Thinker. But the Psych kept going. They all did. Until Jon heard an all-too-familiar laugh.

Rushing forward, they broke past the tree line and into an open area with a chain fence stretching for miles. On the other side was the crazed redhead pushing an oversized cart. Half a dozen burly men watched – laughing and cheering her on.

What's she doing? Hiding, they observed.

Oya loaded rocks into the cart, hauled it to the other side of the clearing, and dumped it, only to run back and repeat the process.

That crazed grin of hers glowed. Each load of rocks intensified Jon's irritation. Those men were large and well-muscled, why were they watching a girl a third their size haul large rocks? Offering nothing more than cheers? And... *What's in their ears?* Jon gagged. A thin silver band was imbedded in each of their left ear lobes. They all had at least one more of those bands along the outer edge of the same ear. And one man had a tiny black rod a little higher up the lobe. Horror twisted his face. *Why're they mutilated?*

A man as massive as Xingho walked up to her and held out his hand. She said something in Oŭndo and clasped it.

That gesture...she did that to Ferdinan when we first met... Jon took in the forests behind them and the fence in front with open lands beyond. He never heard of a place like this. But... Jon tried to think. *What is this place? Why...* Green wrapped around Oya's ear caught his attention. It was a thicker band he'd never seen before, but it obviously hadn't marred her body.

Ferdinan guessed she was from South Chūzo, but they speak her nearly extinct language. Is this the last of her people...? But if that's true, why're they having her haul rocks? And...those metal pieces... Is this where undesirables are sent? What's going on?

The surreal sensation plaguing him for days dissipated. *What's she getting us into?*

Wicked green eyes locked on to where they hid. "Come say hi!"

All four of them froze – not wanting to move. But those alien eyes stayed on him until he did. Tillia threw back her shoulders and poured every ounce of authority into her stride – passing him on the way to the fence. Gongie and Bob kept pace behind him.

"What're you doing?" Jon asked her softly.

"Showing them we're capable of what they need."

"This isn't the kind of place we should be in."

"Little Miss, introduce your philanthropist friends." The giant's deep voice growled pleasantly – five bands shining in the sunlight.

"This is my friend Jon, he's the cook."

The man nodded. "You look strong enough. We'll need you in the mines with Little Miss when the kitchen's done with you."

"Ye...yes, sir. Thank you, sir..." Jon stumbled out. *Mines?*

"These are Tillia and Bob, they're the apprentice hunters."

The man nodded to them. "You're greatly needed. Disease stole three of our hunters last year."

Bob looked at Tillia, but the girl kept her gaze on the man thrice her size and nodded back.

"And this is Gongie. He's the counselor's apprentice." Oya gave the Psych a look of pity and curiosity - making Jon nervous.

The giant gave Gongie a small bow. "We're grateful for your desire to help our afflicted."

Worry creased Gongie's brow. "I hope to help in any way I can."

"This is Mr. Charlie." Oya stepped up to the fence - hands on her hips. "Think of him as the King of this little kingdom."

Her smirk held the same overconfidence she usually bore. But her wild eyes warned them to treat him with respect.

This left Jon confused - and nervous. What person earned respect from a girl who respected no title or position? And one who looked like that? *What crimes involve mutilation as punishment?*

"Little Miss vouches for each of you. Don't tarnish her honor." The man stared at them as if he'd seen them before. "Welick."

A younger version of the giant with three bands approached.

"This is my son. You can always find one of us."

"I'll see them to the front." Oya jumped and latched onto the fence - scrambling up and over with ease.

Is there anything she won't climb?

It was another ten miles to the entrance - and it blended in with the rock wall. If not for Oya, they would've never found it. The trek continued for another few miles - ending in a two-room cabin.

"Pick a mat, then it's time for lunch." Oya leaned on the door.

Distaste twisted Tillia's face. "We're expected to share a cabin? In a place like *this*. That's inappropriate."

"There're two rooms," Oya smirked with great amusement.

131

"Um...Oya?" Jon stepped between them. "Why're we here?"

Oya closed her eyes and took in a deep breath. Their groupmates froze – eyes clouded. "This is a gift I'm giving you. Choose well what you do with it."

"A gift?" Her seriousness amazed him. "How is dragging me to a place run by the mutilated a gift?"

Brow furrowed, her lips pursed to the side. "It's a disservice to you and your country that you don't know about mining camps."

"Why would my country have a place for such atrocities?"

"I can see why yours was the first to fall." Oya shook her head slowly. "Don't call me 'Oya.' I'm 'Little Miss' here."

Before he could ask, she stepped outside and the other three returned to life.

Am I dreaming?

* * *

The first-in, volunteer group Welmher Umagato was perfect. Their ethic and lack of fanfare suited Ferdinan. The information they gathered was invaluable. And their focus for Azuté was on equipment distribution and preparing volunteers to take over abandoned farms. This was exactly where Ferdinan needed to be.

Orientation was held in a comfortable room around a modest table. Annoyingly light and simple duties were explained. But he'd do whatever they wanted for access to information and resources needed to prepare for his return trip. The unexpected donation from Master Fulason's men would let him do more than originally planned too.

But this meeting was boring. Ferdinan's attention drifted to the blueprints lining the walls. Numerous notes attached with red and black lines littered the schematics. *Alterations needed to cater to Azuté's needs? Interesting prototype. Unfortunate it won't work.*

"Son?" Fingers tapped the table until Ferdinan's head snapped up. "Is there a problem?"

He paled – feeling dizzy. *Why's it so cold in here?* Pulling his jacket closed, Ferdinan pointed a bony finger at the wall. "I apologize. An error in the third blueprint drew my attention."

"Error?" Amused, the older man asked him to point it out.

Shaking, Ferdinan approached the schematics – pointing to one of the few spots without notes. "The wiring's wrong – ports three and four won't connect. Half the machine won't get power."

"That's where the trouble lies?" A woman who'd been waiting her turn walked over. She studied the spot for a while. "It looks fine."

Ferdinan traced the lines. "You'll need to rework the terminal and expand the casing to fit the missing connections."

Frustrated dark eyes filled with respect. "How did you see that?"

Ferdinan looked away. Using his family name was inappropriate, but if it got him closer to the information he needed... "My father's Lashi Samultz of North Chūzo."

The adults stood aghast – rethinking the rest of the day.

"I've studied schematics extensively. I'd be happy to help in any way I can." Guilt choked him. *How can I use my family like this?*

* * *

The best way to end a hard day's labor was with a beautiful diamond sky. Alien green eyes searched overhead – knowing she'd never find what she sought. But there was value in searching.

Heavy steps shifted dirt and pebbles. Considering the weight of those steps... Turning, she gave the giant a wicked grin.

"*You look nothing like the Rā-yŭmôn.*" Mr. Charlie gazed at the stars with her. "*If you hadn't visited in the land of visions...*"

"*And you met my mother not long ago...*" Delicate fingers fiddled with the cuff around her ear. "*You had every right to chase me away.*"

"*You're sure they can be trusted? The way they stared...*"

"*The staring... stems from ideological nonsense I'm hoping to break Jon of. At least enough to make my dear friend's life easier.*" Shifting, she craned her neck to look at Mr. Charlie's face. "*As for trust, I put a lock on their minds. I'll never compromise any of you.*"

"*Yet you feel responsible for West Azute's camp.*"

Oya laughed – hard and bitter. "*My responsibility concerning camp Nellappi stems from being there. The others are different.*"

The giant nodded and sat down. "*It's an honor to meet the new Rā-yŭmôn... Or are you actually the Rā-yŭ?*"

"*Unfortunately.*" With Mr. Charlie sitting, Oya could face him comfortably. "*I have a favor to ask and a task to offer. Please listen.*"

"*Always.*"

A delicate hand fished in her pocket before extending to him. On her palm sat a skeleton key with a broken tooth. "*Mom said you were the most reliable and trustworthy.*"

Sorrow clouded Mr. Charlie's face. "*I'm sorry. Only you can hold more than one.*"

It felt as if the world froze – ready to cry. "*I didn't come upon this decision lightly.*"

"*I'm sorry. But—*"

The earth screamed. Below her feet Humawit tantrummed. It yelled. It cursed her. It cursed him.

Oya held out her hand. *Beware the innocents you'll hurt.*

The abomination will never be cleansed if you don't!

Pain twisted Mr. Charlie's face.

"*You heard it?*"

He nodded. "*I'll need time to find and train a keeper.*"

The trembling stopped and Humawit's ire faded.

"*Which brings me to the task.*" Oya bowed her head. "*The other keepers are too old or too new and I don't have time. Would you train those I find? And help the Jinku if she accepts the responsibility?*"

Exhaustion aged Mr. Charlie thirty years. "*How many stories?*"

"*Five.*" Oya giggled. "*Six if you include your own heir.*"

"*Teach me and I'll do what I can.*"

Chapter 19

Preparing rice, picking vegetables, and grinding wheat took all morning. It wasn't easy...but it was better than the mines. It was eerie underground – like something was watching him. Neither were his beautiful new clothes suited to the work. Blistered hands swung the pickax again, jarring Jon's arms and shoulders.

Wicked green eyes glowed as the dirt coated, crazed redhead dashed about. And that Cheshire grin never wavered. Even while gathering and hauling heavy rocks Oya laughed and joked. She did the same above ground – always seeing to the residences' happiness.

Wheeling the cart around, she teased him. "Men younger than you have done ten times as much the last hour."

"They're children, not men. And I'm a Scientist not a laborer." Jon nursed blistered palms – ignoring the desecration surrounding him. "I could fix the equipment. Older tech's fairly simple."

A delicate golden-brown hand patted his arm. "They're...weary of scientists and businessmen. I wouldn't mention either of those."

"Why's that?"

"Give me your pickaxe." Taking it from him, she offered a different one. "Here, I sharpened this one for you."

What? "You know how to sharpen tools?"

"It's easy." She fiddled with the green band wrapping her ear.

"Thank you." Sharpened or not, his hands would bleed all night. "Why are you wearing that?"

A deep growl rolled through stone walls. Mr. Charlie activated a strange device as Jon's heart pounded. No one moved for an eternity. Not until the man shouted something he didn't understand.

"What happened?"

"Sometimes the earth complains." She patted his hand and left to joke with a couple miners.

I don't understand her... She was the least "girl" like girl he knew. Neither did the horror of this place bother her. And... There was something different about her here. Her strength and indomitable spirit had doubled. And... *What is she to these people?*

Laughter echoed through the cavern as Oya put all the weight of her tiny frame into pushing the full cart. *How's she happy doing such dangerous work? Why can't I figure her out?*

A boy tapped Jon's shoulder – pointing to the entrance. Like everyone else, he was mutilated too. But only in the lobe. *How can they do that to their children? But they let them in places like this.*

Bowing a thanks, Jon returned the pickaxe to the tool rack and headed to the surface. At least hiding his disgust was getting easier.

The midmorning sun eased his tattered nerves as he walked to the kitchen – finally making it without help. Finding anyone who spoke Common was a challenge some days. Heat from wood burning stoves filled the room, but the plethora of old women didn't mind. *Mothers and grandmothers too...* There wasn't a single old woman in the kitchen who didn't have at least two bands on their outer ear. And the kitchen Master had six. *Why?*

As he had the last few days, he went to work chopping vegetables only to be stopped. A withered hand tugged at his filthy silk shirt and the plethora of silver bands shone.

"Little Miss insists we let you cook. Show me your skills." She then repeated herself in Oŭndo.

A strained smile curled Jon's lips. *I don't understand. What is this place? Children didn't deserve such abuse. But they all wear those mutilations with pride...* "*Teŭ hi.*"

"*Thank you.*" She corrected.

Blushing, he repeated it correctly. The subtle sounds of Oya's tongue were difficult. *Stop thinking about it!* "*Grandmother Yuma,* how *many* servings should *I prepare?*"

"*Servings?*" A thick eyebrow rose high on her weathered brow.

"To portion *ingredients and prepare the* plates *and* side dishes."

"Silly boy. *Silly boy.*" A withered finger pointed at him. "For dinner, a half deer in the pot. Chopped up – bones and all."

Horror twisted Jon's face, inviting laughter and a bit of teasing.

"Bones make good broth and give good nutrients." The old woman reached up but wasn't tall enough to pat his shoulder. "Pick three vegetables and a root – a basket each."

But... Taking no heed of servings or nutritional balance? How're these people not malnourished? Ugh! What is this place?

Pushing aside his father's lessons, Jon prepared dinner as he was told. The old women teasing him in both Common and Oŭndo.

* * *

"Crime's up twenty percent. Jails can't handle the numbers."

"What sort of crimes?" The Duchess nibbled at a nutrition bar. They weren't terrible. Not particularly filling, but good enough.

The security official cleared her throat. "Split. It's either people damaging property or stealing food. Petty theft has also increased."

"Reassess the needs of those stealing food and adjust rations if warranted. For the rest, select examples at random 'til their actions stop hurting their fellow citizens." The Duchess sat back. Jails were short-term holdings to quickly evaluate offenders and adjust their files for release. They weren't designed for this situation. "The rest can sew treatments into the dying fields until they're producing again."

"Yes, ma'am."

"Next, Mr. Loguan."

"Construction stopped on the suspended railway." Mr. Loguan announced, standing perfectly straight in his immaculate gray suit.

The Duchess's voice lowered half an octave. "Why's that?"

"The resources are depleted, ma'am."

"They quoted the budget. A contract was agreed upon. We fulfilled our end. If they can't manage themselves properly, they'll pay for the rest. Comb through their records to find the problem."

"Yes, ma'am..."

The Duchess waved a hand. "You're both dismissed."

The two exchanged glances before bowing and exiting gracefully.

"Have you finalized the arrangements for our trip to Kidico?" The Duchess turned to her assistant standing in the corner.

Straight and prim, he bowed. "Yes, ma'am. I fixed the itinerary to accommodate the youngest's desires. If you'd care to approve it?"

A soft smile twitched on her lips. "Yes, please."

"Activities are arranged for Trannie and her tutor while you and your oldest are in negotiations. All meetings and appointments are confirmed. Including time to offer respect to the Kal before leaving."

"Impressive, arranging that so quickly." The Duchess smiled.

"Yes, ma'am. Your eldest daughters will meet with North Kidico's Master while you greet the Kal."

"Efficient." Returning the screen to the man, the Duchess thanked him. "You never disappoint me. Dismissed."

* * *

The office was small but remote. Exactly as Ferdinan requested. *No one will bother me here.* As long as he got everything done, he could access most of their systems without questions or disturbance.

It was perfect. But he couldn't get comfortable. For days...

Shivers took over. Ferdinan latched his jacket, wishing it was larger through the shoulders. *What's missing?* Every day he searched for what was wrong. *It's not the room... It's...*

Letting out a sigh, he went to work. He hadn't been alone for a year. Even moments of solitude...there was always someone waiting. Now he was truly alone...on a deserted floor. No one walked past this office. No one bothered him. Just like his life before South Chūzo.

Ringing filled his ears and his heart raced. Shaking hands grabbed his screen to call... *Who? Who would I call? What reason could I possibly give?* There was only one person he wanted to talk to and she was busy at her own site. Ferdinan burned red. *Foolish.*

The screen *beeped.* Thin lips curled and warmth filled his chest. Until he saw the Duke's name. His father forwarded a message from Chūzo's Master accompanied by three words: *"You are required."*

The State of Affairs Conference 'cause of my disks...? They'd garnered attention in certain circles. But enough for an invitation? *Eight weeks... The fieldtrip, travel to and from school... Only two weeks to finish Elbie's apprenticeship. I'm the worst mentor.*

Something solid and cold stuck in his throat. *A murderer has no place at such an event.* But shaking fingers confirmed his attendance. *My nails are blue...* And he was *cold*. Standing, he jogged in place.

Blue crystals latched onto his reflection in the desk's well-polished surface. That evening at Leoniel's shop haunted him. Appeasing the school and the Artimuses... *How angry will the Duchess be when she sees me? If I take the slowest routes...*

Four weeks. It wasn't much time to lose the weight. But... Jon wasn't here and the school couldn't reach him. Four weeks...

Making a plan, Ferdinan tied back his hair and went to work. Each hand worked independently on its own screen – doubling his productivity. Neither did he stop until the lights went out.

The apartment was close, but he ran anyway – down the streets, up the stairs, through the door, and past the four sitting in the common room. They said something, but he didn't stop.

Door locked, he checked that the alley was deserted, opened the window, and slipped out – activating the cuffs on the way down.

Feet firmly on the ground, he bolted.

* * *

Every muscle ached. Bandages held Jon's shredded palms together. Dirt and grime embedded in his skin and under his nails. He wanted to sleep for days. But the Thinker sat on the thin sleeping mat – mind empty... Until his ally...brother drifted into his thoughts. *He's not getting worse, is he? Did I instruct his groupmates well enough?* Ferdinan wouldn't improve, but keeping him from getting worse was vital. A month without him or Oya... *Oya... She belongs here.* Minus the atrocities that didn't seem to bother her.

This place... Jon felt his mind atrophying. There was plenty to do. Swinging a pickax. Food preparation. Cooking group meals... But nothing intellectual. Technology that once existed was in disrepair. Everything beyond the camp was inaccessible. There was nothing to program. No devices to improve. No way to make ideas reality. If not for the old women teaching him their language...

If he put aside imbedding metal bands in their ears, their simple life was actually quite enjoyable. But they had no concept of the things he considered basic necessities.

The door opened and a pale Gongie stumbled in. The Telepath eased onto his own sleeping mat and buried his head in his knees.

"What's wrong?" Jon cleared his mind and scooted closer.

"Everything here... I don't understand it." Gongie rubbed the bridge of his nose. "I'm sorry. Bob had it rough today too. Is still..."

"Do you need anything?" Jon patted his shoulder. "Or I can sit here with you."

"If there's something for nausea..." Gongie offered a shaky smile – paling a little more. "I'd love company also."

Jon squeezed his island brother then left to ask the old women what was available. They treated him like a nuisance, but sent him away with a minty smelling drink and mischievous smiles. *This has to be Oya's home. But she doesn't have a silver band...*

Half way to the cabin, someone called his name. Turning, a one-legged boy ran up – crutch under one arm and carrying cloth secured in his free hand. *What happened to him? He's younger than me...*

Jon hurried over so the boy didn't have to go farther than necessary. "Is something wrong?"

"You forgot this!" The boy panted and held out the small package. "You're as hard to catch as Welick!"

Blushing, Jon took the offering and bowed – chocolate brown eyes focused over the boy's head to keep from staring. Either at his missing leg or mutilated ear. "I'm sorry for...causing you trouble..."

The boy laughed, "Was no trouble. I love a good run."

How? Running with a crutch couldn't be comfortable. Jon blushed harder. Why him? Asking grandmothers to chase after someone was wrong. Neither should a maimed child be told to. Chocolate brown eyes studied scuffed shoes. *What do I say?*

"I hope your friend feels better."

Startled, Jon looked up – then away. "Thank you."

"I'm Maelel and I'd rather you stare at me then past me." Maelel grinned when the bright red Jon finally made eye contact. "Thank you. Gongie's kind of strange. But he's trying."

"He's the best of us all. I'm sorry. I should get this to him."

Chapter 20

Soft thunder shook the caverns. This happened every day and the complaints were getting louder – fiercer. It was unnerving. Tests said everything was structurally sound. But Jon was still apprehensive. If Oya wasn't there, he wouldn't be able to force himself inside.

Heart pounding, he faced the entrance. Something bad was going to happen. He felt it. And Oya skipped inside without a care. "Wait!"

She gave him her most mischievous grin. "Yes?"

"Play in the kitchen." *Am I really suggesting this?* "I'll take your place in the mines."

Laughter rang out loud and clear. "A full day would kill you."

"I'm serious. Please don't put yourself in danger."

Cradling his hand, her smirk turned sincere. "Nothing will happen today."

"Excuse me?"

"I'm still negotiating. Nothing will happen today." Patting his arm, she continued inside.

What kind of joke is that?

* * *

Hitting the floor was an unpleasant way to be woken up.

"Ow..." A boney hand rubbed at his hip. Ferdinan's stomach screamed for food, but he wouldn't give in. Shivering, he looked for the jacket...he was already wearing... *Why's it so cold?* Dry coughs racked his body. Desperate for warmth he stood and jogged in place.

But half-finished blueprints waited for him. And the histories called. Righting the stool, he went back to work. Or...he tried. Cotton filled his head. Grabbing the green mint tin, he opened the bottom. *The full dose gave me excessive energy. But my appetite... Can I stay in control? If I take the larger dose every other day?* Hesitating, he took the larger dose and went back to work until the lights went out.

Then he ran.

* * *

"I...want...do something..."

Gongie's heart twisted. As Ajani spoke, anguish consumed him. Speaking was a struggle. Words would often vanish before reaching her tongue and focusing took twice the effort it should. Always, her hands ached and dark shadows stained her eyes.

The pain didn't bother her. Neither did the limitations she faced.

It was knowing she'd never be helpful. Not in a way she planned. Or in any of the ways she tried since. It broke his heart. She should be angry or tired or have given up. But she hadn't. She continued searching for anything to improve the camp or the resident's lives.

Anything – without adding more burdens to them.

She didn't cry, but her despair was deeper than he could comprehend. Consumed by it – he still didn't understand. Still she didn't cry. He wanted her to, but she couldn't.

And she wasn't the only one. Many kinds of trauma were suffered here. But that wasn't what hurt them. It wasn't what broke them. And he didn't understand. This community... It helped them through death and dismemberment and tragedy. It helped minds broken and plagued with unnatural sorrows. But this...

It wasn't a desire to be needed. It was a need to help others, to improve the community, to make something better for someone else... But the community couldn't fix them. Neither could Gongie.

There was nothing normal about this place. And he was scared his words would make things worse.

"...sorry." The woman leaned forward and took her crutches. Light reflected off five silver bands and a tiny chip of green stone imbedded in that strange triangle of skin above the lobe.

"No! I'm sorry. I want to share your burden. I want to help." Gongie's voice broke. "But I don't know how."

"Seems...are...aren't...different..."

"I'm sorry. Please give me another chance?" He wanted to ask about that stone chip, but worried it might be rude. It didn't take long to realize what those silver bands represented. The one in the lobe marked each of them as a member of this camp. But the ones along the edge of the upper ear were earned. Like Master Daeya's tattoos.

But she was the only one with that green chip in... *What's that part of the ear called?* Coupled with the high respect everyone felt toward her, it made him wonder how significant it was. And if knowing would help him help her.

A motherly smile warmed him. *I want to help her. But how?*

Creepy green eyes appeared beside the woman. *Where did she come from?!* The hollow doll grabbed the crutches and lifted Ajani to her feet. "I need a new light. Show me to the storage?"

A small bit of warmth eased both hearts. "...love to...Little Miss."

"Sorry, Gongie, I'm stealing Ajani now." Oya shifted her back to the woman, squatted down, and lifted the adult before sprinting off.

Excitement faded the further away the woman got.

Ajani was the last for today so Gongie cradled his head and released the building pain. *Why does nothing bother them but that?*

All the voices and minds... He didn't understand. Things that'd bring fury or pity or unquenchable sorrow to others were barely noticed here. And things that didn't matter held grave importance. Being useful and helping people was wonderful, but here it was like...

Gongie froze – mind running through the last few days...

It's what makes them human...

It wasn't about feeling needed or leaving a mark. Improving the community, helping individuals...that was their humanity.

Ajani wants to be human again... Everyone he listened to did. But unlike the others who lost it to age or injury, she gave hers up. *Is that why she has the green stone chip? But why would giving it up earn her the respect they give? Wouldn't it be the opposite?*

But his words couldn't return a humanity he didn't understand. He'd insult their culture and possibly hurt them.

He dried his face. *Would Oya help me or torment me like Ilu?*

Standing, he walked toward the heart of camp and watched – soaking in their thoughts and emotions until alien green eyes and a wicked grin appeared without Ajani. *What's she going to do?*

Unnatural red hair dashed to a group of children. Laughter and foreign words filled the air. Soon they were playing. All save Oya and a little girl who sat holding a mangled, stuffed something. He wasn't sure what they were saying, but the girl's sorrow quickly turned to joy.

Oya chatted with a woman and hugged an old man. Instructions were given to some and others were teased. The mischievousness painting her face was completely hollow. Yet...that empty doll knew what everyone needed to smile. *What is she?*

"Ajani's bored. Ask her to give you tours of the camp. Rest with her when she's tired, walk at her pace, and carry her when needed."

Bored...? He hadn't sensed that from her. "Where is she?"

"Kitchen. The old women are gathering a snack for you two."

"Thank you." He didn't care about a tour, but something deep inside him insisted he wanted one. "May I talk to you this evening?"

"I have negotiations tonight." Wicked green eyes stared at the puffy clouds overhead. "But soon. And...your question. You haven't earned the answer yet. But that doesn't mean you can't."

"Question...?" But his eyes didn't see her anymore. Shivers ran through his body and his heart raced. Centering himself, Gongie found Ajani and carried her wherever she directed. And it was strange. Everyone they passed felt exactly the same toward her.

* * *

Herrard rubbed eyes tired from countless hours of reports and updates, helping Xhou with the Duchess, training Nammie, and preparing for his last block. *I never want to look at another screen...*

"I wish I was six again."

Healer Baer smiled sympathetically. "Last year's always chaotic."

 "Mind if I take a break?" Herrard pushed the screen away.

"That's fine." Baer held up a hand. "But first, Yuyu."

I know... But admitting it. "Her hands won't get any better."

"She should be on partial restrictions already."

"I know. But...then she'll know her limitations are permanent."

"Delaying will make facing those limitations harder."

Pain twisted Herrard's face. Being told her hands would always hurt when she worked and wouldn't be nimble and dexterous like before...seeing that pain... But he didn't want her hearing it from anyone else. "I'll tell her by the end of the week."

"It's hard. Being able to heal like we can – but not being able to heal everything." Healer Baer clasped his hands. "It'll hurt. And the only solace you'll find in the face of her shattered future is knowing she still has one. While alive, she can still grow and create."

"I'm sorry for being selfish." *No one should have to hear this.*

"I'll tell her if you can't or be there for support if you need."

"Ok." Herrard walked to the door, but he wanted something else to think about over break. "Have you ever scanned a dead body?"

Bear's face hardened and he sat back defensively. "Why?"

The incident with Oya...none of it made sense until he recalled she wasn't breathing. Gruesome curiosity had been growing since. Sitting back down, he told the Head Healer what happened.

Baer looked up. "One Healer to another?"

Herrard nodded.

"Even awake, she felt like that." Baer studied his hands. "To me and Healer Raderick. We haven't figured out what it means."

Brow furrowed, Herrard nodded. *Is she a Healer somehow manipulating our scans? Or a Psych altering our perceptions...?* But she was unconscious, so it couldn't be an ability. Could it?

* * *

A boy in dirt-coated, hole filled clothing shouted. Sighing, Jon smoothed his once beautiful attire. *Maybe I should've accepted the work clothes Oya offered.* But they were uncomfortable. And ugly. Frowning disapprovingly, the boy jogged up and took his pickaxe.

"You'll hurt yourself." Smiling, the boy lifted the tool above his head and froze. "I use all my strength – not just my arms and back."

Jon stared but didn't understand. *What does a child know about using a mining tool? Why isn't he at school?* And his ear... This boy was one of the few children with a band in the upper ear. *Why?*

"Watch." The pickaxe hit with a *clunk* – jarring the boy's hands.

"Don't swing like that. Swing like this." The boy shifted his body, bending his knees - melding with the earth. Then he swung again. It sank deep. A small jerk and an impressive chunk hit the floor. The boy returned the tool. "Don't swing, just hold it like you're about to."

Jon bent his knees and lifted the pickaxe above his head. Small hands grabbed his hips and squared them toward the wall - forcing them lower. Nudging Jon's ankle widened his stance. The Thinker's arms twitched and ached waiting for the boy to climb a rock and adjust his arms and wrists. If Oya was here, she'd be giggling at him.

Jumping down, the boy stood a safe distance away. "Now pull it down, not throw it forward."

It didn't make sense, but Jon watched and mimicked the motion. The pickaxe bedded in deep. There was still jarring, but it wasn't as intense - leaving his wrists much happier. "*Thank you*... How?"

A smirk curled the boy's lips. He spoke, but stopped at Jon's confusion. "We learn safety - *safety* - first. The old women said you couldn't cook either. Little Miss vouched for you; prove her words."

"This kind of work doesn't exist at home. And I'm a great cook. There's only one person who doesn't like my food and even he'll eat it..." Jon sighed. *Getting defensive over something so stupid...* "I learned a different kind of cooking. I've never fed a village before."

"A camp." The boy corrected, annoyed. "Villages are bigger."

Jon stared, but the boy wasn't joking. "Uh... I don't understand."

He returned Jon's look. "Little Miss brought someone who doesn't know the difference between a village and a camp?"

"I don't know why Oya brought us. I didn't know this existed."

Disgust coated the boy's face and he gave Jon a hard, angry glare. "You dare call Little Miss that?"

"She told us that was her name. I'm surprised she's letting you call her Little Miss. She corrects everyone who calls her 'Miss.'"

Confusion replaced disgust. A dirt coated hand scratched at fine black hair. "Why would she do that?"

"What does 'Oya' mean?"

The boy shook his head. "Ask her. Call her 'Little Miss here.'"

146

Chapter 21

Thirst strangled Ferdinan. *How long has it been?* There was still work – and information to catalog for his return trip. *Ugh... water...*

A knock danced on the door before he could stand.

After a coughing fit, he managed a rough "come in."

A lovely girl with curly black hair and hazel eyes entered.

"Muntec was right. Have you been here all night?" Disapproval saturated her voice.

"I apologize, Lady Lulia." Ferdinan coughed, brushing strands of hair off the desk. "May I help you?"

Pity. Annoyance. Disbelief. Many things flashed across her face. "I was sent to check on *you.*"

"I apologize for troubling you. I'm working."

"We haven't seen you in days. No one expects you to work this hard." Moving closer, her tone became soft – understanding. "We're worried. Come on, Muntec has dinner waiting."

Ferdinan forced a smile. During the day he worked. At night, he ran. He couldn't afford this disruption. If he didn't lose weight, he'd fail again. *I always fail...* Acid burned through his arm.

"Don't touch me!" Heart pounding, he broke her grip. Scared, worried eyes moved closer. *Why? She should be angry...*

"We cooked the food exactly as Jon told us and you need sleep." She stopped, startled. "Your lips are blue. Are you feeling ok?"

Ferdinan smacked away her approaching hand and shook his head to dispel the black spots. *Don't touch me! Don't touch me...*

"Your hands are ice! Your nails are blue too...how bad's your circulation?"

Ferdinan held his tongue and smacked away her hand another time when she reached for him again, but followed her back. Once there he bolted for his room, locked the door, and climbed out the window. Ignoring the histories pleas.

* * *

Surf rolled over white sand, enticing him. But a run along the beach wasn't a luxury Zephyr could afford. Catching up was simple with the schedule his cousin developed. Now to finish school early so he could help his aunts tame the unrest plaguing his country.

The extra time the fieldtrip afforded him was invaluable. *I've finished half the block's work. Now to stay ahead of schedule.*

A chime interrupted his large-scale military strategies lesson. One hand reached for the screen and the other pressed on his chest. The tightness was back, but it was manageable. *I'll do it again tonight...*

Zephyr painted on a smile. "Denila, how may I help you?"

"You find the most creative ways to steal more vacation." She gave him a wink. "My yearmates are having a dinner party. Join us."

"I'm working hard while you fourteenth years play and feast." This won a giggle from his friend and rival. "Sorry, I'm too busy."

"I wasn't inviting you; I was commanding you. Being alone is bad for the mind. Has your cousin taught you nothing?"

That question tightened his chest more. *I learned what happens when a protector doesn't protect.* "Ok, but only dinner. No games."

"Hmmm." Bringing a finger to her lips, Denila appraised him. "Ok. But you're staying through dessert, socializing, and having fun."

"Agreed." He gave a farewell and put the screen down. "Fun and socializing," what right did he have? It wouldn't earn him forgiveness.

But if it kept his friend from worrying...

* * *

"Enjoyed...the fields?"

Gongie gently placed Ajani on a chair near the fire. Eating every meal around a campfire was strange. "They were more beautiful than I expected. I'd love seeing more tomorrow – if you're not too tired."

Ajani smiled. It took a couple tries to pat his head. "The river."

The embodiment of beauty and serenity mixed with pain and reverence from all those nearby. "I can't wait. I'll get your dinner."

After each tour, Gongie settled Ajani by the camp fire and got her food. But tonight, the girl who brought Ajani to their sessions stopped him. *What did someone so young do to earn two bands?*

Though a head shorter, she looked down on him, sized him up, and defensively clutched Ajani's bowl. "She's *my* Iompa. Your work ends when the sun sleeps."

Thoughts and shared memories... Generations long anger and distrust... Fear... And disgust at what he represented all hit hard. This wasn't the first time. But those thoughts usually came from those who kept their distance and avoided him when he passed.

What happened here? Bowing, he apologized. "I'm truly sorry. I didn't know I was intruding on your time with Ajani."

"How could you not? Someone as old as you?"

"In my culture, adulthood isn't earned. You age into it."

She gave him a hard look and snorted. "That explains much. Spoiled and entitled. And lacking all respect. How did the world continue with such ignorance and sloth?"

He wanted to argue - tell her children working wasn't right. But her surety left him feeling small. *This isn't my world.* No child here worked unless they decided to and proved they were ready. And they could stop at any time. When new interests developed, adults provided opportunities to explore them. There was nothing forced.

"I don't know. But it did somehow."

She snorted again, but gave him a smirk and skipped away - careful not to spill. Sitting beside Ajani, she smiled and they chatted. She helped Ajani eat and watched closely to make sure the woman didn't choke. Tears welled as true joy and love radiated from the girl. And from Ajani... But the woman was also envious.

His mind filled with her youthful days running from elder to elder, injured to injured, sick to sick. The joy of helping. And the pleasure of growing deep bonds... She missed that. Yearned for it again. But she was happy watching the girl enjoy the same love.

Batting tears away, Gongie headed to the cabin and huddled on his sleeping mat. There were too many emotions inside him. His own. The girl's. Ajani's. Everyone else here...

They drowned him and tossed him about. But the most painful were his own. Hugging his legs, he buried his face in his knees. Joy. Pain. Confusion. Bitterness. Anger – everything flowed out of him. *I've always been sheltered...* Home. The islands. Previous fieldtrips... But here he had to endure. Before, the worst was stress or loss. They were easy to handle because he understood them. But not here...

And their emotions... He never felt anything so real before!

An impossibly cold hand reached across his shoulders and squeezed. He jumped...but didn't pull away. It was startling – disconcerting. No one expects a doll to walk into a room and grab them. But whatever Oya was, she showed him how to connect with someone here and was offering comfort he needed.

"Your joys and their joys, your sorrows and their sorrows, aren't the same. But thinking they're miserable, pitying them, isn't fair."

Gongie almost laughed. Before he would've thought that was a lecture. But now, it felt like a lesson summary. "You're right."

"You still feel you can't make a difference. But you have the ability to understand on a level no outsider could hope. Step completely out of your world if you want to help."

"How?"

Oya mussed his hair. "Suffering, sorrow... Pain and grief are abundant everywhere. And all suffering is individual."

He squeezed her back. "But I don't understand these people."

"Even from inside another's head, can you truly understand?"

A realization hit. "You didn't need a lightbulb."

"No. But she needed to show me where they were. And you needed to see differently."

How could a lifeless doll do something so significant? "You're wonderful here. Everyone loves you and you never stop helping. Why not be a little nicer at school? You're more than capable."

"The islands aren't part of my kingdom. They were promised autonomy when they were created."

What does that mean?

***

"May I ask you a question?" Elbie stood timidly.

Smiling, Xhou gestured to a soft spot of grass. "How can I help?"

"You're great at programing." Elbie sat.

Xhou took a bite of lunch. "I *am* great. And it's fun."

Elbie giggled at the silly response. "I'm making a 3D carbon printer and was curious how you'd approach programing."

Dropping his utensil, Xhou faced him. "You're building a *what?*"

"A 3D carbon printer! It'll print on a molecular level."

Xhou was stunned. "Where did you get that idea?"

A sheepish smile accompanied Elbie's story.

"You truly are Ferdinan's apprentice." Letting out a breathy laugh, Xhou offered a cookie to the boy. "May I ask a favor?"

"Thank you!" Unlike his mentor, Elbie *did* like sweets. "I don't have many resources yet, but if I can I'll do it."

"Stay in touch with me - tell me about everything you make. Especially your graduation project."

"Um...ok..." Elbie shyly nibbled at his half of the cookie.

"You're amazing. I'm offering you a lab when you graduate."

Those words made Elbie beam - and his cheeks redden. "I'm not as amazing as Master Ferdinan."

"You will be." Reaching out, Xhou mussed Elbie's hair. "Don't take as long as Ferdinan seeing it - don't let your pride swell either!"

Laughter bubbled up.

***

Diamonds filled the black velvet overhead. *The stars don't have answers. They don't hold my treasure...* Still, she searched.

Wild green eyes studied the lighted cord. She hadn't added to it since leaving the islands. Humawit held dominion here. Holding it back, forcing her will, and seeing to the people of this camp... *I'll collect the rest when we return to the islands.*

Heavy footsteps approached. "*What do you look for every night?*"

Wicked green eyes turned to Mr. Charlie. He looked nothing like Ozar, but they shared a similar height. "*Something I won't find.*"

"*Whatever you told the counselor, Ajani's lauded him for days.*"

"*High praise for an outsider.*" Is he truly an outsider? Stop. I can't afford to be wishful. "*And the others?*"

"*The old women enjoy teasing Jon. And he's growing comfortable.*"

"*He's trying not to insult anyone, but his attitude's the same.*" Oya sat up when he sat beside her. "*I hope he recognizes he shares their sense of family. Hope he can let go of his biases enough to do so.*"

Mr. Charlie laughed. "*The hunters respect Tillia, but she happily stays distant and they're grateful to oblige.*"

"*Yah…she's a fun personality. And Bob?*"

"*Ruco likes him — sees himself in the boy. But the rest are…insulted by his disrespect.*"

Oya laughed long and loud. "*I'm disrespectful. Jon's also disrespectful sometimes. But Bob? Talk to him. You'll be surprised if you're not stubborn now.*"

"*I'm the stubborn one?*" Mr. Charlie gave her a challenging look.

"*Yes. No one asked. Yet you take offense despite my word.*"

"*Four children can't change generations of history.*"

"*I don't expect them to. But I want to create that option again.*"

Mr. Charlie nodded. "*Speaking of, how's Iinami's new keeper?*"

"*Got her to the closest village.*" Oya grinned. "*They'll split to reestablish their fallen camp.*"

"*I'm glad.*"

Chapter 22

Where are you...? Jon was the first out of the cave when work was done, but he waited for Oya. Rumblings continued sporadically throughout the day – putting him on edge. Monitoring equipment found nothing wrong. Neither did Mr. Charlie's hand scans.

But the earth still groaned. It wasn't safe. Even outside the caves' entrance his heart raced. By the time he could breathe again, more grumblings came – throwing his heart back into spasms.

I promised to keep her out of trouble... The trail of men ended, but Oya wasn't among them. *I promised I'd keep her out of trouble.* Voluntarily going back inside... He shook. *I promised I'd keep her out of trouble. Oya's still in there. She's a girl...she's Ferdinan's only friend. And I promised to keep her out of trouble.* Slowly he moved.

Her echoing voice haunted the empty cavern and angry walls growled. She growled back – speaking faster than he could follow.

"It's time to leave."

Slowly Oya turned. Dim light painted her grin with anger and sorrow. But she didn't move. *"You... I was...to the water."*

"Who're you talking to?" Jon looked but it was only the two of them. *What's going on?*

"Humawit."

"Who?"

Oya placed a delicate golden-brown hand on the stone wall. "Once there was a child, younger than you and I. They loved the water. Loved it so much they built a raft to live on it. They told it of their dreams and hopes, and played in it 'til exhausted. The water loved them too. Providing well and protecting them.

"Every so often the child returned to land for what the ocean couldn't provide. On their final trip, they fell prey to wolves. The wolves chased them for sport – overrunning them. Killing them. And abandoning the child's mangled body when they were finished."

A chill ran down Jon's spine and his soul screamed the story's importance, though he didn't know why.

"For days the child's body lay – chased so far from civilization no human would find them. So far from the ocean and lakes and streams their dear friend couldn't reach them.

"With no one to bury them, their spirit couldn't leave. So it seized control of the body to bury themselves. There was only one place the child could rest. The ocean. And it called constantly. It wept for them and they mourned in return." Green eyes sharpened, boring deep into the rock. "The earth noticed – recognizing the child for the monstrosity they were. And it did what it deemed right. Such an atrocity couldn't exist. Rising up, the earth hurtled rock and dirt 'til they were buried deep – crushed to never move again.

"From their forced grave they pleaded. The sea is their home – where they wish to rest. But the earth wouldn't listen. Sorrow and frustration turned to hate. Earth held on and hate became a curse."

Why does this sound familiar?

"The earth demanded the child rest, to let go of their anger. One last time they screamed to be released. Again, the earth refused. So the child unleashed their wrath upon the land. The curse spread – taking in a nation. And because the earth was stubborn, it died.

"To this day, the earth holds them and the child won't release their curse. The land sits desolate – locked in an eternal stalemate." Brushing her hand over the rough surface, Oya spoke in Oŭndo.

She sounds so serious. "Show"? "Weak?" What's she saying...?

"That's how and why the Cradle of the World fell."

It wasn't what he asked. But it felt more significant.

* * *

Shadows seethed – waiting patiently for their targets. Moving forward, grime coated shadows stalked to the docks. Nobility taking lavish trips while they starved? *Let the Duchess reach the ground.*

The group sprang – separating the young girl from the three women and hauling all four to a secluded area.

Hunger fueled the mob's courage. Coated in grime and dressed identically – they pressed in, confident in their anonymity.

"Behold your mother's sin," Their leader dragged the girl aside. "Come out children."

A small hoard of young emerged from the tall grass - coated in muck and bellies grumbling.

"How will you teach a growing noble her proper place?"

Hungry, angry children dragged the Duchess's youngest through the mud and beat her when she struggled. They tore her clothes and hacked off her hair.

The Duchess lunged, but was restrained, powerless to help the screaming girl. Knife in hand, their second smiled, covered in a fury grime couldn't hide. She started with slicing off the Duchess's hair.

"Give us back our food. You don't get lavish meals and grand parties while we starve! Rationing starts with the noble's households!" Her fury raged – stripping hair and clothing from the women.

Shouted demands bellowed.

Now to strip the Duchess and her adult daughters of their pride.

No pity was shown.

Frail bodies withered against their anger. Naked. Beaten. Tossed to the mud. They left the Duchess to crawl to her youngest.

* * *

The dreaded chime sounded. If Ferdinan ignored it, his groupmates would come. He didn't trust them. But causing trouble was counterproductive.

Heading to the apartment, he calculated the miles he needed to run. All conversation ceased when he opened the door. The four stared. It was unnerving. Gaze lowered, he headed for his room.

"There's plenty of dinner left."

"Yes, Lady Lulia." Hand on the knob, he was interrupted again.

"Join us for Oodek. You need a break too," Muntec offered.

Leave me alone. "You don't want me to play."

"Why's that?"

"I win strategy games." *Leave me alone.*

"High and mighty for a Tinkerer," Muntec chuckled smugly.

"I'm not boasting. People don't like playing with me."

155

"Now I have to see for myself."

The histories' screen doubled in weight. "One condition."

"Name it," Lulia chimed hopefully.

"Why?" Ferdinan faced them. "I'm not bothering you and we aren't friends. Why keep doing this?"

Hesitating, Muntec answered, "you're our groupmate, why wouldn't we want to know you better?"

"I hate being lied to." Those blue crystals hardened.

Uncertain glances shot between the four.

Sighing, Ferdinan turned back to the door.

"Is it true?"

"Is what true?"

"You saved Yuyu?" Lojomac stood.

An ache grew near Ferdinan's temples. "I was in the right place."

"Not from what I heard. They say you were burned...badly..."

"They" need to mind their place. "It doesn't matter."

"It's amazing." Mindandi interrupted his third retreat.

Ferdinan kept blue crystals on the handle as the black spots fazed in and out. *How do I escape?*

"I can't believe Xhou's doing so well."

Someone got slugged.

"Excuse me?" That ache thudded harder against his skull. Acid burned across his chest and his heart told him not to listen. "No – I don't want to know."

"You don't know?" Muntec was punched again. "Ouch! Stop it!"

Bickering broke out but Ferdinan wasn't listening.

Burning turned to panic. *I don't want to know!* Jerking open the door, the skeleton slammed it behind him and covered his ears.

The standing mirror caught his attention. *Why am I panting? No...think about something else.*

His reflection... The histories cried, but he ignored then.

He hated it, but he couldn't stop looking. The burning faded as he studied every inch of his image. *How am I doing?* There was no scale...but his eyes said he'd gotten bigger.

No more, he couldn't allow it. *I have to run more, farther, faster.*

And that's what he did.

* * *

Bowing. Apologizing. Bob took the roll - leaving the rest for someone else. It was wasteful taking something he couldn't eat. Nervously, he looked around, but the residence still gave him cold glares. *I'm eating alone again...* He could intrude on his groupmates, but he didn't want them disliked as well.

Moving to the light's edge, Bob took a small bag from his pocket.

"Mind if I join you?"

Startled, but relieved, he scooted to make room for Mr. Charlie.

"Bob? Correct? Ruco's impressed with your progress."

Bob nodded not sure if he should look at the giant or keep his eyes down. With the difficulty he had not staring at their bands, he kept his eyes down. It was odd seeing something so horrifically taboo treated as normal. Amazing. "Thank you. He's a wonderful teacher."

"Yet you're sitting alone." Mr. Charlie pointed to the campfire. To the animated conversation between Tillia and the other hunters, Jon being teased by a bunch of old women, and Gongie enjoying the company of a woman and younger girl. "You understand why?"

"No, sir. Seems I'm not accepted." Bob bowed deeper. "I'll still do my job. I'll get your smokehouse's full."

"Why work so hard to reject the life you've taken?"

"I don't understand."

"You turn down every meal. It insults the land that provided for us and those who prepared it. Denying our hospitality insults us all. They rejected you because you've rejected us."

Ice formed in Bob's gut. Looking down, he clutched the little container. *I see...* "I didn't know your belief."

Mr. Charlie offered the bowl.

"I'm sorry..." Bob looked away. Sometimes he truly hated being a Fighter. Athletes didn't have such a stupid weakness.

"Knowing the insult, you'll still repeat it?"

"I find myself in an uncomfortable position." Bob opened the container and showed the man the mix of seeds and nuts. *They're completely isolated...maybe it's ok.* "As king of this camp can I trust you not to repeat my words or use them against me?"

The giant folded his arms and nodded. "You have my word."

"I was born with a condition that makes it impossible for me to digest animal proteins. I don't like people knowing."

Mr. Charlie studied him. "Strange the double standard your sect holds between its followers and leaders – current and future. But not unheard of. Holding to your beliefs is honorable."

"What...?"

"Stories can give the right outcome when the truth can't be told." Mr. Charlie smiled. "You'll be welcomed come morning."

"Thank you."

"What foods can you eat?"

* * *

It was unnerving seeing Oya's boundless energy spent by evening each day. But she'd laugh when Jon checked on her. Today she laid sprawled on her sleeping mat.

I don't understand her or this place. "You don't like being called 'Miss,' but 'Little Miss' doesn't bother you?"

Giggles poured out of her. "'Li-i-toh Mi-i-sa.' Not little miss."

Her exaggerated pronunciation startled him. "'Leet-oh Mee-sa?' What does that mean?"

Oya pronounced it for him until he said it properly. "What does 'Jon Artimus' mean?"

Jon considered her question. "Is 'Liitoh Miisa' your name?"

"Nope."

"Why have them call you something other than your name?"

Oya rolled over to look at him. "Names are heavy things."

What? "Oya... What does Oya mean?"

"Teno asked if you were lying. I told him 'no.'" A mischievous look glowed at him. "But he's right. Don't use 'Oya' here."

Jon rubbed his temples. "How many have I insulted?"

"None. Not with 'Oya' anyway. Teno doesn't understand yet." Her smirk grew wicked. "Consider it a prank on my part."

A prank? But...she couldn't have known she'd bring us here... Jon shook his head. More likely, Oya was her name and considered important. *But she said she had no title or birth of high standing... Who is she?*

"I'm sorry to intrude," Gongie's voice came from behind. "There's something I need to ask Oya."

The crazed redhead jumped up - grinning at his discomfort.

Jon smiled. *I'm glad you sound better.* "Oya, be nice."

"What fun's that?"

Ignoring her, Jon stepped outside and sat on the porch.

Though muffled, he heard Gongie's question. "Please...show me how to write 'thank you' in their language?"

The air grew heavy. "Those are exactly the right words."

What a strange statement. But it fit this strange place.

The evening air was relaxing. But his mind wandered to Maelel - and all the mutilated ears. These people... Their clothing was boring and uncomfortable. They ate basically the same thing every day. Little bothered them. Children and the infirm worked. And they desecrated each other's bodies as a sign of honor.

I don't understand it. What kind of people were they who could do that to women? And children? That'd think it's ok to put the young in dangerous situations? And had no respect for the body.

It irritated him. But he'd done well to hold his tongue.

"Brooding brings storms." Oya appeared and sat beside him.

"They lack proper medical care but won't leave for children?" Jon sighed, bursting. "Then failing to provide, force them to work? Force activities they can't do anymore?"

"Unfortunate things happen, but these parents aren't neglectful."

"And mutilating their children? Is that simply 'unfortunate?'"

"Don't presume to know what's best for those you don't understand." Oya turned her gaze to the night sky. "Maelel is happy. Nothing stops him. No one forces him. He proved himself an adult to do what he loves. And right now, he loves delivering things. And stop calling the honors they've earned 'mutilation.' The island boss man's tattoos don't appall you. Their bands are no different."

"They're completely different! Master Daeya's tattoos have deep cultural and spiritual meanings that don't leave the body deformed!"

"The bands have the same significance. More. Considering how much harder they are to earn. And a minor hole is less deforming than tattoos covering the body."

"No! It's not! Modifying the body. *Inserting* things in it that're never removed! That's multiple desecrations!"

"What do you think tattoos are? They inject ink into the skin – permanently modifying it. If the bands are removed the hole will eventually go away. But that ink never will." Oya stood – larger than life and scarier than death. "This isn't your world. These aren't your people. This isn't your kingdom. You're ignorant. And closed minded. You've no place deciding anything here. But if you put your blind beliefs aside for a moment, you'd learn something important."

Following suit, Jon towered over her – not caring what she was. There were women and children here suffering for no reason. And he told her exactly that.

Alien green eyes grew frigid. "Why assume your beliefs help anyone? Or your world ever benefited theirs? Though I shouldn't be surprised by a descendent of the first offender. Ask Ozar about its ugliness and its sin. Your country only looks beautiful to you."

Burning cold froze him in place – like her icy hands grabbed his soul and rung it. He stood there, shaken. Realizing what had always been at the edge of his mind. *She's an unstoppable force...*

Chapter 23

Taking down a deer wasn't difficult. Hunting trips to mountain towns food caravans had difficulty reaching were part of her bi-yearly breaks. But the deer here were huge. Securing the rope around her arm and her feet at the base of the tree, Tillia heaved again - but couldn't get it off the ground. *I will not be bested by a dead deer!*

Unnatural red hair appeared. Jon's friend stood on the tree's trunk holding the rope to keep herself from falling. Nearly hanging upside down, crazed green eyes flashed a challenge. "Ready?"

Tillia braced her feet at the base of the tree. "Ready. And. Pull!"

Both girls heaved with all their might. And the deer lifted - a little. Annoyed, Tillia slid her hand up the rope. "Ready. And. Pull!"

It took a few rounds, but they got the deer hung high enough.

Wild giggles rang out as Oya slid down. "Thank you."

"I should be thanking you. Why aren't you in the mines?"

"I'm waiting for the miners to catch up." Smoothing the yellow shirt the camp provided her, Oya faced Tillia squarely. "You don't like being here. But you haven't complained and you show no disgust for their customs. You've exceeded my expectations. Thank you."

Tillia studied the normally crazed girl... Those impossible green eyes were serious, almost regal. She looked nothing like the untamed child pestering the islands' weak. "What right do I have judging a place so separated from my world? Their ways work for them."

"Well said." The seriousness faded and her Cheshire grin set in. "As a reward I'll tell you, your leadership skills won't work here."

Disbelief wrinkled Tillia's forehead. "I'm not here to lead."

"Doesn't mean you can't learn something important."

* * *

The hut Gongie worked in was near the center of camp. While their sleeping cabin was on the distant outskirts. But the Telepath enjoyed his morning stroll. If not for Ajani's tours, he would've never realized the open field with the little cabin was the school. Children played there in the mornings and afternoons. But an entire camp of children getting their education from the same little building? How?

Schooling here was strange. Children came until they decided to be an adult. They chose an interest and proved they could do it. If they didn't like it, they returned to the school. There had to be things he was missing. But it was an interesting concept of maturing.

In the distance, a group of children ran and laughed. Another group lazed about or read. Other children were scattered around chatting. But all were waiting for breakfast.

Except one child. Frustration, anger, and fear radiated. Following those emotions, Gongie found a young boy propped against a tree and holding a torn stuffed toy. It was hard to tell if the stuffing was lost or compressed from years of love.

Approaching, Gongie knelt. "What's wrong?"

Tear filled eyes looked up at him and blinked.

He doesn't know Common... How do I pantomime this? Pointing to the toy and then to himself, Gongie held out his hands. "I'll find someone to fix it."

Little arms squeezed the damaged toy tight and a smiling Ajani pulling out a colorful bundle floated through his mind. "Ajani?"

That startled the boy. More memories of the woman rushed in. Scattered, but happy. Until a dark one twisted the boy's face.

What happened to cause that...? An idea came to him. A likely stupid idea. But maybe... *The exchange cabin.* It was filled with clothes, toys, and blankets – many made by Ajani. *What if?* Gongie repeated the gestures. "I'll take it to Ajani and bring it back."

"Your gestures are nonsensical." A middle-aged woman approached. She had four bands in her upper ear, but her lobe had both a silver band and a black rod.

Gongie didn't know what the rod meant. Only a handful here had them. But four earned honors told him she was impressive by the camp's standard. *Hopefully this isn't rude...* "Would you help me ask him if I can take the toy to fix and bring it back tomorrow?"

"You sew?" An eyebrow rose on her face, wavering between surprise and amusement.

"No.... But I'd like to do something useful during my time here."

The woman smiled. Kneeling, she coaxed him to hand it over.

Holding a damaged toy and sewing supplies the teacher gave him through breakfast was awkward. He kept it out of sight while working. But once the girl from the previous evening helped Ajani get comfortable and left, Gongie retrieved it. Her eyes lit up and beautiful memories filled his mind. *The last thing she made him...*

"Would you help me fix this." Gongie pointed to the torn fabric – lip quivering. *That was her grandson?* "I've been useless. But if I can fix this then I'll know I did something – even though it's small."

Ajani smiled. "Thread...needle."

Sitting beside her, Gongie took the thread and needle and did as instructed. Ajani tried describing how to make the first stitch but what words cluttered her mind and escaped her tongue didn't make sense.

"I'm truly sorry; I've never done this before. Please show me?"

She nodded. Carefully he placed the stuffed toy on her lap and handed her the needle but it slipped through her fingers... Frustration filled them. Frustration and pain at being incompetent to do something she loved. It intensified every time her fingers failed her.

What can I do? There has to be something. He needed this to work because *she* needed it to work. He gestured for her to stop – mind still searching. Until a lame idea came to him. Lame...but feasible. "I apologize, I'll be right back."

Dashing outside, he searched for a stick. One thick enough she could keep her grip but not be awkward. Finding three of various sizes, he ran back inside. *If she has difficulty with the needle, she won't be able to manipulate the fabric on the toy...*

Looking around, Gongie's dark eyes landed on the curtain. Taking it down, he folded it so two ends came together.

"Ok, first, I'd put the fabric like this?" Gongie tugged the frayed edges over each other – making the woman cringe. "That's wrong?"

"Yes!" She laughed. Taking the curtain, frail hands folded each edge and brought the two folds together. "This."

His fingers fumbled magnificently, but he eventually earned her approval. Only...he didn't know how to knot the thread. It was more difficult than he expected, Then he had to battle the fabric again. By the time he was ready for the first stitch, he was bursting with his own frustration and her amusement. Piercing the fabric with the needle, Gongie held it up for her to see.

Again, she laughed. "How...never learned...so simple?"

"This isn't the kind of work I'll be doing."

Nodding, the woman grabbed the folded edges and the stick and showed him how to put the needle in. Which he did wrong. Multiple times. But eventually he got it.

How can something that looks so simple, be this complicated? The proper angles, getting the right amount of fabric, anchoring and tension and not puckering the cloth... He was glad the tear was small, because it took longer than planned.

But by the end of the session, Ajani was laughing and clapping for him. And he felt strangely accomplished.

* * *

Negotiations were complete. Xhou wasn't entirely happy, but that was expected.

Looking around his lab, he sighed. Everything was done – supplemental lessons, his graduation project, every task his mom sent, negotiations. All except naming a successor. And this.

Tomorrow was Rura's birthday.

This time he'd do it right. Metal sheets laid out, ready and awaiting the laser cutter. The Zi double checked the cuts and scoring were properly programed and fed the metal in.

Building the first boxes with rudimentary tools was important. But the last one... He'd do it right

It was time.

To put her to rest.

To move forward.

To be the leader of a new country.

The machine was fast. Heated edges bent easily – leaving the metal undented and scratch free. Welding. Shining. Buffing...

It felt like he was cheating. Cheating himself. Cheating her. But soon he'd have over forty million people to care for.

Whoever he needed to be, he'd become it. Whatever was needed, he'd do it. And he'd do it right.

She loved purple and butterflies... Walking to the general-purpose lab, he enameled the box.

Morning's colors filled his lab by the time he returned. Placing the gift on a window's ledge, he studied it. Butterflies flitted around a field of purple wild flowers...

It wasn't good enough.

If I told her to wait, she'd be here instead of useless boxes. He crushed his mom because he didn't say "after lunch."

Nothing could change that.

"I truly am sorry, Rura. I loved you so much... Can you forgive me for failing you?"

Taking her picture, he placed it inside the box, sealed it, and stacked it in the moving crate.

Time to choose a successor... He knew who he wanted. But...making that offer – starting their training. It made everything feel too final. Too irreversible.

* * *

While the camp slept, Oya continued negotiations. Low thunder followed her bare feet through the cave's entrance – surrounding her inside the cavern.

"Complain if you wish. But you can't have me."

That signature grin turned sinister at the earth's response.

"Humawit, try and you'll lose."

Something light tugged on the loose fabric of her shirt.

"You'll regret hurting any of them."

That threat released her. Oya's grin softened.

"I'll be gone soon. Will you steal your sibling's promise like before?"

165

* * *

Growls cried out. But Ferdinan refused to give in to his stomach.

Denying himself food was difficult after a year of Jon feeding him. But he'd beaten hunger before. He'd do it again. It'd simply take more willpower this time.

Stinging rain attacked as he rounded the lake. Forcing his feet faster, Ferdinan weaved through the trees. The thick canopy provided protection from pouring rain, but made the ground slick.

Faster, faster, onward, pushing forward as far as he could, Ferdinan didn't stop. His stomach twisted and grabbed at his spine and black spots stole his vision. *No! I won't fail again!*

Main roads became visible through the tree line, so he slowed – getting his bearings. *How far am I from the apartment? How far have I run? Twenty miles? That's not good enough. I'll never succeed!*

Judging by the moon, there was six hours before work started. The light splash of shoes hitting standing water kept a steady rhythm. Six hours wasn't enough. *I can run faster in the forest...*

Shifting directions, his stomach grabbed ahold of his insides and threw him to the ground. The knees of his pants tore as he skidded. Clutching at his belly, he shivered uncontrollably. *No! I can't fail!*

"*Ugh!*" Emptiness held him hostage. *I'm wasting time. Move!*

But his body wouldn't listen. No matter how much he demanded! He couldn't get back to his feet.

"Are you alright, sir?"

Light blinded Ferdinan.

"Son? Why's a child out this late? Curfew was hours ago." Kneeling beside him, the officer called for help.

Ferdinan groaned.

"Were you attacked?"

Another groan stole his words, but Ferdinan managed a "No." *Let me disappear.* Causing trouble. Being caught unforgivably weak...

Agh! I hate this!

Chapter 24

Being treated like an invalid - forced to stay in bed, forbidden to work... There was too much to do! Being lazy wasn't acceptable!

Warmth washed over Ferdinan and the Histories pleaded every time his anger flared. He hated it. *I need to work. And finalize arrangements for my return trip over break. Run! I need to run!*

Please stop.

I can't! You don't understand!

Relax. Read. Learn. But stop.

No! You don't understand! Avoiding being seen through the cracked open door, Ferdinan slipped on his shoes.

Stop abusing your body. It can't take anymore.

Shut up!

Quietly, eyes watching and ears focused, Ferdinan slipped out the window. Instead of floating down, he flew to the rooftop, moving unseen from building to building until he was certain it was safe.

Easing himself to the road, Ferdinan ran.

* * *

"Ah! Like Master Ferdinan's pet robot except it looks and acts like the animal?" Elbie smiled. *How adorable. Students could have pets without disrupting the ecosystem...*

"Which animal would you choose?" Yuyu bounced excitedly.

"A bird."

Spinning the toy, pink eyes drifted in thought. "A bird? Really?"

"Yah! They're fascinating! And beautiful! Their songs..." Elbie loved the recordings he'd heard, but... "Please, let me help you!"

Yuyu smiled, but looked away - expression growing strained. "I might need your help for the rest of my time here."

Elbie's own smile vanished. "How bad?"

167

"I'll always struggle with delicate work. My hands will tire more easily. And if I keep working anyway, arthritis will develop faster."

"I'm so sorry." Elbie blinked fast to keep back the tears. She could create within limits that'd grow more restrictive... He couldn't imagine. And didn't want to. "If I could fix it... I'll always help you."

"I'm sorry for asking so much."

"Even if you didn't need my help, I'd still beg you to include me. You have the cutest ideas." Elbie felt helpless watching her lip quiver, so he looked at his hands. Blistered skin...pain... *Stop. They're fine now. I'm fine. We're safe.* For both their sakes, he changed topics. "Has your group decided on their project? For the fieldtrip?"

Frustrated giggles left her. "Finally! Rita and Wahnie are so stubborn! How about you? Excited for your first fieldtrip?"

This time Elbie looked away. "I don't get to go."

"If I can go, you should be able to."

"I don't have medical clearance to leave the islands."

"What does that mean?" Yuyu spun the little toy.

"The Head Healer says I'm allergic to everything off the islands, but I'll probably outgrow it in eight or nine years."

"I've never heard of anything like that."

Elbie hadn't either. But there had to be a reason for such an absurd lie. When he wanted to know, he'd find out. Forcing a smile, he faced her again. "Have fun for me! Tell me all about it! Ok?"

* * *

Screams filled the area around the school. Screams of playing children. They made Gongie smile. As did the boy's joy when the Psych returned the stuffed toy. Anyone from this camp would've done a better job. But the boy was thrilled anyway.

Wading through the sea of energetic children gave Gongie time to study the two teachers standing guard. They were older but still fit and spry. And they both hosted four earned bands each. Imbedded metal hoops and rods were a little off-putting at first. But it was nice seeing at a glance how much respect he needed to give someone. Besides, after years of unintentional exposure to Ferdinan's mind

168

and all the taboos the Tinkerer easily broke, those bands were of little consequence. And...he was starting to like how they looked.

Once he reached them, Gongie bowed. "Thank you for yesterday. I learned a valuable skill and was able to help someone."

The teacher who interpreted for him snorted and shook her head. "Couldn't sew, but wanted to fix a cloth toy? Outsiders."

Gongie bowed again to her. "I know it was foolish. But I want to help someone before I leave. I need to."

Both teachers smiled, understanding him differently than intended. But it could still work. If he approached this right.

"Forgive my rudeness, but could Ajani teach sewing here?"

So many emotions welled up in them - all directed at him. Offence. Irritation. Disbelief. Indignation. Annoyance. And so many others. But it was the pity that confused him. And none of it showed on their faces. It was disconcerting how flawless their masks were.

The woman sighed as that respect and pain everyone held toward Ajani washed over her. "That's disrespectful to Ajani."

"I apologize. But I know she can do this. She taught me how to fix the toy in a few hours - and I'm incompetent at those skills."

The man shook his head and gave a small smile. "All these children - Ajani's mind can't focus on so much."

"You know she has trouble speaking and she becomes frustrated easily. The children would be bored and confused, making things even harder on her." The woman added.

"True. But one or two at a time... At my school, first years - students who recently arrived - are given a mentor to teach them one on one. This is wonderful. We learn so much both as a mentor and a mentee." Gongie wasn't sure how to interpret the mixture of thoughts and emotions coming from them. "If it's only a few, she could do it."

Irritation and gratitude surged inside the man. "You think we haven't considered this? Haven't tried all we could for her?"

The woman patted Gongie's head. "She can't hold a needle or manipulate the fabric anymore. If she can't use words or tools, she can't teach. She'll be hurt again. Every time something she tries fails, it kills her soul. We won't do that to her anymore."

"You're right. She can't hold a needle. She taught me with a stick and thick curtains. Despite my ignorance, she taught me to mend that toy and embroider flowers to hide the seam with a stick." Bowing, Gongie asked one more time. "I know Ajani can help again. If you provide time for them with her, you'd help generations."

Neither teacher showed how impressed they were with what he said. They exchanged a silent conversation before facing him again.

"You'll take responsibility?" The man gave him a hard look. "Be here should something go wrong?"

"Yes. 'Til I leave. Which is all she needs to prove herself."

"There're a couple interested in sewing..." The woman looked over the screaming children. "Bring Ajani after lunch."

Thanking them profusely, Gongie hurried to work. The day passed slowly. But the wait was worth it to feel her excitement.

Like Oya, he carried her piggyback to the school. The teachers provided a small room, supplies, and three children. *Why do the children also feel that toward her? Were they taught to?*

"Bag make I want for dad."

"Carrying harness make I want for mom."

"Teach mending clothes, please."

Joy vanquished a portion of despair in Ajani's heart. He'd never felt such delight. And for a moment he understood.

Being unable to help one person was terrible. Never helping anyone again... *I'm glad it worked.*

He finally helped someone.

* * *

Sunshine was heaven sent and too quickly spent. Ten minutes wasn't enough. Stretching tall, Oya caught a ball in the process. Laughing, she tossed it back to the running children. *Break's over...*

Grabbing some water, she made her way to the caves.

And the earth made its final threat.

Wild green eyes looked around, but no one else noticed. "*You won't win.*"

170

Bare feet flew.

* * *

Herrard's bedroom door opened – startling Xhou. *Was he napping?* "Enjoy the luxury while you can."

The Healer rubbed his face and plopped onto the couch.

"Dinner's almost done."

"Thanks." Herrard leaned over until he was laying.

Pan seared massacre was piled atop a plate and delivered to the dramatic Healer. "Here."

"Wow...this is terrible." Punctuating the critique, Herrard pushed the plate away.

Xhou frowned. It *was* terrible. "It's what's available at home."

"Ah...I'm sorry." Herrard sat up, "You know–"

"Guess I don't get to travel the world while my siblings work." That dream died after the plague hit. Every dream died.

"I was looking forward to abducting you to Kidico." Herrard's face twisted as he blinked back tears. "Instead, dad sent a list of requirements I have to figure out how to fulfill..."

"But there's still one block left." Xhou put his plate down to focus on his distressed island brother.

"I don't want to be a young adult. I'm not ready."

Concern lined Xhou's face. "What's expected of you?"

"I only get one choice. One I'm expected to make quickly so my father can step down." Herrard studied his hands. "I'm scared. In a few months I'll lose it all. Every future I hoped for is now impossible. I don't know what to do. Or *how* to do what's expected of me. How do you find a spouse? How can I know anyone off the islands cares about me instead of my position? Now that... And after..."

"What comes after?" Leaning forward, Xhou squeezed Herrard's shoulder.

"I'll be studded to every major family. Will the assigned wives see me as human? Or only a means to an end? Why do I have to think about children when I feel like a child? And because of the...

171

I'm facing it alone. I don't want to be alone." Herrard closed his eyes and breathed out slowly. "Why do I have to lose everyone I love? Lose them all and be forced into a world of strangers where I'm barely more than an object? Here I'm human. But in a block..."

"I'm scared too." *What am I saying?* But... They used to talk openly – and he missed it sorely. "I'm not ready either. I don't want to lose my island family. Lose you. I don't know what I'm doing, but soon millions will depend on me regardless. I'm scared too."

They sat in silence watching Xhou's attempted meal turn cold. Tears fell freely. There was no comparing their situations – but... Herrard rubbed his eyes and moved to sit beside his island brother. Stretching an arm across Xhou's shoulders, they mourned.

Blue-black eyes turned to the Kalj. "I need your help."

Herrard gave a shaky smile and dried his face again. "I agree to nothing 'til after you've told me *everything.*"

"You'll never forgive me for the Boligo incident, will you?" It was silly, but this was the best way to lighten the mood.

"No." Herrard scraped his plate's contents onto Xhou's heap.

The Zi chuckled before turning serious. "I'm training Norger for Science Lead...and am not sure what to do..."

"I'm having Nammie shadow me through the first half of the block, then she'll take over with me as an advisor 'til I graduate."

"Norger knows the basics... But...there's a new student I don't know how to prepare him for."

Curiosity piqued, Herrard gave his full attention.

"We're getting a fourth Tinkerer."

"Fourth?" Sturdy hands played with long, light brown hair while Herrard processed that. "There's four?"

"I know! Having two at the same time was unheard of...then Yuyu." Xhou winced at the outrageous pile of food. "Tinkerers are... eccentric? That's not quite right, but... Bria didn't have to learn since Ferdinan trained Yuyu. And Elbie was mostly like any other Scientist before I was needed. So how do I prepare Norger for the new one?"

"'Mostly like any other Scientist?'"

"Remember Ferdinan's first few years?"

"His first twelve." Herrard shivered. "Ferdinan would gladly take another apprentice. It's the only joy he gets."

"I doubt the school will let him." Xhou fidgeted. "There're things that don't make sense about Tinkerers – that're frustrating."

"Like what?"

Paling, Xhou considered his words. Leads were given privileged information... "Do you remember when Ferdinan started talking?"

"That was unexpected..."

"Things like that."

"I'm more confused."

"Yah...me too..." Xhou thought. "I can't say more, but... How do you prepare someone to work with people no one understands?"

"Why not have Norger spend time with Yuyu and Elbie? They're easier than Ferdinan so..."

"Have the two youngest Tinkerers train my successor?" Xhou shook his head. But it wasn't a bad idea.

* * *

Sunlight blinded Jon. Glorious sunlight...

A red topped blur flew by – determination hardening her face.

He didn't think – just followed.

"Go back, Jon," she stopped at the opening.

"What's going on?"

"Go back!" She pushed him away from the cave's entrance. "Follow and you won't get out."

The earth shifted and she vanished.

"Oya! Come back!" His heart raced. He couldn't move...

And she didn't return. Breathing became difficult. Letting her die... But going inside...!

Her voice echoed down the rock hall as miners ran out shouting – pushing him back. *If she dies, Ferdinan will too...*

He was supposed to be a brother.

But he didn't want to die.

Tears filled his eyes. Reaching in deep, he broke fear's grip and ran. He ran against the dwindling tide. Ignoring shouts and dodging hands...he ran and didn't let himself think.

A massive hole split the floor – separating him from the miners. At its narrowest Mr. Charlie could jump it. But the man was as tall as Xingho. The rest wouldn't make it. And falling... *How deep is it?*

He needed to run! Leave while he could! But he braced himself and shouted to Mr. Charlie. Jon held out his hand and the giant grabbed the closest miner and tossed her.

Pulling her to safety, he turned and caught a young boy... One miner after another... While Oya pressed her hands against the stone – shouting instructions that made no sense. Until the wall crumbled.

Oya's shouts changed. The crowd split – the largest pushing forward the smallest. And it amazed Jon. Amazed him! Pushing aside survival instincts to give those who could get through the chance. The walls kept crumbling but Jon caught all who were thrown.

"*Time!!!*" Oya screamed. Everyone on Mr. Charlie's side of the gap turned and ran deeper into the caverns. Intense green eyes locked onto him. "Outside or follow Mr. Charlie!!"

Desperate pleas fell on deaf ears. The giant yelled to go back. But he couldn't. Not without Oya. He couldn't face his little brother if he left without her. Or his family...

Jon didn't realize he jumped until giant hands caught him. The rock screamed! Dust choked his lungs and debris assaulted him.

Oya shouted louder. The earth growled – deafening them all. And that crazed girl bowed her head, eyes closed.

"Oya!"

Mr. Charlie grabbed his arm and waist – forcing him in deeper.

And Jon knew...

I killed us. All three of us. I've hurt my family, my Island brothers... Everyone who cares... 'Cause I couldn't get her out...

The earth fell.

Chapter 25

Connecting with Ajani helped Gongie. Each day she guided him a little further past his preconceptions so he could accept their pain without question. Without confusion. He didn't understand – not in a way that'd help. But he was starting to.

Ajani's magnificent... Even struggling to express words, she held the children's attention. Respect and admiration radiated from them. And excitement. They felt... For them, it was like they were chosen to participate in a miracle. Gongie didn't understand. But he felt his own kind of respect and admiration for her. *How do I show her how much I appreciate her? What can I do that'd be meaningful to her?*

Sitting quietly in the corner, he watched her connect with the three using only a stick, curtains, and scattered words. And they were patient. Waiting. Listening. Asking questions. *I'm glad.*

When the three decided to try alone, Ajani gestured Gongie over – a sweet smile blooming on her lips. "Thank you. Ahran'chada."

"Ahran'chada? That's 'thank you' and your native tongue?"

"Yes. In..."

Gongie struggled deciphering the sounds. "Ohu...un...deh?"

Giggles scattered around the room. Ajani repeated the word. Multiple attempts later they were still giggling at him. "Oh-oon-doh?"

All four clapped and laughed. *Guess I was close enough.*

"Everyone here speaks Oh-oon-doh, but only a few speak Common. Are there other languages?"

"No... Common proof... One kind...adulthood."

"Ah..." The three sniggered and one asked Ajani a question before falling silent – almost as interested in sewing as in what the outsider would ask their teacher. So he obliged them. "Other than learning Common, how would I prove I was an adult?"

This time, instead of giggling, the children helped Ajani answer.

War drums pounded in his chest. His heart raced as if running a marathon. Running for his life. Cold sweat consumed every inch of his skin. Screams filled his mind. *Run! Run faster!* Rock fell around him. Imprisoning him. Dust choked his lungs. It was dark and the earth was angry! He needed to run! Run! *Get out!*

We're going to die... Get the young'uns out... Everyone larger than me push the small ones through! Don't stop moving!

Everything collapsed.

Everything was dark.

Frail arms wrapped around his huddled body. He cried. His heart raced. They were still there. He heard them. Their terror...

More little hands touched his shoulders and head.

Run...

* * *

Rocks pounded the inside of Jon's skull. Neither did the sudden light help. Moaning, he pushed himself to his side and Mr. Charlie helped him sit up.

"Are you ok, son? We were thrown hard."

Reaching up, Jon felt something cool and sticky matting his hair.

"Why did you come down? Why didn't you run when Liitoh Miisa told you?"

"Oya!" He scrambled – biting back dizziness and ignoring the pain. "Oya! Where are you?!"

"You'll bring another layer of rock down." Mr. Charlie warned.

"Oya, where are you?" Another unexpected light blinded him. His head throbbed and he swore it'd explode.

"I won't move before you reach me."

"Thanks," Jon stumbled toward her voice – taking her hand once he reached her. "What were you thinking?"

"Don't judge things you don't understand." Oya's voice was soft, but firm. "Mr. Charlie?"

"Water cart's about half full. It'll keep our throats wet a couple days – which is how long the lights will last without recharging."

An ice-cold hand touched Jon's arm. *She pushed us...*

176

Mr. Charlie took something from a miner and slowly moved around the cavern.

Fully dilated eyes grinned. "We'll get hungry, but the water will provide time."

Before Jon could respond, the miners approached. One word passed around them. "*Ṝă-yŭmôn.*" It was clearly directed at Oya. *What's Ṝă-yŭmôn?*

Mr. Charlie knelt beside Oya and spoke quietly. "Digging out isn't an option."

"Humawit wouldn't release us that easily." She glared at the rock. "I'll hold it back. Move closer when I tell you to."

"Understood." Standing, Mr. Charlie patted Jon's shoulder. "Guard her while I check on my people."

"Always." Scooting closer, Jon studied her. "How bad?"

"I've been worse."

The sweetness of her laughter scared him. "That's not funny."

Mr. Charlie called and every miner huddled around.

"What's happening?"

"Don't worry." Oya mussed his hair.

Sorrow and gratitude filled the miner's faces and they repeated that word again, only more reverently.

It made Oya laugh. "*I promise to... my... Forgive the trouble.*"

Scared and helpless, Jon studied her. The strangest person he'd ever known. A trickster god before she was a girl. Dilated eyes held no green. And her body was still... *She's never still...*

Men and women moved in – drawing his attention. Rock half buried Oya... *A couple inches and she would've died...*

"It's ok, Jon. Everything's ok."

His mouth moved, but the words stuck. *Why didn't she run? Why did the men leave her behind? Why didn't Mr. Charlie drag her away?*

I abandoned her...

They all did.

"Enough!" Oya commanded playfully.

"This is wrong!" Jon yelled.

"Everything's ok." Her face turned bright. "You worry too much."

What am I going to do? What can I do?

"You'll hold your family again." Oya was perfectly serious and sincere. "I promise."

* * *

Every hunter bolted when the messenger came.

Keeping pace with Ruco and the others was painful. Bob wanted to run full speed – so did Tillia. But that was an island luxury they didn't have here. They reach the cave's entrance to see billowing dust and miners scattered about.

While Tillia ran through the crowd, Bob moved uphill. There was no unusually tall boy or blood red hair no matter how many times he looked. But an irritated Tillia approached Welick.

The young man shouted commands and quelled the chaos. Dirt coated miners gathered a few feet away. The rest headed to the camp's center. And Tillia argued with the young man. Bob shook his head. *If Mr. Charlie isn't here, he's in charge. Show him respect.*

"Head to the campfire. I'll address everyone there after I've talked to the miners."

"No. I'll not wait idly while my groupmates are missing."

"I understand. My father's missing as well. But I need you–"

"You don't understand. Jon's family is important to my people so he's important to me. I'll not wait idly when I can listen now."

Bob understood. North Oueshi was important to his people as well. But being obstinate wasn't helpful. *At least Gongie's calm... Gongie!* Dashing forward, Bob interrupted the stupid argument. "I'm checking on Gongie."

Tillia paled, responding in Tilkish. **"Get him as far away as you can."**

178

Bob ran. But Gongie's work hut was empty. *Where...? Think!* That stuffed toy came to mind. *The school...* Turning, he flew, passing a small girl a few yards from the building. She was running too. Disbelief and irritation radiated at him when he passed her.

Barging in, Bob found a frail woman on the floor next to the Telepath - fragile arms wrapped around Gongie and humming a soft tune. Three children surrounded them.

Calming himself, he steadied his breathing - pushing everything inside him away for later. The Telepath was being bombarded - he wouldn't add to that burden.

"Are you part Oroskim? I've never seen anyone that fast!" The girl panted, holding her side.

How poetic. Unwittingly comparing a Fighter to that beast. My platoon will laugh. He held onto the amusement, hoping it'd bring Gongie some relief. Carefully he knelt beside his groupmate. "Gongie, you know what happened."

"No! Ajani's my Iompa, not yours."

"I'm sorry...what was your name?" *Iompa?*

"Larasi. What do I call you?"

"Bob. I apologize, Larasi." Whatever an Iompa was, he'd talk to Gongie without making the girl upset. *Can you hear me?*

It took a moment, but Gongie nodded. The Telepath was shaking and panting.

Can you hear Jon or Oya?

Troubled eyes looked away, voice barely audible. "It's too loud."

The girl rambled to her Iompa and the other children.

I'll get you away... "Where's the furthest place from everyone?"

"What a weird question." The girl glared, moving closer to Ajani.

How did he explain? Or did it matter? "He needs someplace far from everyone to calm down. I won't intrude between you and your Iompa. But I asked for the same courtesy."

"All of you speak so weird."

"What's...wrong?" The frail woman rubbed Gongie's hand.

179

"It's not my place." Standing, Bob waited for the woman and children to move and lifted the Psych. "Please? Where's the farthest from everyone I can take him?"

The girl snorted and knelt. Pulling the woman's arm across her shoulder and securing her own around Ajani's waist, she gently lifted.

"We'll show you."

"Just point the way."

"No. He's our jasachi too."

* * *

Damp hair fell in Ferdinan's eyes – making him shiver harder and thwarting his progress on both screens. No one could stop him from what he needed to do. No one. Not even the histories that wouldn't be quiet. *Shut up! Why's it so cold in here?* He jogged in place, desperate for warmth until his office was invaded.

"Why're you out of bed?" Muntec sighed, relieved.

The world bobbed and swayed. "I have work to do."

"You need to rest." Lojomac stepped closer.

Ferdinan blinked but the room flickered. "What?"

"You're going back to bed."

"No..." Ferdinan steadied himself with the desk. "I have work..."

"You need to lie down," Lulia reached out to steady the skeleton, but Ferdinan jumped back.

"Don't...!" His head and shoulders hit the wall. Stick thin arms shielded him. "I...I've three more drawings–"

"No." Muntec stepped closer. "You're translucent. Sit down"

"I'm..." The world spun. "Leave..."

Chapter 26

"*Can we safely move you?*" Mr. Charlie asked.

Grinning, Oya patted Jon's back and eyed the glowing orbs in her peripheral. "*It's definitely there.*"

Miners dragged Jon away. Gently, carefully they dug her out and moved her to a safe spot where the Thinker latched onto her. While Mr. Charlie gave silent instructions, she smoothed Jon's hair.

"*Whatever you need.*" The giant sat beside her.

What're my options? Humawit was fighting hard. The camp's equipment was old and in disrepair but fixable - hopefully. *Ferdinan has the talent to effectively use the camp's resources.* Only...

She was exhausted. Preserving the connections and holding back this small pocket of earth... *I don't have the energy, but...*

"*Your son,*" Oya squeezed Mr. Charlie's hand. "*Would he let in my friend?*"

"*I doubt it. Even you had to prove yourself to him.*"

"*But he believed your dream.*" She grinned. "*I'll need your help.*"

Letting her head roll to her other side, Oya took Jon's hand in her free one. "Mind if I borrow these? And maybe a little energy?"

"*Anything, Liitoh Miisa.*"

"My hand's always yours." Jon put his free arm around her, pulling her to his shoulder. Tears cascaded down his cheeks.

~

"*Welick! Follow my instructions and we'll see you soon.*" A delicate golden-brown hand stretched toward him.

Taking it, he pulled himself onto a twilight beach with a starless sky and giant moon overhead. "*Liitoh Miisa?*"

"*Your father's safe.*"

Relief blanketed him. "*Thank you.*"

"Don't dig. The earth will crush us."

"I have to try!"

"Then allow my friend in. He has the skills to save everyone."

Welick chewed on his lip - unhappy with her command. *"How will I know your friend?"*

"He looks similar to Jon, but his hair is longer and curlier. He's much thinner... much..."

"Tall, skinny children aren't uncommon."

"His torso – front and back – are scarred. As are his shoulders and arms. Healed burns cover his left side, back, upper chest, and arm."

Welick was taken aback. *"How?"*

"Saving a small child from a fire. The other scars aren't my place to say. Neither is it your place to ask."

There was a long pause while Welick thought. *"If such a man appears, I'll let him in."*

Oya lifted her chin and rolled back her shoulders. *"Don't ask questions he doesn't want to answer. Help him even when he doesn't ask. Don't give up on us. Whatever Ferdinan requests, give it to him."*

"Ferdinan? That's an odd name."

"An odd name for an extraordinary child." She winked and released his consciousness.

Now for her dear friend.

* * *

Slender fingers brushed over the stubble atop her head. *If I find them...* But they had every right to punish her for failing them. As long as they didn't hurt their fellow countrymen.

But attacking a child! Her child! There was no call...!

The Duchess pushed those thoughts aside again. *She* failed. But she was furious for her daughters! And that fury was compromising her work. So she stuffed it down deep and picked up a screen.

Data filled one box and the proposed draft another. The third was an expedited schedule to transport volunteers to East Azuté. Now to get the numbers. *They aren't unhappy enough to leave.*

She faced her study's window and the view of the city center below. Lights flashed in the distance. More evidence of her failure to cope with unexpected situations. But in a few months rations would increase. Recovery could start in earnest.

How to contain the discontents for a few months?

A well-dressed man entered and bowed.

"Speak."

"Minnora and Trannie arrived to Queen Am'ria's care safely. Lady Emelica's working with the General."

"Thank you. Has your family decided?"

"Yes, Duchess."

"And?"

"I can do more here. But my sister wishes an assessment for Transition Ambassador in my place. She's assisted Lady Emelica since school and has the knowledge and skills needed for that role."

"If chosen, how much of your family will she take?"

"Her spouse and child and our parents."

"Schedule her assessment."

* * *

"Hello." The elf woman stood before him – long, loosely braided hair shining like starlight.

Why's she here instead of the Fisherman? "What are you... I...I just...did I...?" Humiliation blanketed him.

"I need your help."

"What?"

The elf woman wove a tale about his friend and ally, how to greet the leader's son, and what to expect the man to demand. Even giving him information about the available equipment.

"Where am I getting this?"

"You already know," A sapphire eye winked. "They're still safe."

Why are my dreams so ridiculous of late? "Where are they?"

The magnificent elf placed a long, delicate finger over his heart. "Would you willingly have your eyes opened a little?"

"My eyes are open."

The elf ignored his comment. "How're humans connected?"

"Relationships connect humans." *What do connections have to do with open eyes?*

"And what do humans call those relationships?"

Relationships...are... "Bonds. Threads."

Her grin grew. "Exactly. Just follow that thread to your friend."

"You can't see metaphorical things."

"Not if you're eyes are closed."

He studied the elf. *Why not? It's only a dream.* "I want to see."

"Close your eyes." When he did, she placed her fingers over his eyelids. "Picture your friend. What does the thread connecting you look like?"

"Oya..." It was simple. He saw it clearly. "It's as green as her eyes and vivid as her grin."

The elf dropped her hands. "Look."

Her amusement was focused on his chest. Looking down he saw...it... A vibrant green lighted string.

"Time to wake up." The elf's sapphire eyes glowed in satisfaction. "Save your friends, White Knight."

~

Boney hands wacked away the wasps stinging his face.

"He's waking!" Lojomac called out.

Ferdinan fought to sit up, but those wasps restrained him.

"Lay down. When was the last time you ate?"

"Stop asking me that!" A boney fist threatened to punch him.

Lojomac cringed, but didn't let him up. "Stop fighting."

"Stop touching me!"

"I'll help Lulia find a healer." Muntec rushed out.

"No!" *I have to get away!* Breaking free from the wasps...that beautiful green thread came into view.

It was so real he swore he could touch it.

That...wasn't a dream....?

No. It wasn't.

Urgency filled every cell.

"Are you cold?"

I have to leave. "The floor's cold."

"Will you be ok to move somewhere warmer?"

Ferdinan assaulted the boy with an incredulous look and kicked him and his stinging wasps away. "Water, please... I'm thirsty..."

Lojomac rubbed his stomach – looking torn. "I'll be right back."

Grabbing his bag, Ferdinan slipped away and snuck up to the roof. *First...* He didn't know what he was doing. If he'd finally broke completely. But the information he collected was invaluable. Taking his screen, he sent a message to Grandpa Huey with all the information and data he'd gathered.

Flying mask and goggles in place, he activated the cuffs. Looking at the green thread was hard.

I'm broken or that dream was real.

But if it was, his ally and only friend would die if he was too slow.

Just like in South Chūzo...

Flying, Ferdinan followed that green strand through the evening and into dawn.

Please let me be broken.

Chapter 27

"*Identify yourself.*" An intimidating young man as tall as Xingho demanded.

Cold, tired, and uncertain, Ferdinan stepped closer. *Why is this place real?* If he was broken that'd mean his only friend was safe... And the ally he tormented...

If he failed again... *I can't...not again...*

Heart twisting, Ferdinan brought a fist to his chest. "*Mr. Welick, son of Charlie, Chief of Camp Shenki, I request entrance to your community.*"

Ferdinan offered his hand, the way the elf instructed.

"*What's your name?*"

"*Ferdinan, sir.*" He kept his hand out – lip trembling.

"*And your purpose?*"

"*To help those trapped below. Including your father.*" Ferdinan saw his Prince's apprentice shift uneasily behind Welick. *Please laugh...mock me! Say no such thing happened! Please... Please, tell me I'm mad...*

"*Remove your shirts.*"

Blue crystals closed, he swallowed back a sob. It was better to be broken than for anyone's life to depend on him. This wasn't supposed to be real...

Bony fingers attacked the buttons of his jacket. It was warm during the day but the spring breeze was still sharp. Removing the first shirt, he kept his eyes closed. The second and the third followed. Each were folded precisely and laid neatly on the ground.

Fully exposed skin elicited gasps and stares. One man ran to some bushes – heaving at the sight of him.

I'm disgusting... "*Do you accept my request?*" Shivering, he held his hand out again.

Welick stood stunned. *"Anyone who risked their life for a child has earned a place here."*

The gate opened and the giant shook his hand. *How did he...? No, I have to work.* *"Your monitoring equipment."*

Grabbing his shirts and bag, Ferdinan followed – noticing the silver hoops in the man's ear. *Jon must've had trouble here.*

Old, unkept machines made Ferdinan's heart sink... *"I can start with this, but I'll need better equipment brought in."*

"That's not an option." Welick stood unyielding.

"It isn't good enough," *I'll never reach them in time.*

"It'll have to be." When Ferdinan argued, Welick stated his position and the line he wouldn't cross. *"I want all of them home. I love them. But if I have to choose between a couple dozen or the thousands depending on me. It's not a choice."*

"The treaties..." Ferdinan whispered.

"You've heard of them?"

"I apologize." Ferdinan bowed. *"Bring me what tools you have and I'll make this work."* *Somehow...*

"You're as confident as you sound?"

"Oya's my only friend...and Jon...is important to my country."

"He's quite the important person." Welick pointed to two women and a boy. *"I have duties. They'll assist you."*

Ferdinan bowed and the man left. Turning to the three, he listed the supplies he needed and they dashed away – leaving him alone with technology that didn't exist anymore. And Tillia.

"How can I help?"

Stay out of my way. Pulling the strip of cloth from his pocket, Ferdinan tied back the top half of his hair. "Keep everyone away. Let me work."

* * *

Nervous energy filled the cavern. Mostly from Jon. If he didn't stop fussing, she'd put him to sleep. "What sort of bedtime stories did your mother tell?"

He squeezed her tighter. "Dad told the stories and mom sang."

"I can't sing." Oya waved everyone closer. "But I know many stories."

* * *

Flashbacks to Ferdinan's first fieldtrip haunted Dæya. "What happened?"

"He passed out. While Lulia and Muntec searched for a healer..." Shame coated Lojomac. "I...he begged me for water... It's the first time he asked for anything... I only left for a minute, but he was gone when I returned. We searched everywhere. And contacted local authorities and the chaperone."

"Then you did everything you could." Superintendent Dæya kept the frustration off his face. He wasn't upset at the boy – he was angry at himself. Next time he'd overstep his authority and contact the General. If he had the opportunity in the future.

"I really am sorry." Lojomac's voice broke. "We tried. We did everything Jon told us – everything you told us. But nothing worked. And..."

"You did *everything* you could. I'm sorry for putting you in that position. If I had a choice..."

"He's really sick. If we don't find him, I'm afraid he'll die."

"I worry about that every day." That was going too far. Burdening a student with his responsibility... "Don't worry about Ferdinan. Focus on finishing your projects and caring for yourselves. Master Lindra and I will take care of things. This wasn't your fault. Make sure you and your groupmates understand that."

Dæya doubted the boy believed him, but Lojomac nodded anyway.

* * *

The scans looked terrible. But he found a path through. And the drill... Ferdinan grimaced. It took tearing apart three others to get this one working. *I'm bringing updated equipment and manuals here.*

Chasing everyone away, Ferdinan started up the laser drill. He wasn't confident in the tool or the cave's condition. Putting anyone else in danger – he refused.

Machine on, he double-checked the scans. If not for the controls being intuitive the lack of manuals would've been problematic. Securing it in place, he started – running scans constantly. Everything went well.

Until it didn't.

An alarm blared and the drill did something it wasn't supposed to. His mind took in everything, memorizing every detail...trying to stop the drill. But he wasn't fast enough.

Earth screamed. Grating rock deafened him – buried him.

If it crushes me... Finally... But if he gave up, he failed.

That warmth came again, only this time it felt like a shield. And Ferdinan swore he heard the histories scold the earth...

Too much rock covered him to push away – but the crushing weight lessoned considerably. *If I move wrong...* Slowly, testing each piece and bracing himself as best he could, Ferdinan worked.

Muffled voices and haphazard digging grew louder. More than once rocks shifted – pummeling him. But eventually fangs, crushing tentacles, and acid dragged him out.

"Stop! Don't touch me!" He begged Welick and the two Fighters. Burning acid kept melting his skin... "Please don't touch me..."

Chapter 28

Elbie slid a small screen to Xhou. "What do you think?"

Picking it up, he scanned every inch of programing. *Simplistic but impressive for a second year.* Simple or not, the true test was running it. Loading it into the simulator, Xhou accelerated the cycles.

Unfortunate. He turned the screen to the Tinkerer. "Better. But it glitched on cycle fifty. A diamond takes more than fifty layers."

"Ah! I thought I had it!" Snatching the screen, Elbie gave his fill-in mentor a grateful smile. "Thank you. May I watch a few times?"

"Of course." But Xhou snatched the screen before Elbie could restart the program. "Before that. Yuyu! Thank you for waiting."

"I'm sorry!" Mismatched eyes wide, Elbie bowed to his island sister. "I didn't know you were waiting."

"It's ok. I'm early." Pink eyes glowed and her fingers absently played with a little toy.

Xhou gestured to an empty chair. "Let me get my bribe."

The Tinkerers giggled as he dashed to the fridge in the corner of his lab. Their unusual eyes lit up at the ice cream and fruit pie.

"Those lessons with Jon Dinta worked." Yuyu giggled – reminding him of the monstrosity he attempted a couple days ago.

"Thank you." Elbie looked at the dessert, then Yuyu, then Xhou. "But why're we eating pie?"

"Why?" Xhou flourished his spoon with a giant grin. "'Cause I need to make sure you two don't forget the important things."

"Important?" Yuyu smirked.

"Yes! Look at that pie – best murtilas you can find!"

"Berry pies are the most important?" Elbie snickered.

"Don't forget ice cream!" The feigned indignation sent the two Tinkerers into a fit of giggles. "I need your help, but I've no right asking. Children your age shouldn't be put in that position."

Both of them dropped their spoons and gave their full attention.

"Most students only have one mentee. Some two. Never three."

Yuyu turned an excited smile to Elbie which he returned tenfold. "Four Tinkerers at one time? That's never happened!"

"It's exciting! But after this block, I graduate. I respect Ferdinan, but he' needs to focus on his health. Which makes things awkward." Xhou bowed to them both. "Norger will replace me – he'll fill in for Ferdinan. But I've no experience helping a Tinkerer through their first year. Please help me train Norger to mentor a Tinkerer."

The two exchanged looks – carrying on an unspoken discussion.

"You don't think Master Ferdinan'll be able to be a mentor anymore?" Yuyu asked directly.

"Teaching's his greatest joy. But his health and everything happening in his country..." Xhou leaned back.

"We could mentor them." Mismatched eyes didn't waver.

Xhou laughed at that beautiful offer. *He always reminds me of Ferdinan's best parts.* "Neither I nor the school can allow that. Ferdinan was too young to mentor Yuyu, but he'd earned his lab."

"Elbie isn't wrong," Yuyu frowned. "If the new Tinkerer can't have Ferdinan, then one of us should be there with Norger."

"That's our demand in exchange for training him." Elbie smiled and took another bite of the delicious dessert.

Xhou laughed again. "I love you two so much!"

* * *

Empty bellies grumbled and parched throats begged for relief. In her peripheral, the orbs drooped. But they weren't enough to keep the connections, hold back Humawit, and sustain those trapped.

Darkness grew stronger as lights died. And the water was almost gone. *If I kept Û-ya'in it could've subdued the land. Maybe...*

Humawit's refusal to bend was forcing her to make a choice. One she didn't want to make. She knew the right path. But...

"Jon." Oya whispered.

The growing giant flinched – voice strained and dry. "Yes?"

192

"Give me a happy song."

"What?" Confusion twisted his face.

"Normally, I'd dance and prance around. But unfortunately..."

"There's no piano." He looked desperately at the failing lights.

I told you to go back... But it was done.

Wild green eyes looked at the colorful threads she put so much work into... Giving it up... What would she do? A delicate hand tugged at the steel chain around her neck.

"*Liitoh Miisa?*" A young miner interrupted her thoughts. "*I know a happy song.*"

She beamed, giving him the light and warmth of the noonday sun. The young man called to his fellow miners with renewed energy.

Five dry voices sang. Oya laughed heartily. And every time a song ended, she demanded another. Until the last light failed.

I'm trusting you, my dear friend.

* * *

This little haven beyond the camp's struggles and worries was perfect - despite the trek. If only Gongie could escape his own...

His throat always felt dry. Hunger pains mixed with nausea and fear. Even under the sun everything was dark. And Jon...he wanted to help his island brother. It wasn't just the fear of death or the darkness closing in. Something was wrong with Oya.

If Ferdinan knew... *Ugh...* Ferdinan... Despair, fear, and worry from thousands was bad. But the Tinkerer crushed his soul.

Breathing out, Gongie focused on the stream's light burbling and the rustling leaves. For hours. Until Welick came. He still had duties. As did the other two. But staying in camp too long made him sick.

The young man also needed the break to think and the long stroll here provided the opportunity. "It's time."

"Thank you." Gongie bowed. "Thank you. I apologize. I came to help and provide comfort. Instead, I need it."

The giant shook his head, "we see you're close to Jon. And how deeply you feel the camp's suffering. You should need comfort."

Those words matched the young man's deep empathy. And with it came fear. Welick looked strong, but was terrified of losing his father and his friends. Of fulfilling his father's role. This camp was his family. Their pain and loss haunted him as much as his own.

This Gongie understood.

"I'm considering having Tillia help with the children. If you join her, their innocence and ignorance could provide a break for you."

A shaky laugh escaped Gongie. "Tillia doesn't do well with children. Her expectations are...unreasonable. But I'm taking Ajani to the school today, I'll happily help while she's teaching."

Just mentioning her name elicited reverence and pain.

* * *

Please!

Turning, Ferdinan bashed boney fists against the stone wall. Why did this keep happening? Every path was safe until he made progress... Every option was good until he dug a few inches! No matter how deeply he scanned before! No matter how many times he double checked! Tested! As if the earth was changing to spite him!

The world faded in and out and his heart pounded erratically. Dry coughs racked his trembling body. And the fatigue...he was so tired. Exhausted, he slid down the wall and huddled on the floor.

Please...

"Stop this." Those words barely escaped his strained throat. "Work. Keep working. They'll die if I don't keep working!"

And if anyone caught him being so unforgivably weak... It wasn't just the three assigned to assist him, children would wander in randomly too... Standing, he moved the drill and programed it for a more intensive scan.

Only...

The machine powered off after a few minutes and wouldn't return to life.

Ferdinan screamed.

Chapter 29

Resignation was settling in for everyone but Ferdinan. The camp residents were accepting their loss. This eased some tension, but brought many worries. One of the outsiders was buried. Did they hold the others here or risk the outside world coming in? *Why's that such an ardent fear?*

Then there was the darkness coming from the mines. It grew stronger, angrier every day. The fury made Gongie shudder.

Larasi arrived and situated Ajani comfortably, but didn't leave. Multiple thoughts crowded her mind. Though he didn't understand them, the bag on her back and Ferdinan's face accompanied them.

Smiling, Gongie sat. "You're welcome to stay if Ajani agrees. Or is there something you need to discuss too?"

"There's a couple things." Gently squeezing Ajani's shoulder, Larasi continued. "The skinny boy... Kitchen masters are trying to figure out what to feed him that he'll keep down. Any suggestions?"

That wasn't a pleasant question. "I don't think there is anything."

"What does that mean?"

"You can't tell by looking at him?" That was rude, but there was nothing these people could do for Ferdinan. And he shouldn't know either. Not that it was his place to talk about... "There's only one thing he tolerates well. I'll tell you how to make it before you leave."

"Ok." Larasi wasn't satisfied, but she slipped the bag off her back and handed it to Ajani instead of pushing.

Pride and gratitude radiated from Ajani. The pleasant happiness was perfect. He didn't say anything – just enjoyed the beautiful respite.

Frail arms held out the bag. "Thank you."

"I'm here 'cause I want to be."

"And Ajani wants you to have it," Larasi countered.

How do I argue that? Smiling, he took it. Inside was an outfit of simple fabric – lovingly worn but in great condition. Holding up the shirt brought a smile to Ajani's lips and her son's delighted face filled their minds. "May I try this on?"

Ajani gestured to a door at the back of the hut. The cotton slacks and extra-long tunic were strange. And too big. But wearable. Orange suns and yellow flowers filled a maze of greens and reds embroidered on the collar. *I know what to do...* But to do it... Taking his nice shirt, he tore the front hem. *Sorry, Leoniel Kyo. It's for a good purpose.*

Stepping out, he gave a twirl for the two waiting on him. "It's magnificent! I love it! Thank you."

Ajani laughed and clapped while Larasi giggled. "It's so big!"

"He'll grow."

"Thank you." He knelt and showed Ajani the torn hem. "I snagged it a couple days ago. Please teach me how to re-hem it?"

Larasi gathered the curtain and sticks when Ajani nodded.

The lesson took longer than it should've. *Why do I have such clumsy fingers?* But he got it and only made them a little late.

While Larasi packed the teaching materials, Gongie took Ajani's hand. A lovingly crafted outfit she made for her son – then gifted to him. He understood the significance. "Thank you for your lessons. Your patience, love, and generosity. Thank you for accepting me."

Frail arms wrapped around him. Her warmth and joy and love were unlike any he'd experienced. The purity and sincerity... The gratitude... The unbridled joy of this moment – he'd never forget.

* * *

This pace was killing him. If Ferdinan could triple the speed... The green lighted string constantly reminded him of every failure.

How much time did they have left? Food? Water?

How did all the tunnels become completely filled? Multiple paths in and out of that cavern – all collapsed.

And for nine days he failed to progress. Nine days... Nine days and he was farther away than before. *What am I doing?!*

"*Have we gotten any closer?*" Welick interrupted Ferdinan's panicked, despairing thoughts.

"*I can't...I'll trigger another tremor! I'll kill them!*" Ferdinan screamed. Scans mocked him. They were fine, then flaws appeared that weren't there before. "*I can't lose them to a stupid mistake!*"

Taken aback, Welick stood frozen when Ferdinan bowed low.

"*I apologize. I had no right. I...I'm scared. ...I don't want to see anymore death.*"

Tentacles crushed his shoulders. Ferdinan broke away but faced the man. If only he could brush off the histories' undeserved warmth.

Voice calm and deep, Welick asked how close they were.

"*I don't know. The scans change every time I make progress...*"

Welick took the boy's shoulder, only to be shrugged off again. "*You haven't slept in four days. Sleep deprivation leads to mistakes.*"

Ferdinan hid his twisting face. Sleeping terrified him. But he was tired. So tired... "*Don't let anyone touch this...*"

"*We'll shoo the young'uns away.*" Welick walked Ferdinan to his father's bed – growing more worried each time the boy stumbled.

* * *

How long had it been? Days? Weeks? In this timeless black abyss? Jon couldn't see his hands in front of his face. Couldn't see Oya to check how bad her leg was. It was buried in rocks seasoned miners had trouble moving... She had to be sick – her leg infected, rotting from the inside... She needed it removed before it killed her.

When Ferdinan found out... When his family...

Tearless sobs choked him. His throat was so dry! He'd never known thirst. And he didn't want to think about it. Or his family...

How hard was losing a brother? Losing two? Two sons... That's what'd happen. He and Oya would die here. It'd kill Ferdinan and crush his family. He didn't want to hurt his mom and dad and brothers. He didn't want to hurt anybody!

And he didn't want to die.

But it was so dark. So dark...in this spacious tomb.

When Oya took his hand, he refused to let go. Refused to stop holding her. Because if he did, he'd lose her in this dark.

197

This terrifying dark...

Closing his eyes couldn't make it go away. And if he let go of Oya...she'd die alone. Her energy was gone... *How sick is she?*

He didn't want to die. Buried alive. He didn't want her to die.

And facing anyone if they reached him in time but not her...

But he wasn't a god.

The only thing he could do was hold her.

* * *

As odd as it was being summoned by the Superintendent, it was more disconcerting sitting there staring at each other. Whatever the man had to say, he didn't want to say it. And Zephyr wasn't sure what he should do. So he sat. Waiting. *How much trouble am I in if he can't find the words?*

It wasn't until the golden Prince started fidgeting that the man found his tongue. "Your cousin often travels to East Azuté. Does he still have contacts there?"

Pink tinged Zephyr's cheeks but his hands moved. *I'm a terrible cousin.* "I wasn't aware he spent much time there. I'm sorry."

Frustration lined Dæya's face. "How about West Azuté?"

"I wasn't aware he often visited that continent." Tired of wasting time, the Athlete asked directly, "What's happened?"

Though unsurprised, the Superintendent was hesitant to answer. And Zephyr... He hated himself for the hope filling him. For thinking he wouldn't have to face what he did to Ferdinan's soul.

Suffocating goo grew more oppressive until he jabbed his freshest wound. "Tell me."

Nodding, the man offered an unsettling account of Ferdinan's disappearance and asked a dozen more questions. But in the end, neither were any closer to figuring out where the skeleton went.

Golden hands danced again and again before his tongue found the words. "Let me be the one to contact my family. Please."

"Considering the circumstances, that's probably the best course."

Chapter 30

It's time. The water was gone. Everyone laid lifeless – awaiting the inevitable. *I know your pain and racing hearts, cramping muscles and chills. I know your hearts' suffering.* And she knew it'd get worse until it stopped. For the thousandth time she looked at the lighted strings wrapped around her palm. A light only she saw in the endless dark. *A few dozen or hundreds of millions?*

It wasn't a choice.

There's always another way, right? Oya turned to the orbs laying on the ground around her. *Too bad the Fisherman's on the islands...* Reaching out to him meant losing her grip on the stone. *There's no guarantee he could come anyway.* Or that he could do anything.

She knew the right choice.

Jon shivered – his grip weak. She smoothed his oily hair. Death wouldn't end here, but it was still dozens versus hundreds of millions.

She knew the right choice.

But she knew these dozens with her. Was watching them suffer with what dignity they had. While hundreds of millions was unfathomable. A number without faces or histories or dreams.

Oya knew the right choice.

"Friends. Come close and lay comfortably." She waited for the shuffling to stop. Her voice was soft and calm.

The dead must move verily on – what was must waste away.
But those that linger sadly search, seeking yet to keep.
One small shred, something of the dead in their lives.
The living know the loss will be filled by those still among them.

Opening her hand, Oya released the lighted strings.

The dead may cry, confused, clinging to those they knew.
But those who survive move onward, pain of loss fading.
One old ache, replaced by passions and life and creation.
The living know life leads onward, ever walking among them.

They slipped away, beyond her reach. All but the silver thread.

The dead may linger near those they loved in life.
But their presence prolongs the pain, hurting those who remain.
One must, to stay alive, learn to love and fight and strive.
The living know the dead have no place among them.

The right choice...there was no doubt.

But it wasn't the choice she made.

The orbs moved. Energy welled up. And she used it to claim every miner. They each slipped away. *I'll hold you as long as I can.*

"Know this, Humawit. Every death is on you. Every curse given 'cause of your actions will come upon you. Every tear and drop of blood. Every consequence'll crash upon you 'til you're nothing more than the beasts that run across your face."

* * *

Between age, disrepair, and inferior technology, the drill needed constant repairs. Though Ferdinan's little audience was fascinated. He didn't mind the children watching while he made repairs, but sent them back to school when it was time to work again.

Except when one of their teachers came. This time it was a man. All but one jumped up when he called. The last didn't hear him – and pretended not to notice her peers leave.

Pointing to himself, then Tansu, he tapped his temple and wiggled his fingers – moving them to the side. She giggled innocently. Her hands leapt around, asking a dozen questions. *I'd love to teach you properly.* But people were dying...if they weren't already dead. So he promised to answer and ask one question each day she came.

Grabbing the repaired power cell, he placed it between them. Tapping his heart, he moved his hand as if turning a dial – then told her to repeat it. Her bright smile was blinding as she repeated the gesture multiple times – asking what else had the same name.

Tansu pouted when he reminded her it was only one question a day and asked one of his own. Boney hands danced as he asked why some had a rod in their earlobe as well as a hoop or two different colored hoops.

Her eyes doubled and her hands moved so fast he had to ask her to slow down. Apologizing, Tansu explained that they were born in a different place and accepted into their camp. And that there were people born here who left to join other groups.

A dozen follow-up questions filled his mind, but he had to work. Thanking her, Ferdinan told her to go back to school. An impish little smirk shone as she jumped up and dashed away – reminding him of Oya. Pain twisted his heart. *Please don't let me kill her...*

His screen *beeped* while the drill ran scans.

"Ferdinan!" Healer Yahmo looked truly startled. "What's wrong? Where are you?"

"I need your help." How much longer did they have? How bad was their condition? If he failed again... *No. I can't fail.*

"Anything." Healer Yahmo leaned forward expectantly, worried.

Boney fingers scratched the back of his head – freeing a worrying amount of hair – as he explained what he could. Ferdinan's heart raced and jumped. Black spots wavered in and out. He was so tired...

"That's terrible. Are you ok?"

"I'm fine." Ferdinan closed his eyes, holding back frustration and black spots. "I don't know when, but I'll need transportation soon. I'm sorry for the unreasonable request. But I trust you."

"I'll have my pilots on standby. Anything else? Anything at all."

He was incompetent...a murderer. He'd fail like always – because he wasn't fast enough...good enough. He couldn't see what was in front of him. Couldn't dig a hole. Couldn't do anything...and more people were going to die because of it. Because of him! "No."

* * *

Fire shot from his leg to his brain. The stub-nosed blade freed the blood beneath his skin – forcing the tightness out. Wiggling the knife made his nerves scream and drew that suffocating goo faster.

Removing the blade, Zephyr watched red bubble up and run down his leg onto the white shower floor.

Why...?

All the records...everything – useless. His cousin thoroughly traveled East Azuté, but every contact Ferdinan had was dead. *I've stopped - why run now? Is this about his twisted sense of duty?* It was his fault. *What I did to him, his soul, he ran 'cause of me...*

At least the Superintendent agreed to let him contact his family. How long could he avoid it? And... *The Duchess - how much will this hurt her?* Then there was aunt Tenalia...

Rinsing off his leg, he wrapped it. His screen chimed. Dressing quickly, he hurried to answer the waiting call.

"Hi, layabout." Denila grinned playfully. "Give me a race!"

"Just got out of the shower."

"You can take another! I need to win as many matches against you as I can before being kicked into the adult world."

"There's plenty of time," Zephyr grinned. *I want to be alone... But I don't want to worry her...* "Ten minutes. General Studies."

"Five," she upped the challenge.

Dropping the screen, he slipped on shoes, ran down the stairs, and out the door - nearly colliding into her.

"So slow! I came all the way here to find you!"

"Ha! Cheater. You won't beat me to the jumping cliffs!" He bolted, though her reflexes were as keen as his.

"Good luck!" Going full speed, she kept an eye on the Prince.

Miles flew by and she pulled ahead. Worry twisted her face - a Fighter couldn't outdo an Athlete long distance. "What's wrong?"

"Nothing."

Grabbing him, she forced them both to a stop. It took a minute to slow her breathing. "Why're you limping?"

"It's nothing, a mild injury."

"And you didn't go to a Healer?"

"It's not that bad."

"If you're-" Looking down - she paled. "What happened?!"

Blood soak through his pants' leg. Unfortunate. He enjoyed the relief his jarred nerves brought. *How should I answer?*

* * *

The more time passed, the more Gongie felt powerless. But at least there was something he could do. Every day he threw himself into helping Ajani teach the children. Being around them couldn't drown out everything, but it helped.

The language barrier was a fun challenge, but he quickly realized pictures were extremely helpful. He was a lousy artist, but he tried. When he wasn't helping Ajani or working, he thought of ways to adjust materials and strategies to make teaching easier for her.

But keeping his mind occupied wasn't easy. He didn't want to think about the passing days, the miners dying underground, and Ferdinan dying above. Or how they should be heading to the islands. He didn't want to imagine the conversations he'd have to have with his island brothers and Jon's family... How to tell them...

Larasi's arrival signaled the end of lessons. Everyone disbursed, but Gongie stayed to clean up. Normally Larasi teased him before taking Ajani home. But today she and her Iompa sat waiting quietly.

A strange kind of pity he couldn't comprehend filled them. It was genuine and sorrowful, making him feel loved instead of pathetic. That strange pity took root after Larasi showed him the safe haven.

Now they intended to address it. *What're they going to do?*

"It's not Miisa, so it must be Jon." Larasi's gaze didn't waver.

"I don't understand."

Larasi turned to Ajani a moment before addressing him again. "We're sorry your Niompa is trapped."

"I don't know what that means." Gongie searched the surface of her mind, but it was something she knew beyond thought.

"Your companions, the hunters, they worry for selfish reasons. But their emotions are disconnected from them." She considered her words. "It's a sad thing. But they aren't sad. It's different for you."

Thirst. Hunger. Pain. It all drained away... Gongie heard Larasi's voice, but none of her words reached him.

All of it was gone. At once.

They're all gone...

Is this what death feels like...?

But... Dozens fading to nothing at the same time...? How? Dizziness...and the world warped... Warmth ran down his cheeks.

They were gone. Their voices, emotions. They vanished.

"I'm sorry..." Gongie pushed away the arms reaching for him. "I'm sorry. I'll be back."

No objections reached his ears as he ran for the caves.

All he felt there was something unnatural.

Something dark and angry.

* * *

Dæya's head throbbed. *Jon's group?* "How's that possible?"

"I don't know, sir. All locations were submitted and approved by me in person. But I can't find theirs and don't remember their site. I remember getting them situated, but not where..."

Fists clenched, Dæya sighed. Ferdinan's disappearance he understood. But not noticing a group was missing? For a month? Master Lindra's memory was excellent – she was meticulous and organized. *I should've made them all stay.* "How long can you wait?"

"Two days. The port needs to be vacated for supply shipments."

"You've informed Masters Zeni and Nii of the situation?"

"Yes, sir."

"Tell them to situate the students and to implement a visual check each evening. I'll contact the Nuwa. Bring your students back to the islands and keep rumors in check." Adding more burdens to chaperones...and right after the second group of students arrived.

The Superintendent rubbed his face. *Is Ferdinan searching for Miss Oya? Her influence over him...and the chaos surrounding her!*

I feel helpless. Useless...

Chapter 31

Being unhappy about an assignment doesn't preclude fulfilling it... Tillia's heart pounded when over fifty children surrounded her. Children who defied and teased her. And the teachers smiled and told her to play nicely! *Why're normal children so obnoxious?* The youngest were annoying, but the older ones purposely irritated her.

Lowering her stance to fight, they quieted down – calling to each other in their language. But they weren't looking at her. They stared at the edge of the school grounds where a half-dead Ferdinan stood on a stump. Long, unruly hair mostly hid his strained, awkward smile. Neither did he move when the children migrated toward him.

"Having fun?" Bony hands moved as he spoke.

An older boy shrugged and said something. Ferdinan responded – tapping his temple, extending fingers on both hands, and swaying them back and forth.

The boy looked at Tillia. "Everyone knows how to play."

"Not everyone. But they can learn."

Seeing someone other than Zephyr use hand language was odd. And it almost distracted her from that insult. *When did he learn it?*

Grumblings came as older children translated for younger ones. Stepping down, Ferdinan sat on the stump. A little boy studied the skeleton then ran into the schoolhouse. Though perplexed, the Scientist focused on the others until he returned with a small bag.

"What's this?" Blue crystals eyed the bag, but he didn't take it.

The boy spoke and put it on his lap and the others nodded.

Why do they flock to him? Give him gifts? Listen! Why...?

Ferdinan tried returning the bag, but the boy looked at him incredulously – saying something that hit the skeleton hard. Tillia swore his lip trembled before hiding behind overgrown hair.

"Break taking?" A younger child leaned on Ferdinan's knee – making him grimace.

"It's almost over." Ferdinan poked his palm and swiped away.

Excited words came from a one-legged boy carrying a box. Until he looked at Tillia. "Gran-ran said you're Little Miss's friend."

"She's my dearest friend."

That hand language isn't the same as Zephyr's... Tillia knew the gesture for "friend" and Ferdinan didn't use it.

"You're getting her out, then."

"Yes."

"Good. Then you'll get everyone out."

"Amazing said. Wonderful a storyteller." A girl grinned - getting the younger children excited. "Sea bird story...you told your sister."

Ferdinan blushed, but nodded until waving arms caught his eye. Hands dancing, he smiled at her. "What would you like to hear?"

Tillia offered an escape. "Don't you have work?"

The children objected and begged.

"Ten minutes." Strain and worry dimmed nearly colorless eyes.

Cheers broke out as an adult appeared from the tree line.

"What do you want the story to be about?"

A number of suggestions were given in both Common and their tongue, but one caught his attention. Whatever it was, it came from a tiny voice Tillia was surprised he heard. Addressing her, the girl shook her head. Only their language and hand speak was used after.

Every child listened intently - laughing and cheering.

How can someone so miserable tell a happy story?

The adult approached Ferdinan as he tied back the top half of his hair. A cup was handed to the skeleton and the adult waited while he drank. Giggles and chittering spread among the children while the pale, shaky Tinkerer sipped at the cup before waving goodbye.

And Tillia was left entirely lost. *How did he do that? Why do they flock to him but defy me?*

* * *

"What should we do?" Elbie watched his island sister spin the little toy. Xhou's request was exciting. But they weren't ready. He hadn't finished his apprenticeship and Yuyu was still working through basic classes. Neither were close to earning a lab.

"If Master Ferdinan can't, then we should start her training." Yuyu looked around nervously. "We don't know where she's at..."

"Yah..." Having another Tinkerer was amazing, but how much harder would it be to keep their secret? "What if she's still *trapped?*"

"Then Norger will need one of us there." A gloved finger tapped against Yuyu's chin. "How did a Thinker mentor Master Ferdinan?"

Ferdinan was in Elbie's earliest memories...but... "I don't think they did anything useful."

"Oh?"

"There's rarely one Tinkerer on the islands and there was no manual or instructions Xhou received for us, or to give to Norger."

Yuyu sat for a long time thinking. "Explains my mom. And Lashi Samultz and Eirie Napala."

Elbie nodded. *Why do we suddenly have so many?* "Jon Dinta might have some ideas after all his time with Master Ferdinan."

"Yah... But have you seen him?"

Elbie didn't want to think about that. If both Jon and Ferdinan didn't return, something bad happened. And since he and Yuyu were young children, it was unlikely they'd be told anything.

* * *

Every scan looked fine until they weren't. Yellow lights flashed. Immediately, Ferdinan shut down the drill. Another scan revealed a micro fissure, invisible until he was on top of it. Recalibrating the equipment, he did a deeper scan. *Please! I can't kill anyone else!!*

The fissure hit a key spot he needed to avoid. *When?! Why does this keep happening...?*

Random weaknesses appeared out of nowhere. *Why do I miss everything? Why am I incompetent?! I hate this!!* His heart jumped and twisted. *How much time have I wasted!? Again!!?*

Despair dragged Ferdinan to his knees. Useless samples...they'd been Minjing's death sentence. Just like useless scans were for those trapped beneath the rock.

My uselessness killed so many...and now... I'm killing them all!!

He screamed.

◊

Normally Bob waited outside – keeping the children away and listening for any problems happening inside the cave. But when that scream echoed out, he bolted in and didn't slow until he saw Ferdinan doubled over retching, barely able to inhale.

Checking the drill, he knelt beside the skeleton. A boney hand grabbed his shirt and held on. *Will he disappear if he let's go? What should I do?* Gongie warned him not to touch Ferdinan but the child was deathly pale and barely hanging on. Even a monster would comfort someone in this much pain.

Gently, Bob held the skeleton's hand and steadied the trembling body with the other. *How much pressure is crushing him?* Eventually the heaving stopped. Ferdinan gasped, fighting to calm himself.

"You need rest." Bob tried helping Ferdinan up but was pushed back with unexpected force.

"No." The shaky word was definite. Ferdinan climbed to unsteady feet and dragged the drill up the tunnel.

"What's happening?"

"I can't go that way." The drill turned at a steep angle to the wall and roared to life.

"Wait!" Bob grabbed Ferdinan's arm.

"Why?!" The skeleton screamed – trembling, teeth chattering.

Squaring his shoulders, the Fighter hooked Ferdinan's gaze, forcing him to focus. "Calm yourself. Or you'll make a mistake."

Paling, Ferdinan closed his eyes until he stopped shaking.

"Ok." Bob stood by the drill – ready to shut it off.

Lips twitching, pleading eyes fell on the machine. It hummed to life and Bob secured the goggles Ferdinan gave him.

Light filled the hall, bringing attention to something Bob hadn't noticed before. The rock... Something dark like rot crept along the stone. Slowly. Watching, he noticed it spread.

Chapter 32

Gongie froze when the voice came again – accompanied by flames. Bolting up, he kicked Bob scrambling to his feet.

"Where are you? I can't find you," floated through the window.

"Whoa?" Scanning the room, Bob watched Gongie force on shoes. "What's happening?"

"I won't leave you, but I can't find you." The voice came again.

"Do you hear Ferdinan?" When Bob nodded, Gongie opened the door, "I don't know, but fire's everywhere."

Eye's wide, Bob leapt up, searching wildly. "What? Where?"

"Tell me where to find you." Ferdinan pleaded as bare feet stumbled blindly across dirt.

"Get Tillia." Gongie dashed out. Fire consumed everything.

This feeling... Emotions and delusions... *Where am I?*

"Come back!" Gongie's words weren't what Ferdinan heard. *"Don't leave me behind! I don't want to die!" I didn't say that...*

"I won't let you! I'll find you!"

What is this....? When he grabbed Ferdinan's arm, the burned, twisted corpse of a girl held where he was clutching. With all their might they pulled. And when Gongie let go, she ran off. *How....?*

"No! Don't go that way!" Ferdinan bolted after her.

What's happening? No matter where Gongie looked, there was no camp, only a burning science building. Crumbling walls, flames, Ferdinan, and that running corpse were all that existed.

The girl vanished. Anguish filled every ounce of this dream – this hallucination. It twisted his soul and weakened his knees. *What do I do? I haven't been trained for this...*

"No! Come back!" Ferdinan yelled. "I have to find you!"

Gongie followed the Tinkerer – hoping he wouldn't hurt himself on things he couldn't see. *Can I make myself a part of this?*

Every restriction concerning Ferdinan made him hesitate. *But... He'll get hurt if I do nothing... We both will.* "I'll help you find her."

"Do you know where she is?" Dull eyes devoid of life pleaded.

That worked? Ok, keep going. How do I end this dream?

"Oya, where is she?"

Oya? His only friend... "The lab. Be careful."

"Fire's everywhere." Ferdinan's head turned, bringing an engulfed hallway into view.

Which way back to the cabin? Where's Bob and Tillia?!

"Move! I have to reach her! I have to save her!"

"She's already dead." *Why did I say that!?* Those terrible words felt like they were put there by someone else.

"No! I have to save her!" Ferdinan's face contorted. Pure desperation forced him on. "I can't leave her behind! I have to find her! I have to save her! Oya! Help me save her!"

Smoke bellowed in, whisking them to Ferdinan's lab - Oya's voice echoed around them.

"When you lifted the beam, I saw her. She was under Yuyu–"

"Why didn't you tell me?! I would've held it longer!"

"She was already gone."

"I don't believe that! That can't be right! I should've gotten her!!"

How do I understand those words? "Ferdinan, you did all you could. It wasn't your fault." Gongie searched. *How do I end this?*

Ferdinan's mind screamed - rejecting Gongie's statement. The world shook and they were in a hallway.

"You saved us." A little boy swallowed hard - mismatched eyes filling with tears. "Xhou understands Rura couldn't be. Please don't blame yourself."

"Huh?"

"She died instantly..."

Everything faded. Cruel, grating laughter deafened them.

The world changed and Gongie found himself aghast. *Is this the creation of a galaxy?*

Lights and materials flew. Sometimes they combined – forming something different, sometimes they danced – looking for the right pieces. It was amazing. And in the midst were two small lights flying erratically – thrashing about, damaging everything in their wake.

Gongie approached what looked like the inner workings of an ancient gear clock. Something grabbed him from behind – spinning him. Bob's terrified eyes pleaded for him to answer. Where Bob stood were rocks and trees. Whipping his head back, Gongie found Ferdinan in the midst of the galaxy being torn apart. The skeleton was on his knees, cradling his head, rasping out in pain.

"What's going on, Gongie?"

"Where's Tillia?"

"She's next to Ferdinan." Bob's face darkened. "What is this?"

"I don't know." One of the lights caught his eye. Gongie focused – willing it to him. And it obeyed. Like a puppy starved for attention it charged, leaping into his arms. Elbie's words rang out. It felt so real – a vivid memory he couldn't forget. "Where do you belong?"

"What kind of question is that?" Bob shook him.

"I'm not talking to you, Bob." Lifting the orb, he watched it fly to one of two small, mangled holes near each other. *They were torn out...? Who'd do such a thing?* "Bob. I need you and Tillia to go."

"You're half a foot from a cliff. We aren't going anywhere."

How long has this been killing you? How did you not break? "You can't be here."

"Why?"

Turning back to Bob and the dark forest, Gongie chewed his lip. If anyone found out... *They never gave us consequences...* Meaning, he didn't want to know. "I'm going to scan him."

Bob paled. "You're not allowed to do that – especially to him."

A few feet away Ferdinan moaned and yelled while Gongie straddled two realities, ready to commit a terrible offense.

"Ok." Bob guided him to Ferdinan. "This never happened."

Thank you. Gongie turned back to the wonderous world the skeleton knelt in. "You need to take those lights."

"Why do strange things haunt my dreams?" Ferdinan asked the blood red hair and unnaturally green eyes standing between them.

"'Cause your mind's wondrous. Now, grab those. They're hurting you." *Why's he seeing Oya?*

"They aren't real. They don't belong here! They aren't real!"

"Yes, they are." Gongie scooted closer. "If they continue, they'll break you beyond repair."

"They can't be real."

"You see where they belong."

"They aren't real!!!" Ferdinan screamed. Blood filled the world.

"Why?" *Will this make it worse?*

The carmine grew deeper. "I can't... No more... There's too much blood on my hands..."

What? "You haven't killed anyone."

"She died 'cause I didn't reach her in time."

"She died instantly."

"I should've gotten there sooner. My incompetence killed her..." Blood poured down faster. "I killed her family then I killed her..."

"Killed her family?" The plague killed them... No. I don't want to know. But his wants didn't matter when another's need was greater.

The scene shifted to the hallway with a pale Elbie. Only, this time there was a third voice with no point of origin. It was grating and cruel and tore Ferdinan down every chance. Though the Tinkerer flinched when it spoke, Elbie didn't notice. *That's Ferdinan's voice...*

"Please don't blame yourself."

Ferdinan died a little. Grating laughter filled the air. Tears stung the Psych's eyes. And that voice continued berating the Tinkerer until the skeleton screamed.

What happened? Why're there so many people?

Gongie studied Ferdinan's face. It was hard – radiating anger and self-loathing. *He yelled at an internal voice...* Things that'd troubled Jon since South Chūzo...

...he was already broken...

That realization...

Gongie didn't notice they were back in Ferdinan's lab until the Tinkerer screamed at Oya.

"I don't believe that! I should've gotten her!!"

Then everything stopped and they were in that Wonderland again. Gongie fought back tears. *If he doesn't reach them in time, it'll kill him.* The skeleton looked like he'd die at any moment... But knowing the reality... And none of it was Ferdinan's fault.

But...if he succeeds...

"Doesn't that make more sense?" Those words came from Gongie's mouth, but they weren't his.

Rejected blue crystals gazed at blood covered, bony hands. *"I'm so dirty. How can you stand being near me?"* Agony screamed out of the Tinkerer.

"Ferdinan." Again, the boy looked surprised to see him – to see Oya. "Rura died in that fire. Oya saw Rura's body when you lifted that beam. She died instantly."

"I don't want that to be real." Collisions echoed around them – like dozens of children flinging themselves into a locked door.

"What else have you hidden away?" Gongie stepped toward the pounding wall. A door appeared and sorrow filled him. There was only anguish on the other side. Anguish fighting to get out.

When it burst, death poured out. Death and decay. All around them names and bodies filled the room. Faces and memories. The ground trembled and a chasm opened between them. Something warm and bright held him steady and whispered directly into his heart.

Help him. You know how.

"Please! No more!" Blood and bodies piled into existence, soiling the magnificent galaxy in angry red.

"Rejecting them doesn't make them go away, Ferdinan."

"I don't want them to be real..."

All around echoed the thoughts racing through the skeleton's mind. *I failed again. I murdered a child. I was incompetent to reach her. I wasn't fast enough.*

"No. You didn't fail. You saved everyone still alive. You didn't kill anyone. You didn't do anything wrong." Kneeling, Gongie took those boney hands from Ferdinan's head. "Not everything is your fault. This isn't your responsibility."

"I *am* responsible. You were there – you saw." Shame forced Ferdinan's eyes down. "I killed so many. I'll kill you and Jon and everyone trapped underground."

Pretend to be her. What would Oya say? "I know you'll reach us."

Utter defeat crushed Ferdinan. Blue crystals closed and the world changed one last time.

Gongie knelt in a small clearing – not far from a hard fall. Bob and Tillia stood on either side of them, pale but watchful.

And Ferdinan was unconscious.

"Can you hear me, Gongie?" Tillia's voice came, strained and tired.

"Yes."

"What was that?"

"I'm not sure." Sunlight peeked over the horizon. "How long have we been here?"

"All night." Bob breathed out slowly. "Is it over?"

"No." Gongie needed to fix the damage before Ferdinan rejected those memories again. Closing his eyes, he delved deep into that terrifying mind and carefully stitched the torn memories back in place. *Seems I'm sewing even in my dreams... Well, not mine.*

It was a choice he wished he hadn't made.

But he'd never regret it.

Chapter 33

Sleep was unnecessary. Neither did thirst nor hunger bother Oya. But even under her protection, the miners wouldn't last long.

"With my last breath, last thought, with what little soul I have left, if you continue thwarting my friend, I'll curse you into oblivion. 'Til your myths are forgotten. I'll command the elements to rise up and destroy you for threatening our continued existences. With what shreds are left of me, I'll keep returning – cursing you every time."

A deep growl crawled along the rock she held back.

"You'll choose to bow before me or lose everything."

Silence. And an air of uncertainty.

"Choose." Once green eyes tripled in size. What was left of Oya's soul unleased a hatred that blackened the stone around her. *"Now."*

The earth trembled.

* * *

How much practice 'til I stop jabbing myself? Gongie sucked on the needle's freshly inflicted wound while comparing his work to the symbols Oya wrote for him. Taking out stitches was a pain. But the luxurious fabric which was once his shirt was unexpectedly forgiving.

Desperate thoughts and despairing emotions bombarded Gongie – even from this distance. *How is his mind so loud?* It took all he had to focus on the comforting burble of the river. And yet... The wave lasted longer this time, but Ferdinan's voice eventually faded. *Bob's impressively good at helping him down.*

Breathing slowly, he went back to work – mind ruminating on the last few weeks. Ferdinan arriving right after the cave-in. Every voice disappearing at once. And that strange angry darkness...

Every time the skeleton made any kind of progress, something stopped him. Then there was the rotting stone Bob described...

Slipping it inside out, Gongie tied off the thread and moved to start the last line. *I didn't think there'd be time to finish.* But he would. And he didn't know how to feel about that. *Four weeks without light or food...* No one knew how much water they had, but it wouldn't last this long. And their voices vanished two weeks ago...

What do I do when he reaches them? The thought of two-week dead bodies made Gongie nauseous. And he'd experience it from every person who saw them... From the skeleton...

There was also Jon's last request. *Being a brother to Ferdinan... How do I keep him alive long enough to return to the islands? No. He needs the Artimus's.* The islands couldn't help Ferdinan and Gongie would never return a child to a family that abandoned them.

And Oya? Ferdinan wouldn't leave her behind, but if this wasn't her home, these people would know where to send her.

Larasi's worried mind interrupted his thoughts. Quickly, he put his project away and leaned back to wait for her arrival. When she came into view, he waved. "Normally Welick gets me."

"I told Welick he was busy and I'd come in his place."

Gongie laughed. That was exactly what she told the young man. "It's ok to speak to your leader like that?"

A small finger pointed to her ear. "We're equals."

Ah...they've both earned two bands. "How can I help you?"

Shrugging, she sat down and leaned against the tree. "Don't know why you ran off that day. But you're worrying Ajani."

And you. "I'm sorry. I'll apologize to her again."

"Maybe we should apologize."

Gongie blinked. "Why? You've been more supportive than I deserve. You've made all of this easier."

"I didn't think mentioning the boy would upset you like that."

"Jon?" Sighing, he bowed forward. "That didn't upset me. I..."

"No. I understand. Losing a Niompa is devastating."

That word... He searched her surface thoughts again, but it was the same as last time. If he wanted to know what that was, he had to ask or scan her. "I don't know what a Niompa is."

"*Niompa...* In Common... I don't know the word. It's like an Iompa, but fairly balanced."

That isn't helpful... "I'm sorry, but I have no idea what an Iompa is. I assumed it was something like a grandmother."

Giggles bubbled up. "I forget how ignorant outsiders are. An Iompa..."

Words he didn't understand accompanied some of the sweetest images he'd seen. It didn't help him understand. But it was nice.

"Ha! An Iompa is one of great importance you dedicate yourself to. You love them and..." Her throat tightened from a deep pain. Taking a moment, she breathed out and continued. "You love them and choose to stay with them. Helping them. Making them smile..."

That pain came again – forcing her to stop. Only, it wasn't pain. It was reverence and respect and love so deep it hurt. *She'd truly do anything for Ajani...* "I understand. It's all those things, but both choose to do that for each other. Balanced."

She chuckled. "Balanced isn't always equal. But close enough."

Pain and joy twisted inside her – inside him. *What could cause anyone to feel this intensely?*

"Regardless. I understand the pain of your loss. Not fully, but better than many. You don't have to hide here when it's too much."

"I..." It amazed him how right and wrong she was at the same time. *If she knew people like me existed...* That was a scary thought. "I do love Jon. We've spent most of eleven years together. And I'm terrified of what Ferdinan will find when he reaches them. But... That's not why I come here. And that's not where my worry ends."

"I'm surprised you chose here instead of helping...Ferdinan was his name?" She waited for Gongie to confirm. "Instead of helping Ferdinan in the caves. That's where I'd be if Ajani was trapped."

"Ah...well..." She leaned in close when he trailed off. "He wouldn't be able to work if I was there. And I... We both have difficulty being around each other."

Dark eyes studied him for a long while. "You don't hate him."

"No! No, I don't hate him. I... I feel similarly toward him as the camp does Ajani. I respect him and wish I could help him so deeply it hurts." Gongie closed his eyes and exhaled. *That's how I feel.* He'd never tried putting his feelings toward Ferdinan into words. They always felt too complex and overwhelming to label. But they were unexpectedly simple. "Can we talk about something else?"

"What would you like to talk about?"

"I've figured out what a band or rod means by its placement in the ear, but why's it only your left ears? Especially the few like Ajani who have so many."

She grinned – emotions turning light and simple. "Everyone who lives in the nine western countries wear their honors in the left ear. Those in the eastern nine, use the right."

It took a moment, but Gongie laughed. "Really? It's really that simple...? Wait. Your people span the world...?"

"Of course. Each country has a camp, a village, and a charge. It's our duty. Or...it was..." Frigid hate flared up.

"What happened?"

"Outsiders." Her gaze shifted to the canopy. "They lied. And they stole. They destroyed precious things that are forever lost. And when we thought we'd hidden well enough, they slaughtered us."

Gongie's heart pounded. "I'm so sorry."

"A new topic."

"Yes! Um..." There was one thing he'd been trying to figure out. *Oya said...but...* It was fine if Larasi refused to answer, he needed to ask or he'd regret it. "I'm sure I haven't done enough to earn the answer, but the green stone chip in Ajani's ear...what's this called?"

There were no giggles when he pointed to the little flap above the lobe. She knew exactly what he was going to ask.

"I'm sorry. That was rude of me–"

She interrupted him with a hand. Assessing him. Making her decision. "Tragus. Ajani earned the protection stone."

"That was a terrible thing to earn...?"

"It's the greatest and worst of honors." A memory bubbled up, but she pushed it away. "Those who earn it die or worse."

"Worse?" *Ajani's too happy for death to be better than her life.*

"Sacrificing yourself kills you one way or another. But if everyone else survives, then it was the right thing." Her lips trembled, but she fought back the tears. "Dead or the living dead, they're the ones who need the protection. So they're given the emerald chip to ward off any more that'd tear them apart from now into the eternities and lead them to the happiness they've earned."

"What happened?"

"She led the slaughterers away. They weren't even human enough to end the torment they inflicted. They just left her for the beasts." That memory came again, and this time she let it play. And mourned at the end.

Tears fell, but closing his eyes didn't stop what he saw. Everything Larasi saw. *She wasn't the only one broken that day.* "I think I understand. Thank you."

"Really?!" White heat flared up, but she pushed it back down before speaking again. "How can someone like you understand?"

"'Cause I've been forced to hide while watching someone break as well. Hide and watch, when I desperately wanted to help."

Surprise filled her. Those beautiful dark eyes shifted between studying him and contemplating his words. *All* his words. "Ferdinan."

She'd be a truly terrifying Psych.

A shudder ran up and down his spine. That darkness surged. It grew and consumed the earth.

Then it vanished...

Larasi gave a sympathetic smile. "Seems we aren't so different."

What just happened?

* * *

Forty million people? That was reaching double East Azute's original population. *Ask the Duchess to train me in negotiations next break.* The agreement she secured was impressive. And her plans – amazing. Zephyr couldn't wait to see their fruition. But...

How to quell possible riots over the lottery? How do we maintain our international position? Losing their position was better than letting countless millions starve. But it'd be his responsibility to shore up their world power. There was time. Not much, but some.

And he had other duties he was shirking. But how did you tell a mother her child was missing?

It took a few tries to compose a message. But he did.

Sending it was the most difficult thing he'd ever done.

* * *

Gently as lifting a butterfly by its wings, Ferdinan carved in.

Stunned... *It broke through...* But what nightmare waited on the other side? The machine's light filled the cavern. Nothing moved.

Please be alive. Please be alive. Please be alive.

Ears and eyes strained beyond that of his heart. *Anything, please! Be alive!* A scream was in his throat when a groan hit his ears.

"*Stay back! I'm widening the hole!*"

Twenty excruciating minutes later, Ferdinan rushed in. Men staggered around as if they just woke up.

"Oya!! Jon!" He dodged the miners escaping their tomb until a giant pointed to hunched shadows. Running, Ferdinan didn't stop until he was squeezing her tightly.

That perfect consuming void was the most comfort he'd ever felt.

Jon wiggled awkwardly to get out of the way but a stick thin arm wrapped around his neck, pulling him in. Stinging needles and an endless void! A tsunami surged, taking over. "*Never again! I thought I'd lost you... I killed you...*"

"*You care so much.*" Oya grinned.

"*Of course I care!*" Sorrow, regret, and painfully embarrassing sobs strangled him. "*You think I don't...?*"

"I love you too." Oya reached an arm around her dear friend.

Jon mirrored the gesture. "As do I, little brother."

"*I'm sorry...*" Ferdinan wept. Tears fell against his will. An erratically jumping heart twisted itself in half. And he couldn't let them go. The needles hurt and the void was overwhelming. But he couldn't let go. He couldn't let them die. Not like that.

"Oya's hurt." Jon whispered after a long while.

Control yourself... Ferdinan needed to regain control. Needed to get his ally and friend to safety, to healer Yahmo. Dizziness and exhaustion broke across him in a cold sweat. But the tears wouldn't stop. They wouldn't stop. "*I'm sorry for being so weak...*"

"*Never be ashamed of tears, for only the living can cry.*" Her mischievous voice danced in his ears. "You never fail to amaze me."

Everything inside Ferdinan magnified. All he could do was hold onto them. *I didn't lose them. I didn't fail them...not completely...*

He was out of control. But they didn't rush him.

"Are you alright?" Ferdinan squeezed them tighter.

"A little thirsty, a little dirty, but not hungry...is that bad?" Jon squeezed back.

"Oya?"

Laughter hit their ears. "I won't be dancing anymore."

"What?"

"It's ok."

Moving back... The limited light showed one pant leg thoroughly torn. But no blood. Tearing back what little fabric remained revealed unscratched, unbruised skin. But her unmarred leg didn't look right.

Oya grinned. "*Guess you've uncovered my little secret.*"

"*I don't...*" Recognition hit.

She laughed at her misshapen leg. "I'll miss dancing, but climbing...I'll miss that most..."

The giant walked over and helped Ferdinan lift her – securing her leg awkwardly. Though Oya grimaced, she didn't complain.

"*Mr. Charlie! This is my dear friend.*" Joy filled Oya's face.

Mr. Charlie bowed his head to Ferdinan. "*Thank you for saving my people. I'm deeply in your debt.*"

"*Are there any who need medical attention? There's room for twenty.*" It wasn't enough, but it was all he could offer. "*The healer I'm taking them to owes me, he won't ask questions.*"

Mr. Charlie chuckled and helped Jon to his feet. "*Thanks to Lütoh Miisa, there were only minor cuts and bruises.*"

"*I'm glad.*" *She's amazing...* "*I've left instructions with your medicine women. Follow them and you won't get sick...*"

"*Thank you.*"

Ferdinan nodded and moved to the tunnel.

"*Wait,*" Oya whispered.

"*Why?*" *Does it matter? I'd do anything for you 'cause I need you.* Ferdinan froze. *...I feel this way...?* It surprised him. And scared him. He never needed anyone before.

With a wink she shouted for Mr. Charlie to take Jon out.

"*Thank you.*" Mr. Charlie guided Jon forward.

Once they were out of sight, Ferdinan followed. Each step reminded him of every agonizing second. Would he find them alive? Did he kill them? Would he kill his only friend?

When did I come to need her? Everything was easier before he met her – when he was alone. But the pain and fear of the last month was better than the seclusion he suffered in that office...and his life.

Solitude never bothered me, why should it now? It's safer. And no more painful than this... He looked at Oya's bright face – dirty as it was pale... Her toothy grin outshone everything. If there'd been any trace of green in her eyes she would've looked fine.

Alone is safer. I can't hurt anyone. I can't fail them. So why do I want this? What makes this better? What makes this desirable? They stepped into the sunlight. Tears streaked down every face. Joyous cries and weeping filled the air.

Oya laughed so exuberantly...! So filled with life and excitement! Resting her dusty cheek against his shoulder, she laughed again.

There's no joy in being alone.

The cavern collapsed.

Chapter 34

The volunteer campaign wasn't garnering the hoped-for response, but that was fine. The Duchess could wait a few more weeks before implementing the lottery. Slender fingers ran over the growing stubble... Making it a consequence for rioting was tempting, but she'd do this fairly. Including placing her third and fourth daughters in the draw.

"Find out where the hesitation's coming from." The Duchess instructed the three standing before her. "The southern regions are volunteering at higher rates than expected, but the capital and my dukedom aren't. Find out and we'll make adjustments."

"Yes, ma'am." The three bowed and left.

Why wouldn't disgruntled citizens flock at this chance? Protests she understood. But why riot then not take the opportunity for more favorable conditions?

This didn't bode well for the lottery. It'd be effective. And the next excuse for violence. Whatever caused this shift in social responsibility... *Why didn't I notice it sooner? How do I fix it?* And if it couldn't be fixed, then how did she guide her people back to not hurting each other? Keeping leaders and nobility in line was their right. But it was her duty to keep them from hurting each other.

A *beep* interrupted her useless contemplations. *My Prince? This is an odd time for him to call.* Smoothing her shirt – a hand ran over stubble...reminding her she didn't have hair to adjust. The Duchess rolled her eyes at herself, then answered her Prince's call request.

* * *

It was odd being squeezed like a stuffed toy. But once Jon escaped the caves, his island brother latched onto him and didn't let go. All day. All night. And most of the morning. But it was the only thing Gongie could do for Jon – so he wasn't about to stop it. "It's ok. You're safe."

Whenever anxiety flooded his island brother, the Psych repeated those words, bringing a sense of safety and security Jon desperately needed. Long arms randomly squeezed him tighter, making sure he was real. That he wouldn't disappear. And Gongie didn't resist – he simply rested against Jon's long, trembling body, providing the connection his island brother needed.

If they were on the islands or Jon's estate, the Thinker would've dragged every person and pillow into one room and found a way to smoosh and be smooshed by all of them. *I'll get you home soon.*

The day passed and the sun faded. Visitors came. Food was delivered...if the milky drink could be called food. And by the time Larasi's mind grew close, Jon was dozing. Gongie gently patted the arms holding him hostage. "Are you ok with one more visitor?"

If we don't have to move.

Leaning harder against his island brother, Gongie soaked in the comfort washing over Jon. "Welcome."

There was a pause while the girl reined in her pounding heart. Slowly the door opened and she peeked inside. "That was startling."

"I'm sorry. I heard you coming."

Stepping inside, she studied the two of them. Amusement and the joy of cuteness radiated from her. "We weren't wrong."

When Gongie didn't respond, Jon looked at her. "About what?"

She knelt and offered her hand. "I'm glad you're safe."

"Thank you. Me too." Jon squeezed Gongie tighter – making him squeak. Dark shadows swirled around the Thinker's mind.

Gongie's lips tightened. He wished he knew how to clear those shadows. It was possible they'd fade away. But if they didn't...

"It's time to get ready." Larasi stood and offered a hand to each boy – wondering if she weighed enough to pull the giant to his feet.

Dread fueled anxiety seized Jon and he squeezed tighter.

"You..re...safe." Gongie gasped. "You...'ll break...my ri...bs..."

I don't want to be alone...

What could the Psych say? Gongie knew Ferdinan wasn't capable of giving Jon the comfort and help he needed. Even without Oya to worry about. "I know... Come with us. I'll get you home."

Jon buried his face in the back of Gongie's shoulder. *I can't.*

"It's a three-hour walk. The mornings are still pleasant, but it'll get hot carrying back supplies after mid-day." Giving the boy's a little smile, Larasi moved toward the door. "If he's changing his mind on leaving with Liitoh Miisa and Ferdinan, I'll find another set of strong arms to carry things back."

"No..." Jon kept his face buried, squeezing harder. "I'm going."

"I assume you're walking with him, Gongie?" When the Psych nodded, she continued, "What should I have the kitchen hands pack for you for the round trip?"

* * *

I almost lost her. Almost killed my ally. I almost killed them all... Ferdinan finished writing a meal plan for those who were trapped then checked the transport's progress. *How can she look ok with those injuries?* He knew what that kind of damage could lead to when left untreated. And it'd been six weeks. *Thank you for still being alive. I'll do everything I can for you.*

"Are you ready–" Tearing claws pushed him away. "I'm sorry, but I need to finish helping her..."

The incredulous look the older woman gave him ground his objection to a halt. It was the same look she gave last night when he was trying to stabilize her leg with the materials they had here. That look ended in him being dragged away from his friend.

Considering Oya was clean, in fresh clothing, with her leg fully braced after he was allowed back, he couldn't be upset. But he didn't want to be separated from his friend again.

"*She'll be ready. Go get the supplies the kitchen masters prepared for you.*" When he didn't leave, she gave him a pointed look – the morning's light glinted off her five silver hoops.

Ferdinan painted on a smile. *I don't want to leave her.* "It'll probably take three hours...or so...to reach the transport."

Oya looked at her leg. "Ambitious. I like it. I promise I won't leave without you."

Pink tinged his cheeks. Steping out of that little cabin was the hardest thing he'd done. But there wasn't time to agonize before Tansu and Maelel ran up. Static electricity wrapped around him and held on until Tansu released him to talk.

Excited hands didn't stop moving on their walk to the kitchen. Neither Tansu's nor Maelel's. Ferdinan mostly watched – responding when they insisted on his input. *It's impressive how well he speaks with his hands while using a crutch...* But... Gears turned.

How hard would it be to make him a leg? Ferdinan already had the diode that adjusted artificial bones as a child grew. Adapting it–

Static electricity and a gentle breeze encircled him. Startling him. Tansu's touch was unusual. But the gentle breeze... Nearly colorless crystals stared at Maelel. *People can feel like this?*

"We promise." Maelel pointed to the kitchen. "You'll like this."

What did I miss....? Boney hands expressed his thanks.

Tansu pointed from her mouth to Ferdinan's ear.

What...? In his search for clues, the skeleton noticed Mr. Charlie standing at campfire's circle. Ferdinan felt himself pale. Black spots scattered at the edge of his vision and the world swayed.

That gentle breeze enveloped his shoulder – steadying him. "Are you ok?"

"Yes... I apologize." A boney hand rubbed his tight chest as he made his way to the giant. Bowing deeply, "I'm sorry. I'm so sorry."

Tansu zapped his shoulder to get his attention and scolded him both for bowing and apologizing. Then told him to sit.

Frozen, Ferdinan stayed half-bowed as he looked at them all.

The giant chuckled and sat down – Tansu and Maelel following. Not sure if standing or sitting was ruder, Ferdinan sat.

"Thank you for saving us. Your sacrifice wasn't unnoticed." Mr. Charlie's deep voice shook their bones and his hands danced. "By saving the One, you saved all of us. I can't thank you enough."

"No. I almost failed you. Any longer and you would've died." Leaning forward, Ferdinan bowed again. "I'm truly sorry."

"Lift your head. A Hiyon doesn't need to bow to any of us." There was a pause and Mr. Charlie repeated, "Lift your head."

Ferdinan obeyed, but kept his gaze down.

"You sacrificed yourself to save us."

"And you almost died...you still could. If I had sacrificed-"

Tansu smashed the side of one hand into her other palm – stopping him from arguing further.

"We didn't die. 'Cause of you, we didn't die. You saved us." Mr. Charlie's tone and hands were firm and unyielding. "My son. Those who assisted you. Even young Tansu who kept bothering you while you worked all stand witness to your struggles. Your suffering. Not all sacrifice ends in death. Neither is death the greatest sacrifice."

"Anyone here would've done more if they had my knowledge."

"That's not true." Maelel interrupted so Tansu could speak.

Bringing both palms down, she breathed out. When her hands moved again, she made it clear the camp accepted their loss two weeks ago. Two weeks before reaching them, they would've stopped and prepare to move the camp to a more stable location.

Those were hard words to hear, especially from one so young. Boney hands moved. "You underestimate what a person will do when they are the only one present who can do it."

In rebuttal, she told him he overestimates most people's limits.

"You saved us. And by saving the One you saved us all." Those massive hands moved reverently. "Thank you, Hiyon."

I saved them. I didn't fail... Lip trembling, Ferdinan shifted to his knees and placed his forehead on the ground. "Thank you."

* * *

"Nephew! How are you?" Tenalia's smile faded quickly. "Have you lost weight?"

Every muscle in the Prince's face was strained. Poking, prodding at his wound set his nerves aflame – helping him through this. "Do you have time?"

The General shooed away whoever was off-screen and gave Zephyr her full attention. "Speak."

The conversation with the Duchess was...unexpected. Telling her Ferdinan rescued a dozen people and was flying to a hospital in Chūzo...all she said was, "*he'll be back as ordered. That's fine.*"

The Duchess was busy. And she knew Ferdinan's capabilities best... But...he felt he was overreacting next to her.

"Zephyr?" Tenalia prodded at his silence. "What's wrong?"

"I apologize..." Jabbing his thumb hard into the freshest wound, he continued. "I felt I should inform you."

Carefully choosing his words, he laid out what he knew concerning Ferdinan's disappearance in East Azuté. "He's taking his friend and Jon Dinta to a hospital in Chūzo. I don't know which, but based on when he left, they should arrive soon."

Tenalia looked astounded. "How did all that happen?"

"I don't know."

"I'll notify my soldiers to search for him."

"Thank you." Bowing, he closed the screen and jabbed harder at the wound. *How did any of this happen?*

* * *

Not once during the three-hour trek did Jon let go of his hand. Even the difference in their strides wasn't enough to give up what little comfort he had access to.

"We're almost there." Gongie squeezed his island brother again. This wasn't best for Jon...but there wasn't much he could do. *I hope those dark clouds go away.* "You can still come with us. We'll go to your estate. You can get everything you need there. All the help you need. We can even arrange to finish the block's work at your home while you recover."

"I want to go home. But with what Oya's about to go through... And all the progress I made with my brother is gone..."

Gongie nodded. Self-abuse was killing the Tinkerer's heart and his hair was falling out. "You need help too."

"I want to go home..." The desire for home and family – a desperate need for comfort he wouldn't get from Ferdinan or Oya battled with responsibility and duty. Long arms pulled Gongie into a hug. "Call my mom. I don't know if I'll be able to while traveling..."

"Anything for my brother." Gongie squeezed back – offering what comfort he could. "You need to know, Ferdinan needs more help than you can hope to provide. You both do. If you can't get help where you're going, call me."

* * *

Zephyr stared at the screen in his hand. He'd done his duty – had informed his family...despite the different reactions. But... Neither the Duchess nor Aunt Tenalia were best for Ferdinan. If they were, none of this would be happening.

But he knew who did care. Who could help.

Slowly breathing out, Zephyr placed a call request to the Queen Mother.

* * *

"Are you sure you'll be able to carry all that back?" Ferdinan's hands moved as he addressed Tansu, Maelel, and Bob.

Tansu looked at the pile and snorted – telling him if he could carry Liitoh Miisa ten miles, they could manage a few boxes. The three moved to secure the carrying straps, but Ferdinan stopped Tansu, asking if he could talk to her.

Holding his hands palms out, Ferdinan tapped his temple and rested his flat hand against his chest. He apologized for not having time to teach her properly and asked if she still wanted to learn.

A bright smile shown and her hands danced excitedly.

Nodding, he offered one of the screens he brought with him. After showing her how to work the device and access the lessons, he warned to study them in order. Supplemental materials were explained. As was the program he'd made to help Oya learn Common. Since they only used hand speak, he wasn't sure how well she read it. Those lessons would improve her Common regardless as while teaching basic mechanics.

In her excitement, she wrapped him in static electricity before running over to Maelel. *They're close...are they siblings?*

"Bob Dosi." Ferdinan bowed.

Looking at Ferdinan and the Fighter, Maelel grinned and motioned Tansu to a shady spot to show him her new toy.

"Yes?" Bob approached and returned the bow.

229

"A Dosi shouldn't bow to a lord."

"It's clear how we rank here." Bob shook his head. "Everything you did earned my respect. I'm glad I learned you're not the person I thought you were. And I'm sorry I couldn't have done more."

"No!" An uncomfortable sensation tightened Ferdinan's chest and ran down his arm. Bowing hid his grimace. "Thank you. I wouldn't have reached them without your help. Thank you for saving my friend. Thank you... I apologize for the trouble I caused."

"You didn't cause me trouble. But you better go."

"Thank you for helping them carry supplies back."

Bob grinned and shooed Ferdinan to the transport. Bowing one last time, the skeleton hurried in and told the pilot they were ready. Jon was asleep...surprisingly. And Oya grinned and removed the green cuff she'd been wearing.

"What is that?" Ferdinan resynced Jon's monitoring diode. *How do I increase the range of these?*

Oya held up the cuff. "This? It distinguishes me as a Miisa."

Ferdinan tried, but couldn't recall the word. "What's a Miisa?'"

"A kind of traveler."

"And Liitoh?"

A grin was his answer. Blue crystals studied his friend and the green string that didn't quite connect them. It stopped a foot from her. *I'll earn your friendship... I'll do anything for you.* The wicked saint who'd run and fight with him... *I'll make sure we fight again.*

Then there was Jon. *What would his string look like...?* Ferdinan stopped himself. After everything he'd done to his ally... *I should've fought harder to make him give up...* Then the last year... All the stress and frustration, unreasonable expectations – being buried alive...! He should've mercilessly forced his ally away. What consequences would Jon face because he didn't? *What do I tell the Queen Mother? She'll definitely hate me now...*

Chapter 35

It wasn't the best – couldn't compare to Ajani's skill before the incident... But Gongie made it. Wrapping it in leftover fabric from his fancy shirt, he headed to Ajani's cabin.

Larasi opened the door. Looking him over, she smiled at the beautiful outfit he'd been gifted. "Any later and she'd been in bed."

"I apologize." He bowed and showed the gift he brought - earning him deeper approval and an invitation inside. This cabin was a little bigger than the one they'd been given. But it was still simple. A modest size common room and three doors in the back.

Ajani sat in a worn chair. Joy filled them both. "Welcome."

"Thank you." Gongie knelt and offered her the small bundle.

Once Ajani conquered the knot her eyes filled with tears. Frail fingers ran across sloppy embroidery spelling "thank you" in Oŭndo. Unsteady hands pushed back the flap closing. Inside were a bundle of sticks and a thick cloth. Ajani beamed. "Thank you."

He took her offered hand and sandwiched it between his own. "Thank you for teaching me sewing and what it means to be human. For giving me the most beautiful gift I've ever received. And opening the door to a new family. I can't thank you enough."

Ajani pulled him into an awkward hug and Larasi gave him a playful whack between his shoulders.

"Thank you, Larasi. For everything." Gongie shot her a smirk.

"Well...you caused so much trouble, the quiet won't feel right anymore." Larasi teased. "We expect to see you soon."

"As soon as I can." Gongie hesitated, but decided to ask, "If I wanted to bring a friend, what would I need to do?"

Larasi looked at Ajani, lips tight. "Ask Liitoh Miisa first."

It didn't take a Psych's abilities to understand Larasi's warning. "I won't tell anyone about here without her permission."

They chatted until Bob arrived. Three 'goodbyes' latter, Larasi started pushing him toward the door.

"Thank you...helping me reclaim..." The rest of Ajani's words were lost between her mind and her tongue, but Gongie heard them.

* * *

"Yuyu! Elbie! Thanks for coming." Xhou stood next to an incredibly handsome boy. "You know Norger?"

"We've talked at some events." Yuyu bowed and Elbie followed suit - forcing his hands behind his back and shaking his head.

"I apologize. I didn't think I'd be useful to a Tinkerer. Xhou insists I'm wrong."

Elbie nodded. "Xhou's been a wonderful fill-in mentor."

"Can't compare to Ferdinan, though!"

"No one compares to Master Ferdinan." Yuyu smiled - fingers spinning the little toy she always carried.

"True." Xhou motioned for everyone to sit.

"I appreciate your time. Even if Ferdinan isn't called away the next two years, I'd like to understand Tinkerers better." Norger gave a winning smile, but Yuyu sensed a hidden strain.

"We're happy to help." Elbie's smile was pleasant, but guarded.

And Yuyu understood. *They don't think Master Ferdinan's returning. Elbie will finish his mentorship with Norger... No, that's not what's happening. Elbie's losing the rest of his apprenticeship to train a Thinker.* Pink eyes glanced over. Her island brother nodded. Pulling out a screen, she gave it to Norger. "These're the primary rules when meeting a Tinkerer. Memorize them."

Confusion warped Xhou's face. "There're rules?"

Yuyu nodded. "'Cause Ferdinan did everything, you didn't have to know about it."

* * *

Ferdinan knew his ally's beliefs better than his own. *I'm sorry, Jon.* Forcing the Thinker to swallow the milky drink he prepared assured Jon was out by the time they landed.

Healer Yahmo waited with a few nurses and two stretchers. Wild, dilated eyes soaked in every ounce of mayhem. But her wicked grin was comforting. As were her dancing bare toes – five of them anyway. *Why does she detest shoes...?*

"Heal-healer Y-Yahmo, th-th-thank...thank you..." Ferdinan managed a bow – swallowing his leaping heart and instinct to run. *Healer Yahmo's a good man. He won't hurt me. He won't touch me.*

"I'm honored you sought me." Yahmo brought his arms in front of him, palms up. "Let's get your friends inside."

Swallowing hard, the skeleton scrambled back as far as he could. *Yahmo's a normal healer. He won't hurt me. He can't scan me.* "Th-th-at's Jon Dinta, he needs t-to be refed. Oya...I t-t-t...eg."

"Hello, Oya. Mind coming with me?"

Wicked grin glowing, she shifted into Yahmo's arms. The healer gave her to and intern then returned for Jon.

There was something Ferdinan needed to say. Needed to tell the man, but all he could think about was how close the healer and his interns were. The skeleton squirmed – wanting to crawl inside the cockpit and run out the pilot's door.

Carefully, Yahmo lifted the awkwardly long, unconscious Jon and passed him to the waiting men. Halfway between the transport and the entrance the healer waited. Given space to escape, the skeleton followed from a distance.

Jon was taken away and they continued to the pristine room he used when visiting. The perfect cleanliness made Ferdinan acutely aware of how dirty he was. A year of showering wouldn't cleanse him.

"Th-the laser?"

"Over there, son." Yahmo pointed to a door on the far wall.

Taking the requested ultraviolet laser, Ferdinan donned protective goggles and went to work rigging it. Once modified properly, he dashed back.

"What's that going to do?"

Ferdinan's heart burst. Long limbs leapt to the other side of the table. *Focus. It's ok. Everything's ok...*

Focus. The second skin... I met her then... But he never would've guessed... It actually worked. She moves and plays easily.

But what does she look like? It was wrong... Seeing his scars didn't give him the right to see hers...

"Um...do...do..." Pushing up the goggles, Ferdinan blushed. "...*erm*... I...c-can leave if it'd make you...more comfortable."

Oya laughed. "I'm not pretty. If you're ok, then I'd prefer you stay. I trust you completely."

Unnerved, he steeled himself and retrieved goggles for Oya and Yahmo. *I can't fail her...*

Even pale, her face was lovely. Ferdinan held onto that image as he worked. "Heal-er Y-Yahmo, p-please wa-tch care-c-carefully."

Pinching the skin, Ferdinan slowly sliced into it with the laser. What looked like flesh split apart – bloodless flesh. He worked up to her knee, not letting the ends touch. Offering the tool, he gestured Yahmo to finish removing the Second Skin. And...

Ferdinan's stomach churned. Large sections of skin were missing. Not just missing, but carved away in odd designs. Along the calf was what looked like...a chain? Improperly healed gashes ran from ankle to hip attesting to repeated stabbings. *Who'd do this...?*

When Yahmo sliced off the Second Skin it turned black and gooped into Ferdinan's waiting hands.

"Tell me about your invention later." Yahmo looked astonished.

"Y-yes, s-s-sir."

"The requested materials are in your lab."

Ferdinan nodded. "Healer Y-Yahmo will pre-p you for s-surgery. I'll b-be there once I-I finish."

"I'll be waiting." Oya gave her signature grin and laid back.

"That machine you sent is a wonder, but for an entire limb... I'd rather the Master Crafter made this one."

Ferdinan shook. Blue crystals fixed on his only friend.

A perfect void squeezed his hand – shocking him. An impossibly comfortable void... "I trust you completely, my dear friend."

Chapter 36

Oya ran through grassy fields and open sky – keeping her eyes up. If she looked down...if her leg was gone here, she'd never run again. How would that effect her promises?

Losing her leg felt less significant than releasing those connections. But she hadn't faced that yet. *My dear friend...* This would hurt him worse than it would her. His soul couldn't survive another wound. She thought she'd seen the ugliest soul, but his... There was barely more than infection left. Could she salvage what was left? Or was cleaning it beyond even the Fisherman's abilities?

The Fisherman... Could he help expedite Yuyu's training? And Keepers. She needed to search harder... *Or...should I make them...?*

"What do you think?" Oya winked at the orbs in her peripheral. They were sweet following her here. Especially after what she put them through. "I also need the Fisherman..."

But no matter how hard she tried – how long she called, he didn't come. "Would one of you retrieve him for me?"

The orbs froze in place and a perfect seriousness washed over her magnificent dream.

I understand.

All she could do was wait and enjoy this beautiful dreamscape. Her last run. *I should find some cliffs...*

* * *

Sunlight woke him... Jon rubbed his face and sat up. *When did I fall asleep?* Pajamas and a comfortable bed...he'd never seen... *Where am I? When did I...?*

Cotton filled his brain. Everything was fuzzy. *Ferdinan made me drink that milk-water...then...*

"He drugged me!" Jon leapt out of bed and nearly fell over. Once his head cleared, he dressed and left to find his little brother.

The halls were pristine. And empty. Until he reached the hub of intersecting paths. In the center was a man sitting behind a simple desk. "I'm looking for my brother and my friend."

A barrage of questions later, Jon learned Ferdinan was with a healer Yahmo in surgery. "Where?"

The man pulled up a map and drew a path to the observation room.

Thanking him, Jon hurried away. *Please be exaggerating how long they've been in surgery.* That long and Ferdinan was there... *What complications arose?*

The first two observation decks showed empty surgical rooms. But the third...

The room was like a glass crow's nest. A giant screen showed crushed bone being fished out of mangled meat. In the corner was his trembling little brother – jumping whenever someone got close. *How's he around so many healers?*

Minutes stretched. Healers continued fishing bone fragments. *What're they doing?* An amputation didn't require this much preparation. Her leg was crushed and without medical attention for a month. It was a miracle she was alive.

Jon watched – analyzing. Ferdinan kept his eyes glued on the screen – gesturing now and then... But nothing they did made sense.

How did he find us? Or know we needed him....?

And...

He drugged me to keep me out of the way...

Terror consumed the skeleton below, but his brother didn't budge. Ferdinan stayed next to his greatest fear to help a friend.

He's a scary gent.

* * *

Dæya waited nervously. Two messages came in earlier. One from Ferdinan and another from Tillia. Ferdinan wouldn't accept his call request, but the Athlete did.

Finally! His screen chimed. "Princess Tillia, you reached the Nuwa safely?"

"Yes. We'll take a transport to the Grasslands. From there, we'll drive to North Oueshi's nearest port and boat to the Queen Mother's estate where we'll wait for a supply transport back to the islands."

The Athlete squared her shoulders and faced the man unblinkingly. "As for your other questions, we've told you everything we can. I'd appreciate you not pressing."

"You were missing for six weeks. I need to know where you were and what happened."

"We were helping a group who needed our abilities. There was an accident trapping a number of people. Lord Ferdinan freed them and is taking Oya and Jon to Chūzo for treatment." Her dark eyes narrowed. "As a matter of honor, that's all you need to know."

They all said that. "Which country?" *Please not North Chūzo.*

"I don't know, sir. Lord Ferdinan didn't say."

"Thank you." He hoped to give Zephyr more information... "Travel safely. Send daily reports of your progress."

"Yes, sir."

* * *

Surgery was taking forever. *Her leg can't be saved...* Jon knew Ferdinan had to try. But it made the inevitable worse. And watching alone... So he left to contact his family. How worried were they?

Terminals were all over the hospital. And none connected to an outside system. It wasn't possible to completely isolate a business. Confidence grew to desperation as he searched for an external line.

Please...I need mom... To hear her voice... He needed his dad and brothers too. A month underground... Trapped by rock and endless darkness...

Jon's heart raced and breathing became difficult. *I need my family!* Rushing back to the room, he grabbed his screen. But there was no system to connect to. No locked ones. No remote ones. Nothing. *Please! I need them!*

There has to be somewhere or Ferdinan couldn't have contacted them.

But aside from breaking into offices... *Think. Offices...where else would external systems be necessary?*

Records...no. Supplies...ordering was done from an office... Surgery... Can I hack in from the observation room?

Returning, Jon checked on the operation that was a day longer than it should be. *What're they doing? Stop delaying the inevitable...*

Removing panels and fixtures... Scouring the room... There was no port to manually connect to. No cables to make a port. Nothing! One attempt after another failed. He could contact anywhere inside the hospital. But nothing granted him access to the outside.

None of them... Jon's heart raced.

It took all his self-restraint to not throw the screen. Putting it down, he beat away every tear. *I need my family...*

Pacing burn off some of the anxiety consuming him. How was a hospital completely isolated? Nowhere was completely isolated! Even at the camp Ferdinan managed to remotely hack Azuté's grid.

Hugging himself, Jon turned to the observation window. His little brother was below. So was Oya. He couldn't talk to them, but he could see them. *I need my family... I miss them... I need their comfort...* Frustration leaked out of his eyes.

A skeletal hand flew up. Everyone froze. Drawing Jon's attention... *What's that?* Something metallic shone where bone once was. Leaning forward, he watched more intently.

Is the metal's what's been taking so long? But who'd do that to a child? What kind of monster would desecrate a girl like that? Ferdinan stepped forward and back and forward and back, over and over until he was close to the operating table.

Shaking, he pointed from his screen to her leg. There was no sound and everyone wore masks. *Is it difficult to remove? Dangerous? Get that out of her! No one should have their body so grossly defiled.* They continued, until the screen above Oya's leg changed. The skeleton nervously pointed to the hip socket.

Breath held, Jon watched...hopeful...then confused. Splaying open the meat of her upper thigh and lower hip, the healers went to work – not removing the metal, but adjusting it. Reattaching ligaments and tendons...

Disgust churned his insides and dizziness forced him to sit. *No...* Ferdinan regularly skirted taboos. But desecrating a living body...?

He wouldn't go that far...

Pale and shaky, Jon pushed past the dizziness to watch again. Begging to be wrong. But they moved to the metal knee and did the same thing...

◇

They carried her out.

It was over.

Two days. Ferdinan was never in a surgery that long. Black spots ate away the swaying room. Swaying became spinning. If not for the wall...

Rest now. Thank you for helping her.

Despairing thoughts consumed the histories' warmth and pushed Ferdinan to his knees.

"Please, get some sleep." Yahmo looked just as tired.

Sleep. Oya was surprisingly difficult to put to sleep. Neither did she bleed as expected. And other things that didn't makes sense... "How was-s th-there no in-in-fection...no p-p-poison?"

"That saved us hours. Before waking her, I'll run scans to check we got all the bone fragments."

Ferdinan withered further – too tired to tremble anymore.

"My secretary'll take you to a prepared room." Yahmo tried coaxing the boy to his feet.

"Pl-p-please..." Shying away, Ferdinan leaned against the wall. Stress knotted his insides. Draining tension left him nauseous. He had nothing left.

I'm not presentable for the Duchess... But his energy was gone. Ice imprisoned him. His head hurt. Breathing was a struggle. And the black spots were growing.

Coughs doubled him over until his face rested on his knees. Every trouble swooped in.

All the guilt.

All the shame.

All the failure.

Each pained breath he took stole a good person's life. *Why did this happen? When did everything go wrong? How do I stop it?!*

Sobs filled the room.

Chapter 37

The lighted green string wrapped behind him. But Ferdinan already did what he could for Oya. Now his ally... *He'll need his family...* The Tinkerer wasn't family, but he'd do what he could. The brilliant glow of exotic green emphasized his blue nails – reminding him how cold he was... *A run would warm him up... No, you have a duty. Jon needs his family, but he can't reach them here.* Half a dozen plans ran through his head, but they all felt hollow, superficial. Why was he doing this? Jon deserved better, but...this was all he could do. *If we were friends...what would Jon's connection look like?* It was stupid to imagine, but Ferdinan tried. And the image wavered between blue and purple in his mind. Neither was it bright, simply existing out of a sense of duty.

Looking down...there wasn't another string. Why would there be? They were simply two people trapped with each other – one constantly tormenting the other. That wasn't a connection. It was terrible and shouldn't exist. So why wouldn't Jon go away?

Finding the right number, Ferdinan activated the chime.

Swollen, tired eyes appeared and changed to vitriol. That expression startled him.

As did the lighted string protruding from Jon's chest, stopping a foot from Ferdinan. Gray swirled around faded purple. But when Jon saw him, black infected it – consuming the entire length.

"Um..." *I'm completely broken...* "Are you ok?"

Jon shrugged him off and slammed the door.

The world crumbled.

It was an odd turn. Ferdinan easily ignored Jon...never the other way around... *Stop being selfish. It's better this way... A nurse can tell him Oya's ok.*

Turning, Ferdinan almost bumped into an intern. Panicked reflexes saved them from colliding.

"Are you alright?" She approached.

If not for the wall, he would've fallen when he recoiled away.

Realization dawned and she stepped back. "I apologize, Master Ferdinan. You're coming from your friend's room, was he asleep?"

"N-no, Miss." Clutching the bar running along the wall, he fought to slow his heart and steady the swaying room. "H-he's awake. But... h-he's in a mood I've-ve never seen."

"Still?"

Ferdinan startled, blinking away black spots. "S-s-still?"

"He was agitated 'cause there're no external lines."

"Ah..." Bony hands rubbed at his pounding chest. "His f-family...is ex-tre-e-mely important to him..."

"Our patients are just as important."

Ferdinan nodded. "Have him...write a n-note for...healer Ya-Yahmo to s-send."

"I will, thank you. Is there anything *you* need?" The intern gave him the same look everyone did.

Ferdinan shook his head, waiting for her to leave. Those black dots swarmed. Moving faster. Closing his eyes, he slid down the wall to sit on the floor. Jon's rejection was unexpected... And...

Hugging his legs, Ferdinan rested his head against his knees pushing away the histories' warmth. *How poetic...*

Stop being weak. I was alone before. Forget everything. Forget and go back to my previous life. Ferdinan hoped he was right about Oya. She said she trusted him. *Please don't be angry with me...*

If she was...

He'd rewind further to that complete isolation.

It wasn't like he deserved a friend.

* * *

Jon sat on the bed hugging a pillow. He needed out of here. But it was dark outside – and there was Oya. He couldn't abandon her to a pit of monsters. But being disconnected from his family...he might have to leave to get help.

Tears fell, adding to the ones already soaking the pillow. He was tired. And scared. And the darkness mocked him through the window. *Nothing makes sense... I need to sleep.* Maybe a rested mind could figure out something...

Drying his face, Jon turned off the light. Darkness stole the room. Desperate fingers clawed to bring the light back. Ice encased him and his heart pounded. And on the other side of the door were monsters.

Double-checking the lock, Jon crawled back to bed. Lights on, he wrapped a blanket around him - hugging the pillow.

I want to go home.

* * *

Acres of wooded land surrounded Yahmo's hospital - allowing Ferdinan to run as fast as he wished.

Ignoring the black spots and swaying world, the skeleton sped up. Heart pounding against his chest urged his feet to fly. *Faster. Faster. Faster.*

Why won't Jon talk to me...look at me? His ally was desperate for family and comfort - and sought them from him before... What changed? Being buried alive...wouldn't the Thinker be clingier?

Ferdinan shook his head. He had a week to shed the weight the Artimuses put on him. To get home. To arrange transportation for Jon and Oya back to the islands. *...I should send them to Jon's. He needs his family...* And Oya...they'd care for her like their own.

Slick leaves jarred his thoughts. Regaining his footing, he scanned the path, and increased his speed.

They'd be better with Mother and Father Artimus. After his run, he'd give Healer Yahmo a message to send to the Queen Mother.

Moving faster, Ferdinan ignored the black dots and dizziness.

Only one week.

The sway of each step intensified. And the world vigorously danced. But he wouldn't stop. He wouldn't give in.

◊

How do I keep him from dying? Not being able to help someone in desperate need was painful. For years Yahmo tried. The healer squeezed his arm as he watched the skin wrapped skeleton fly

243

unnaturally fast. Drenched clothing made it undeniably clear... Ferdinan had no body fat. Most of the muscle was eaten away. Once thick hair was thin and scraggly. Pure desperation drove unsteady steps.

It wouldn't be long. If he could, Yahmo would keep the boy here. Though that'd extend the child's life, it'd ultimately assure Ferdinan's death.

So he waited. Every time the skeleton fell, he waited for the boy to not get back up.

Disk in hand, he stepped into the rainy night and walked to the fallen child.

Scans confirmed everything he thought. And added a concern he hadn't considered. Yahmo lost count of how many addicts Ferdinan helped, but now the boy's blood was saturated with a strange chemical. *What're you doing to yourself?*

Lifting the disturbingly light child, Yahmo carried him inside. Attaching a neural blocker, he drew blood to study the chemical and inserted an IV. The nutrients wouldn't do much, but if it kept him alive long enough to reach home, maybe they'd finally force care on him. It'd look bad for any family to have a child starve to death when food's available – let alone the main branch of the world's most powerful country. *Please don't die. If I could, I'd place you with a loving family as well.*

Chapter 38

The very sight of the skeleton disgusted Jon, so he waited until the monster left to check on Oya. *How dare he go near her after what he did!* Knocking on the unlatched door, Jon peeked in.

Life and energy glowed from the crazed red head as she grinned at her ten wiggling toes. "I'm surprised you weren't here earlier."

"May I visit?"

Sharp, penetrating green eyes sliced through him, but Oya smirked and gestured to a chair.

I'm glad they look right again... How do I tell her? Should I not? But everyone has a right to know when atrocities are committed against them. Or...is it too soon? Should I wait for her to recover? But...wouldn't it be better to tell her now so she can have it removed?

"I wonder what has a Thinker thinking so hard." Giggles spilled out of her, but they didn't feel carefree like normal.

Again his mind raced - wavering back and forth, until an unquenchable desire to speak consumed him. "You were told how your leg was saved?"

"Yes. My dear friend never ceases to amaze me." Those alien green eyes grew soft - then challenging. "I was worried, but he did exactly what I wanted him to."

"How...? How could anyone want that done to their body? Want someone to chop them open and implant things inside them? It's improper. Sacrilege." At least losing her leg was dignified. "How could you possibly want anyone to desecrate your body?"

Disappointment radiated from her. "If you were to lose your hands, wouldn't you do anything to keep them?"

"That's not...! But... Not that! 'Cause I value my body!"

"How's hacking off parts less defiling than inserting something to keep it whole?" Wild green eyes asserted her full authority - the authority she so easily held at the camp. "You don't determine my beliefs and values. Just as I've never questioned yours."

"Wrong is wrong!"

"Not all things deemed improper are incorrect." Disappointment returned to Oya's face. "Following blindly leads to unnecessary pain."

"I don't understand you..." Jon fought to keep his voice in check as frustrated tears ran down his cheeks. "I don't understand! This isn't acceptable!"

"Then you've rejected the gift I gave."

...what...?

"Is this all it takes to reject the suffering? To abandon your duties as a noble? To turn your back while a child dies alone?" Shifting her gaze to the window, Oya grinned – a bitter expression. "Take a walk and think. Ponder those questions and any more you find presented to you. When you're finished, answer them to yourself. You're the one who needs them."

~

A million thoughts bombarded Jon – each saturated with frustration and anger. And humiliation. How was he in the wrong? They were the ones breaking basic...!

Long legs carried Jon around the building. Inside. Outside. With the sun, it made no difference. So long as he couldn't see them.

Looking down at his hands... *If I were to lose them...*

Did that terrify her? She's so active... Never running or climbing or dancing... But it was still wrong! The body deserved respect. Alive, dead, it didn't matter. Again Jon looked at his hands.

He hated her question. He was a Scientist. Losing his hands... But he wasn't in that situation! *I haven't faced that horror...so how can I judge her?* But that didn't justify Ferdinan's sin!

The longer Jon fumed, the more his mind fixated on that question. And the more he wavered. He hated it. Giant blossoms filled the trees, but their beauty offered no relief. *If I woke up with them still there, thinking I'd lose them, would I be angry?*

"It's you."

The utter awe in those two words made Jon turn. A boy his age and no taller than Gongie stared up at him. Gratitude and respect glistened in those dark eyes. "I'm sorry?"

"Master Ferdinan, I'm Azil – from Yurranie..."

Yurranie...? The hospital in South Chūzo?

"Healer Yahmo warned I might not get to speak to you, but I needed to try." The boy scratch nervously at fine dark hair. "You look much healthier than your picture. And taller..."

"I'm sorry, but–"

"No! No. I'm sorry. I know you're busy but... Thank you." Azil pulled a small screen from his pocket and tapped it. An image of him with an older couple appeared.

"I'm not Ferdinan."

"I know. I know. Healer Yahmo told me about...yah..." He handed the screen to Jon. "Thank you, Fer...uh... Yeri. Thank you for my life. What I threw away...was torture. I never thought I'd be happy to wake up. That I'd have anyone happy to see me wake up."

Yeri? And... Jon looked at the image. A couple stood on either side of Azil – each with an arm around him.

"Thank you for the second chance. I'm healthy now. The Nari's are wonderful. They love me even knowing..." Taking the screen back, Azil smiled at the image. "When I catch up on the schooling I missed, healer Yahmo will sponsor me in a Medical Institute."

What did Ferdinan do to him? "May I ask what happened?"

The boy looked around nervously. "...you wouldn't have saved me if you were like everyone else..."

After a long, slow breath, Azil told Jon things he didn't know could happen to a child. The abuse was different, but Azil's distress reminded him of his ally. What the boy did was appalling...but... *"Following blindly leads to unnecessary pain."*

But...

His parents did that to him...? For years... Hugging himself... *Azil was wrong...* But it felt wrong considering that sin his.

"I'm sorry. Thank you." Tears filled those dark eyes. Azil blushed, wiping them away. "I didn't think I'd get to be happy. Thank you. Thank you."

247

What would Ferdinan do? Say? Condoning this...but... *Why did I meet you? I don't need this to think about too...* Bowing, Jon closed his eyes. "I hope your happiness continues growing."

Ferdinan would never say that... But the boy smiled – and that was good enough.

So many shades of guilt and shame filled him. It was bitter. *Why would he do that? Why waste resources on one who...* Thinking it disgusted him.

The world was easier to understand when everything was black and white.

What did he do with these unsettling hues?

◊

"*Impressive.*" Ferdinan gave her his best smile.

Oya laughed as he eased her onto the bed – wondering if Jon was learning what she needed him to. *Prove you're flexible or risk breaking.* "*Hand walking along bars is impressive?*"

"*You practically flew. Are you wearing the cuffs?*"

"*There'd be no question if I was.*" A wry wink made him blush.

Ferdinan knelt on the floor beside her. "*Everything's arranged. You and Jon'll travel to the Artimus estate after completing therapy.*"

"*And you?*" Oya searched for the string that used to mostly connect him and Jon, but it stopped farther from Ferdinan and was blackened on Jon's end. *What caused so drastic a change?*

"*I was summoned home. Please do something for me?*"

She gave an obnoxious smirk. "*Anything for my dear friend.*"

Hiding his burning face behind overgrown hair, Ferdinan sculpted his own mischievous grin to return. "*Make sure Jon's family understands what you two went through.*"

"*I will.*" Sincerity softened her features. "*Race you to the islands?*"

Chapter 39

"Ferdinan? May I talk to you?" Yahmo stepped back when Ferdinan pressed against the wall.

Keeping his distance, the skeleton faced the healer.

"There're two things..."

Dread filled him – egging on his heart and bringing black spots. "Is Oya ok?"

"Oya's fine. This has nothing to do with her." The man waited for Ferdinan to nod. "You're traveling home from here?"

"Y-y-yes, s-sir."

"Can I convince you otherwise?"

"I-I've b-been s-sum-moned."

Yahmo sighed. "Travel under your pseudonym. The conditions there aren't safe for you – please take precautions."

"N-n-noted." Breathing out heavily, Ferdinan relaxed slightly. "A-and th-the oth-th-ther th-thing?"

The healer offered a disk with disturbing results. "If you keep doing what you're doing, your heart will stop."

He scanned me? When? Fire flared across his gut.

Pain warped the man's face. So many kinds of pain. "I know what you're doing. If you lose any more weight, you'll die."

* * *

"Such a beautiful day!" The elf stretched tall and long – smirking at the Prince.

"It's the same as always." *She's unusually happy...*

"You think I live here?"

"I'm uncertain how real you are." Zephyr smirked, hands dancing.

She snorted. "You've heard about your cousin?"

"I was told he flew to a hospital in Chūzo." Zephyr tapped two fingers against his forehead. His hands danced before crossing and slashing down. "I assumed he went to one in North Chūzo, but my aunt can't find him."

"Chūzo's huge," the elf sympathized. "I'm feeling generous."

"Offering me some dried fruit?"

"That's an idea." The elf looked up smirking. "Ferdinan's at a private hospital preparing to travel home."

That straight, useful answer stunned Zephyr. And the message troubled him. "How's he traveling?"

"Train, I believe." When Zephyr's face darkened, she paused. "Is this a bad thing?"

It wasn't simply bad. *Everything with her has revolved around my cousin. He was even there...* Zephyr pushed away the memory of Ferdinan's soul. *If I warn her, she can help him...* "He should fly in directly or not at all."

Her beautiful face hardened. "They'd direct their pettiness toward a child?"

"The unrest and animosity has bled to the Duchess's children. I would've helped, but all my mothers insisted I return to school."

The elf's expression softened. "Your desire's right, but you're execution's wrong."

"What do you mean?"

Kneeling, she poked at his leg. "I see the damage you've done to yourself."

"There's nothing there." The Prince stepped back.

"The guilt, shame, and regret o' past years will fill us 'til we drown. We hope and swim 'til we reach the shore, and there we come to groun'."

"What?" He hadn't heard that poem before.

"It's a warning and a solution. To reach your goal, I suggest you take it to heart." That smirk returned – glowing. "I'll bother you again another day."

"I'll be waiting."

* * *

I'm not wrong! ...am I?

But...the more Jon thought, the less he felt he was right.

What do I do? His parents and brothers weren't here. And... *Have I followed blindly all my life? I've never thought about it...it's just wrong.* Chocolate brown eyes studied his hands as he meandered the woodland trail. Though mostly straight, roots and rocks made multiple attempts on his ankles.

It was beautiful. The spring breeze was sweet with pollen. And the sun was warm through the leaves. But his thoughts grew more confused.

Taboo or not. Improper, monstrous...or not... Oya would run again. And Azil...he was happy after surviving...*that.*

Jon studied his hands. If he were to lose them, but woke up with them still there...would he be upset? Or relieved? Was providing a normal life truly monstrous? But...condoning the means because it gave desirable outcomes wasn't right. Countless atrocities were committed because of such justifications. But...could a desire to help unleash such evil?

They're happy... And I disparaged that joy.

And this morning... When Oya summoned him, he thought she'd demand an apology he couldn't offer. But she acted like nothing happened. Telling him something terrible instead.

Now he had to decide.

Crunching leaves and snapping twigs caught his attention. Spotting the running skeleton was difficult. Stick limbs flew – coming closer. *How can he look worse?*

The pale, shaky, sweat-drenched skeleton was a terrifying sight.

Stick legs slowed – stopping out of arm's reach. Clothing that fit a couple months ago draped on him. Heavy, unsteady breaths doubled Ferdinan over and the gent had to use a tree to stay upright. "You'll get lost...if you wander...too far from...the hospital."

"I need to speak." Jon looked away, unable to bare the sight.

251

Ferdinan panted, but kept his gaze on his ally. "I'm listening..."

"How many have you defiled?"

Ferdinan was silent for a long time. "You found out."

"How many?"

"Twenty-three arms and seventeen legs. I've overseen the replacement surgeries for thirteen of them." Ferdinan's gaze didn't waver. "Every person requested it."

Jon's lips twisted. "How did you force a healer to allow such a monstrosity into his hospital?"

"His arm. He was my first client for bone replacement." Ferdinan squared his shoulders as if shielding the absent healer. "That taboo's wrong. Its whole reason for being created doesn't exist anymore. And because I ignored it, healer Yahmo saved hundreds of lives. I won't stop. I won't apologize. Not for keeping people whole."

"There're things you don't do. Implanting objects in the body... That level of desecration...! Even if Oya's ok with it, I can't be. And all the people you've defiled? How many were children? How many weren't old enough to understand how wrong it is?"

"I'm sorry, Jon... I won't apologize for doing what I believe is right." Face hard, Ferdinan stood as tall as he could.

"But you'll apologize for not apologizing?"

"Just 'cause something's taboo doesn't mean it's wrong." That scraggly mass of sweat-drenched hair lowered. "Most of those I've made bones for were children. Young children... An eight-year-old losing her arm 'cause of someone else's actions is wrong. I don't regret it. Saving a couple arms and legs is the only good I've done."

There were no words. Not for a long time. But something thick and uncomfortable filled Jon's gut. "You honestly can't see the good you've done?"

"I'm tired of arguing. I'll keep doing this as long as I'm able."

And how long'll that be? A myriad of strong, conflicting emotions overwhelmed Jon. He needed more time to choose. *Talk about something else...* "There was a boy looking for you but found me and assumed your picture was outdated."

Jon recounted the conversation and apologized. "I told him I wasn't you, but he didn't believe me."

"It's better he found you. I didn't do anything."

Why does he always lie like that? Jon closed his eyes. *I don't want to decide.* But he couldn't walk away without giving a warning. "Don't go home."

"It's not your concern." Pained blue crystals stared at Jon's chest.

The conversation between mom and Ferdinan's sisters replayed in his mind. "Why would you go there?"

"I was summoned."

"That!" There was too much Jon couldn't tell his family. Now... he couldn't tell his ally this... *I hate all these secrets.*

"What?"

"Travel to the capital. Ask your aunts for an escort to the conference," Jon persisted.

"There's no time. Even if there were, I'm not impinging on my aunts. And I won't waste resources." Bony hands scratched at messy, overgrown hair – losing more than a few strands. "You always want me to go home, why are you opposed now?"

"It's not safe," Jon blurted – then cringed.

"My dukedom's fine." Teeth clenched, the skeleton panted – a bony hand pressed against his chest. "I can't miss the Duchess's instructions prior, either."

Don't make me choose... Do what was right, what he wanted, and take Oya to his home where they both could heal. Or drag an injured girl to a toxic place to stay with his stubborn, unreasonable, improper ally... Chocolate brown eyes drifted to his hands. "Two days."

"What?" Surprise replaced confusion as those blue crystals locked onto Jon's chest again.

Jon looked down, but there was nothing on his shirt. *What's he looking at?* Standing tall... *I want to go home and cuddle with my family... But I promised myself I wouldn't abandon a discarded child.*

Even one as broken as the skeleton. "The healers will have Oya ready for travel in two days. We're coming with you."

"No. You're not." Ferdinan shook his head and crossed his arms. "I'm leaving in the morning. Everything's arranged for you to take Oya to your home in *three weeks* when she's ready."

Jon stepped closer. "Samuel and Sorah are representing at the conference. He'll heal Oya quickly." *I hate this...*

"So will Father Artimus!"

"Samuel already offered to list me and Oya on his travel party."

The skeleton shook – grimacing. "Why? You can go home! You can be with your family! Just go home!"

"Someone else will travel in your place tomorrow," Jon held his gaze steady. "The three of us will leave the next day. That'll be safer for you and allow Oya to prepare for a long ride."

"Why are you so stubborn? You want your family. You hate me." Boney hands clenched tight. "Go home. Be with your family and heal."

"Why're you so stubborn?"

"'Cause if you'd left...! This year of misery wouldn't have happened for you." Dry coughs forced Ferdinan to balance himself with the tree. "Be with your family. Enjoy what you always want. They love you. Be with them."

Jon couldn't interpret the dozen expressions flashing across the gent's face. "They love you too."

"No. They pity me." When Jon argued, Ferdinan cut him off. "No! They *have* to pity me! 'Cause they aren't mine. They're yours. *I* don't get to have them. Go be with *your* family."

"Love isn't finite." Jon looked closer. Every bone protruded painfully and the gent's face... There were mummies with more substance. He wanted to be with his family. Loved hearing Ferdinan say they were his and they loved him. "Two days. If you sneak away, Oya'll drag me to find you anyway."

Epilogue

Everyone stared at her dear friend. It wasn't every day a living skeleton boarded a train. Oya's blood red hair and crazed green eyes also attracted significant attention. As did Jon in his tattered fancy clothing...

Ferdinan ignored the crowd with practiced ease. She made the gawkers uncomfortable by grinning back. And Jon squirmed, unaccustomed to this kind of attention. Every eye judged. Many ushered children away – giving them plenty of space.

I didn't know they were capable of breaking their word. What should I do? Humawit's betrayal changed everything.

Months of work was gone – stealing her option of brute force. If she could recover the energy...the parts of herself she invested...

And her dear friend's soul was wasting away. Infected. Bleeding. Withering. Jon's feelings toward him were agitated, conflicted... *He's internally conflicted too...* It was a sign the Thinker was pondering. Maybe her gift wasn't wasted.

What're my options now? There wasn't enough information to form a new plan. The Fisherman was beyond her reach until she returned to the islands.

She couldn't walk – so finding Keepers was impossible. *Focus on preparing Yuyu to step up as Jinku...?* If the girl chose.

What do I do with my dear friend? Six weeks without Jon and Ferdinan was worse than she'd ever seen. *He depends on Jon more than I realized.*

Get Ferdinan stable and into Samuel's care... Were the two brothers enough to keep Ferdinan from stepping over that ledge?

...then there was the damage she caused...

So many choices could've changed that outcome. Insisting Jon work in the fields when he wasn't in the kitchen. Spending precious energy holding the growing giant outside the cave. Giving up hope sooner and putting them to sleep before dark shadows took hold. Shadows which weren't dissipating for Jon.

Looking down, she concentrated on her leg – demanding it rise. It didn't listen. Neither would her knee bend.

"*I do love a challenge.*"

About the Author

Psychologist, writer, crafter, and colored hair enthusiast... When CR Saxon isn't coming up with new and terrible things to subject various characters to, she can be found attempting projects with more ambition than skill, getting lost in random research, or catching up on chores. Her life is generally one of chaos and glowy screens – all while mentally living many lives in the name of fun, adventure, and storytelling.

C R Saxon

Pain of Darkness

ISBN: 9781955644044

www.ingramcontent.com/pod-product-compliance
Lightning Source LLC
Chambersburg PA
CBHW060407180626
46817CB00007B/2545